THE MAN
TRAPPED BY
SHADOWS

THE MAN
TRAPPED BY
SHADOWS

A ROOKER LINDSTRÖM THRILLER

PETE
ZACHARIAS

THOMAS & MERCER

Published by Thomas & Mercer, Seattle

www.apub.com

Amazon, the Amazon logo, and Thomas & Mercer are trademarks of Amazon.com, Inc., or its affiliates.

ISBN-13: 9781542039673 (paperback)
ISBN-13: 9781542039680 (digital)

Cover design by Zoe Norvell
Cover image: © Anastasiia Smiian / Shutterstock;
© plainpicture/Willing-Holtz / plainpicture

Printed in the United States of America

For my lovely agent, Victoria Skurnick.

Though some scholars estimate there have been tens of thousands of executions in unsubstantiated cases of witchcraft, to this day, the true number remains unknown.

Prologue

Her name was Malin Jakobsson. Twenty-six years of age. Strikingly ordinary features with dull, cloudy brown eyes. Eight years had gone by since her family reported her missing. She'd been dead for each of those. Now, what was left of her bobbed steadily back and forth, slow as the waning tide.

The postmortem examination would echo what he'd done. His *ritual.* Dark markings where she was struck over and over with stones. The exposed fibula blackened from targeted burns up to her femur. Hyperinflated lungs from drowning. Her throat mangled from the hanging—he'd left her suspended for days.

For eight years, he'd preserved her in ice, slowing the decomposition so he could admire his work again and again.

Why now? the police would ask themselves. As he sat in the padlocked basement, fixated on the newspaper clippings from the Gregory Sadler case, his face twisted into a smile.

In the time to come, they would call him a number of distasteful names.

Serial killer. Monster. Murderer. Freak. And then two monikers that would be published in the newspapers: Wiccan. The Peekaboo Killer.

◆ ◆ ◆

Two lamenting tones reverberated through the trees. A white cruiser raced through the early-morning mist. She lay there on the rocky shore of the lake, wet moss and sunken hills of earth all around her. The tiny bones in her fingers snapped. Steepled. Beneath them on her milky chest was a black envelope sealed shut with wax—a purple symbol. It was addressed to the police in ugly white scrawl. But inside was a note to a very certain someone.

Over pebbles, the tires hissed to a stop. A hound barked. The slam of the door echoed. Footfalls crunched.

After eight long years, they found her.

Chapter 1

The dead man's eye hung open. The shadows this time of night mutated the arctic-blue iris to black ice.

Prior to finding the body, it had been an ordinary evening for the guard. One laced with a wintry smell. Outfitted with a vest, a twenty-four-inch side-handle baton, and a canister of triple-action police pepper spray, Garrett Peters bounced on his toes. Under a brisk wind that whispered through the branches and rattled the foliage, his skin prickled with gooseflesh. A shiver coursed through him. Though Peters had only recently entered his midthirties, his hair was graying and thinning like a fifty-year-old's, straw-like and lifting in the gust like a sheet of paper. The park was empty. He'd been ambling through his rounds, slurping grotesquely on a ninety-nine-cent coffee from a Holiday Stationstores and thinking about the Hostess cake smooshed in the back pocket of his green khaki pants. Then he'd felt the hairs sprouting tall from the nape of his skinny neck.

The amber circle from the flashlight at his hip illuminated a pale face on the park bench. The dead man's body was contorted. He'd never seen anything like it. The right arm dangled to the ground. One leg was bent underneath him; the other stretched out over the rail. The boot was nearly kicked off the heel, where swiss-cheese holes sprouted from the back of his gray sock. *Damn tweaker,* the guard thought. But then he saw a clear bottle and an empty brown bag. *Nope, just another drunk.* One who smelled somewhere on the spectrum between homeless dead and the walking dead.

He was looking for a place to set down his coffee so that he could call it in when the man's bent leg shot forward and a gurgle erupted from his throat.

◆　◆　◆

Rooker Lindström blinked at the blob of light bouncing around. *Is someone talking?* His brain spun in a darkness that unraveled before his eyes. *Where in the hell am I?*

Then the smell of piled city-street garbage hit as powerfully as an aluminum-bat crack across the face, and things started to come into view. Trees. Darkness. His body confused the peaceful September night for a molten July day. The hem of his shirt was wet. Sweat- and booze-soaked. A foul brew of stenches: musty clothes, cheap liquor, and puke. Rooker imagined watery chunks and webbed slobber dripping from his mouth.

A violent exorcism belch erupted from his throat without warning. His head snapped forward. He swallowed hard. The taste when the belch climbed out of his mouth was wretched; he could smell the bile burning hot in his throat. He had hurled at some point, and the taste only made him ready to heave once more.

For the second time, he heard the gravelly voice. "Hey, man."

He tried to focus on it, but his eyelids were still heavy—suddenly, not sure why, he thought of Amy's Café, a diner in Riverside County off Magnolia Avenue. The blueberry syrup was a thick goop oozing out of the glass dispenser but delicious on chocolate-chip pancakes. Now it was as though his eyes were coated in it.

"Hey, buddy." Maybe it was the grim reaper. Maybe the light was death finally taking him, walking him toward the afterlife. The voice wasn't quite as mystical or otherworldly as he'd imagined. He pegged death as more of a James Earl Jones type, but this was higher pitched and slow with a Minnesota accent. "You can't sleep here. C'mon, get up."

Rooker squinted behind the shield of his hand. It was just a flashlight's piss-yellow stream waving down in his face. Still, it forced his eyes to well in the corners, nearly welded shut. He could make out a large, shadowed mass around five feet ten, two hundred pounds or so.

Rooker hung off the bench, his hand dangling limp to the cold ground. He'd made an effort to drink less. Nothing as drastic as throwing out all the liquor in the cottage, though. He'd even yet to move the bottle of Absolut from plain sight into a cupboard, and he grimaced as the tips of his fingers brushed against the cold glass of a handle of cheap vodka. He could hear the bottle clunk as it spun on concrete. The sound made him thirsty. He shifted his weight; a few bones creaked. After a few seconds of groaning and getting his stiff joints to do as his brain commanded, he sat upright and looked at the burly man beneath a military salute to block out the light. He still wasn't sure where he was.

"This isn't my bedroom?" he asked the man. His voice was hoarse. He scratched at the straggly hairs coming in black and gray and patchy where his beard connected to his mustache. His disheveled waves looked matte black in the dark, but now the flashlight gave them a shampooed, silky sheen.

"Get up," the man said, irritated. "Don't make me call it in." Rooker appraised the man's aggressive stance, the pumped-out chest, and the spindly fingers that had inched toward the black pepper spray canister. Rooker didn't move. He wasn't entirely sure that he could yet, but it was also his stubbornness kicking in. If he wanted to sleep the booze off on a . . . was this a park bench? Who was this guy to tell him he couldn't?

"Up," the man commanded, and Rooker felt the man soccer kick the sole of his boot as if it were intended for a net just beneath the crossbar. Rooker's foot fell off the side of the bench, his heel thudding to the ground. He felt his stomach filled to the rim, mostly alcohol sloshing left and right.

"Buddy, you touch me again and you'll wish you didn't," Rooker said. The former *"drunk charm,"* as he'd call it, was lost from his voice. "I don't get paid enough for this shit, man. Just get the hell up."

Rooker listened to the man call it in over a small, handheld black walkie-talkie. He imagined him as a boy at a sleepover playing cops. He stumbled to his feet. The ray of light shined bright in Rooker's eyes. He closed them, but it was just as bright behind his eyelids.

"You wanna shut that off?" Rooker asked. But the man didn't. Instead, he stood and waited for his backup to arrive. It was probably a few security officers or park patrol. Rooker lurched toward the man, headed for the light he was drowned in. When he was close enough, he ripped the flashlight out of the guard's hand and football spiked it into the ground. The sound reminded him of the crack he'd heard when his bare knuckles clocked Gregory Sadler in the jaw months ago. The thin bottom cap broke off; the batteries flew somewhere far from them. The front bezel and the bulb shattered. The light was gone. But Rooker could still see the man standing before him, a streetlight not far away, eavesdropping. The man suddenly looked ready for a scrap, and Rooker couldn't help but smile.

Rooker noticed the hand balled tight in a fist at his side.

"Your stance is too wide," Rooker told him straight. "And if you're considering it, that right hand is going to take too long to come up from your hip. You'd be flat on your back by the time it does."

"Fuck you," the guard growled back.

If there was one thing Rooker didn't want, it was to hurt this man. But at the same time, he was in no mood to be bothered. Best to let sleeping dogs lie. In his mind, it was best not to wake a man who can't sleep.

Sure enough, the cavalry arrived. Two uniformed men spilled out of a white vehicle and rushed in his direction. Rooker endured the next couple of minutes of being dragged up by his clothes and wrangled as though he were a dead horse.

As a patrol car parked at the curb, an officer grudgingly stepped out and put him into the back of it. The door shut quietly. Rooker watched the cop scribble something on a small pad and flip it closed. When he was done with the group of men, he sauntered back to the car and slumped into the driver seat. Sitting perfectly still, not so much as glancing at Rooker in the rearview mirror, he jabbed the key into the ignition and sighed.

◆　◆　◆

Manacled in cold steel to the small rectangular table, Rooker sat covered in grime and sweat. The chair reminded him of one of those stackable, flimsy-plastic white ones, but this one was ice and metal and even less comfortable. But at least the tabletop felt like an ice pack against his throbbing head. On his way in, he'd seen two squabbling meth addicts: pustules resembling cigarette burns, teeth rotted. An anorexic hooker with a chest as phony as a cheap toupee. A man he guessed was a DWI. His head was split open where Rooker imagined it had jolted against the steering wheel, his neck erection stiff, his eyes Cornell red and heavy. They were the eyes of drunken guilt.

The officer took Rooker's California ID and the leftover change from the booze he'd bought. It had rattled in his pocket when they searched him. They knew who he was, so Rooker knew what it was they were doing. They had to make a call, see what they would do with him. He was like a lost dog, only the neighborhood wasn't lined with his Scotch-taped photograph. He didn't come with a reward.

It wasn't long before a veteran officer lumbered in. Rooker raised his head just enough to see his silver beard and parted hair. He sipped from a piping-hot paper cup and had a newspaper football-tucked under his left arm. He looked to be only a couple of years shy from retiring with a full pension, yet his arms showed the lean and toned symptoms of the police weight room. Rooker put his head back down and listened to the man take a seat, gulp from his steaming coffee, and place the newspaper in front of Rooker for him to read.

Rooker took one look, saw the headline, and turned it over. "You did a great thing," the man said and cleared his throat twice.

Rooker stayed silent as the dead of night. Not a chirp from the katydids, not a slamming door or car horn, nothing. The officer could probably tell he wasn't going to get anything out of him. "If you don't talk, I have to just put you in a cell." A few minutes later, the man tilted his head back and finished his coffee, went to the other side of the table, and told Rooker, "C'mon." Rooker stood up and was marched into a six-by-eight cell of his own—more of a box with a windowed door— and the door locked behind him. He lay down on the bench, a narrow concrete slab not much wider than he was. He locked his hands behind the crook of his head and closed his eyes.

Sleep didn't come. Instead, he concentrated on the sounds of the place. He listened to the rattle of keys, the hushed voices, the yelled names, the innocent pleas, the drunk-tank slurs, the snoring sleepers. He knew it would just be a matter of time before they let him go. At least he hoped. Otherwise, he'd be fighting a hangover soon, wishing for the silence that haunted Lindström Manor. He typically hated how quiet it got. When it felt as though his perception of time was blurred and his hearing was gone. About an hour deeper into morning, Rooker heard boots stomping down the hall toward him, the jingle of keys, and his door unlock.

"Free to go," the man said and moved out of the way.

Rooker looked up and saw Tess. She wore a grayish-blue jacket over a gray V-neck and the look of a disappointed parent on her face. He'd seen the latter too many times to count from Gunner. He couldn't remember his mother wearing that expression even once.

"Come on." She turned on her heel, and he stood up and followed her. Her hair had changed. It was shorter. Just past her collarbone, chestnut-brown waves trickled to thick strands of yellow hair, like honey dripping down her shoulder.

The officer handed Rooker his ID and change. Rooker told him to keep the latter, closed the man's hand over the crumpled dollar bills and sticky coins, and smiled.

They spent the drive to his cottage in absolute silence. He didn't look over at her once. He didn't care if she was looking at him. They just drove along like a couple married too long, the love gone, with nothing left to say. The heat droned. When she stopped the car, she turned off the engine and stared at the cottage a long while before saying anything.

"This is the last time." She shook her head. He sat there, stubborn as can be in the passenger seat. He went to open his door, but she kept it locked, childproofed. "You helped us when we needed it, but I can't keep pulling favors for you."

He stared straight ahead as though she were a ghost. Like he couldn't even hear the faintest bit of her voice or smell the perfume lingering on her petite wrist. He thought maybe she'd taken his comment to heart, about her wearing men's cologne. Her scent was different now, something more floral, maybe lilac or lavender, and something that reminded him of blackberries.

"Is that it?" he said. He didn't look at her. He didn't acknowledge her.

"Yeah," she said. "That's it."

The door clicked, and he knew it was open. He couldn't let her get the last word in. He was too stubborn for that. He let out the heavy precursor sigh. It hung over them, looming like the bright crack that flashed in the black sky, his words the booming thunder and the pelting rain. "Next time you can't find a serial killer who sits feet away in your office, don't come begging me to find him."

She cracked a smile. "You keep hiding here in your house of horrors." She turned to face him. The gold flecks in her eyes burned nuclear holes right through him. "Curled up in a ball. *Afraid.*"

Rooker smirked and said nothing else. And neither did she before he got out and sulked back to the cottage. The Interceptor kicked up dust and dirt, two faint clouds of exhaust vanishing on the long trail back past the gate to the main road. Before he shut the front door behind him, Geralt weaseled inside, the gold orbs for eyes reptilian, pupils the shape of fine black diamonds—but it was the shade of gold that instantly reminded him of Tess.

Chapter 2

Fragments. Her memories of that morning played in fragments. The way a high-velocity bullet splinters upon entry, bits and pieces spiraling through flesh and tissue and bone, designed to inflict maximum damage.

The moment the line went dead. She remembered the crackling before it disconnected.

The sirens cried. Flickering blue and red as the world faded to black. Her foot slammed down against the gas pedal. Tires spinning past the wrought iron gate. The hiss of sprayed gravel. A world on fire.

The front of the cottage was a ball of flames. Deer Lake Fire Department stormed the driveway. Four men in bunker gear spilled out of Engine 212. Her perception of time slowed, but she hurried toward the chaos. Men in sand and reflective mustard-yellow gear—turnout trousers and coats, overalls, puncture-resistant rubber boots, hard-shell leather helmets, and Kevlar gloves. Their boots clopped like Clydesdales. A long gray hose in tow. Censorious eyes on her as though she didn't belong. Like she was in their way.

They ordered her to stand back.

The sizzling house engulfed in a red-and-orange blaze.

And Rooker standing off to the side, perfectly still. Watching. One man hollered at him, "Is anyone inside?"

He didn't answer.

Hours after the fire was put out, restoration companies flocked buzzard-like to the cottage. She'd helped him pick one that had SERV in the name; she'd forgotten the rest. Later, she'd understand why he'd flinched. It was what was found in the wreckage. *Bones.* The cleanup crew reported the skeletal remains of a body—female—wrapped in an old sheet beneath the floor. She'd watched his face when he got the news. It didn't change. There was no shock, no surprise, no questions. He knew. He'd known all along she was there.

Tess had felt sick to her stomach. The girl from the story. The one he'd written. An overwhelming feeling of dread inside—one that'd infected the tissue and cells deep in her bones—that he'd killed her.

That day changed everything for her. In her mind, if the woman beneath the floor truly were one of Gunner's victims, she'd be missing her head. She wasn't.

The two of them hadn't been on speaking terms since. Really, she'd been avoiding him like the plague.

◆ ◆ ◆

Plunk. Plunk. Plunk.

Water dripped from the spout. It brought her back. She'd been drifting again, this time into thoughts of the two men who had raped her mother. Pushed her mother into silence. Drove her father to commit suicide.

Now her mother wallowed in her own filth until a nurse came to wash her. *It's for the best.* She tried to steel herself in her words. It had been nearly a year since her last visit. And if she wanted to visit her father, there was only a grave that housed his broken body decomposing with the seasons. She closed her eyes but saw them: Jan Cullen and Clyde Miller. She opened her eyes in anger. Lifted the Sig Sauer P226 from the rug beside the tub. Pressed the magazine release and cleared the chamber. Cleaned it. Lately, she found herself keeping it close. Letting her arm hang over the edge of the tub with it clutched in her hand. Leaving it holstered to her hip even when she was off duty. It used to stay in the bedside drawer. Now she left it on top. Loaded.

Her hand served as a snuffer to a flame, extinguishing the hammering in her chest. She pulled the drain on the tub and let it empty. After she wrapped a towel around herself, she raked her damp hair with her fingertips and pulled clothing from the drawers. She threw on a pair of black jeans, a black tee, and an olive bomber jacket. She clipped her badge to her belt. In the mirror, her reflection glared back. Her cheek indented, teeth gnashing the flesh inside. Anger painted her face.

At 6:45 a.m., she sauntered into the station. The only person who'd ever beaten her in was Millie Langston. Sometimes she wondered if Millie had slept there. But now that Millie had quit the team and run off to do God knows what with Rooker, Tess was always the first one in.

She tossed her jacket onto the back of her chair. She reviewed the scant report on Nora Vandenberg, a woman who'd been reported missing a few days earlier. They had nothing to go on. And they were working on something else that had them all far more worried.

Martin Keene ambled through the doors in gray trousers and a white dress shirt. Xander Whitlock followed, making a less impressive entrance in a blue dress shirt and black pants, his top shirt button undone and a solid black tie hanging unfinished around his neck. He gave a quick nod and took a seat at his desk without a single word.

Soon the new guy, John Riggs, was headed to his desk. Shoulders hunched and head down, Riggs wore faded blue jeans and a tan polo shirt along with the same brown cap he wore daily—a frayed and discolored brim—to hide his thinning blond hair. He had a lean, muscular build, and though he was only two years out of the academy, he looked the part of someone with a decade of experience. Tess had given him Elias Cole's desk. Tess still found herself scowling at the desk, envisioning Cole twirling his pen and playing the part of the good cop. She'd run through all the mistakes she'd made. She could beat herself up for a lifetime. She probably would.

She had run an extensive background check on Jonathan Riggs that bordered on stalking. But for her sanity—and the team's—it needed to be done. Riggs checked out, but so had the man who'd once sat there in between killing women, and Jonathan Riggs was more a stranger to her than Cole ever was.

Last to make it into the building was Vic Sterling, with his perfectly sculpted hair, creaseless designer black Henley tee, black pants, and black boots. At least Vic's vanity could always make her smile.

"Circle up," she told them. "The body we found yesterday. The woman who called it in—Elyse Lopez. She was out for a stroll and saw the victim in the water. Doesn't seem to know a thing. Never saw anyone else. Definitely didn't see someone dump the body."

"Even if we didn't find that note on her . . . that ain't no ordinary homicide," Sterling said.

"Agreed. There's something wrong. *Really* wrong."

That's what scared her most. Everything about this was off.

A death like this . . . with signs of torture . . .

Tess's day had only just started, and the thought of being sucked into another investigation like Sadler's made her want to crawl into a hole and hide. There was a pit in her gut that made her shiver; she was headed back there all over again, searching out evil, as if she'd been blindfolded and left in the dark. "I know," she said over her grumbling stomach. Then she thought of the blackened fibula, and her hunger subsided. "Hayes has the body. I just got off the phone with him."

"What kind of sick son of a bitch . . ." Keene stopped himself.

The Man Trapped by Shadows

"World's chock-full of sick sons of bitches," Sterling said. "We wouldn't have jobs if it wasn't."

Tess put her hand on her hip. "We don't know *what* happened to her."

Keene cleared his throat. "Victim looks like she's been dead several years but preserved. Why would the body surface now? What did Hayes say?"

"*Unusual. Strange. Curious,*" she quoted. "That's most of what he said. He has a preliminary report. He still needs more time with the vic. But he said despite the severe burns on her body, he believes her death was caused by asphyxiation due to submersion. Said he's never seen anything quite like it."

Riggs fidgeted in his chair and pulled his cap low. For the first time this morning, he spoke. "She drowned?"

"Did you see what I saw, boss?" Sterling shook his head. "Her legs looked so badly burned that the bone disintegrated. You think she drowned?"

With her fingernail, she picked at the scar etched into her fingertip. The skin around it whitened. "That's what he says."

Chapter 3

Rooker wandered the woods like he used to. They were once his friend, his ally when his father wanted to dish out a beating. He zipped his blue plaid jacket up to his neck. The sweatshirt collar stretched, the stitching coming loose, but it was comfortable and warm. Gravestone-gray clouds loomed in the sky. A storm was coming. Rain would be falling in buckets soon. It served as a reminder to make sure the five-gallon linoleum pails were empty and out. Leaves and twigs crunched, snapped beneath his brown leather boots. He slipped a long black bag off his left shoulder and leaned it up against the base of an old tree. His initials were still there, barely legible in the crumbling bark that flaked off beneath his fingertips in strudel-size pieces. One night when he ran from the house, he'd chosen the tree, hidden against its cold embrace, and slept with his back to it through the night.

He unzipped the bag and pulled out the Winchester Model 70 hunting rifle. It was a 1951, .270 Winchester caliber, with a Leupold VX-2 2-7x28mm scope. Rooker didn't have the slightest clue what any of that meant. He just cared whom it had belonged to and that it fired.

He felt along the stock and traced the initials that had been carved into it with a knife: GS. It was the rifle that had nearly ended his life, the rifle belonging to the one and only Gregory Sadler. Once the dust had settled and the paperwork was boxed, Rooker had convinced Sterling to help him liberate the rifle from Evidence. He still couldn't quite fathom Gregory Sadler's file sitting downstairs in the basement room with his father's—though he imagined Sadler would be thrilled to be so close to his mentor. Rooker considered the rifle a parting gift, one that Gregory wouldn't mind him having.

He swung a smaller backpack off his right shoulder and sat on the cold ground. It was an old military pack that he'd found in the basement of the cottage, in Gunner's kill room. The pack was torn in places; a patch had been ripped off the olive drab camouflage. He'd slapped the dust and tattered webs and dead spiders from it. Rooker put the pack in his lap. He had stuffed it to the brim with old rags and towels and an ancient wool blanket he found in storage. It was his shooting rest; some people called them cheater bags. The person on the receiving end probably wouldn't. He placed the rifle on top of the pack and manipulated it left and right a few times until it felt secure.

He peered through his scope, the standard reticle with a thin center, at his personal firing range. He had markers in place, circular and silhouette steel targets all at different distances from one hundred yards to eight hundred. He'd jury-rigged them so that each was standing six feet off the ground attached to thick wood and secured to the ground with the weight plates from his bench press. He saw a family of deer at about six hundred yards and took aim. He watched them feeding on berries and bushes. One of them cocked its head, and Rooker thought it was looking at him, possibly even sensed him there. The storm was nearing, but the wind hadn't picked up yet. It was virtually perfect shooting conditions, and Rooker wondered if this was how it was when Gregory shot him in the chest. That was a night Rooker would never forget, feeling alone, hunted, bleeding, dying.

He peered down into his ice-water hands. The scar from Sadler's knife leafed a powdery crack through his palm. The doctors said it had healed well, but the scar was still rubbery and pink. But he had plenty of scars that he'd wear the rest of his life, so what was one more?

Just then, a gust whistled low, sent a shudder through him, and vanished like a cold voice from dying lips. His fingernails scratched up and down the dark scraggly whiskers on his face, the sound of a slow card shuffle. He took a deep breath. Filling his lungs with the cool air, he made two fists and blew warmth into the balls of each.

While his calluses fell into place over the rifle, he took in the smells of the morning. It was a concoction of damp earth, animal droppings somewhere nearby, and the bright scent of pine. The smell of steaming-hot cocoa and vodka wafted from a thermos beside him. A few cups of water, a packet of instant cocoa, a generous splash of Absolut, and a scoop of Nesquik chocolate powder—he'd bought a tub of it online, one of the best purchases he'd made in quite a while. He swirled the thermos and drank from it.

He took aim at the target at one hundred yards and clicked the button to start the timer. He exhaled slowly, squeezed the trigger, and the rifle cracked—jolted like a bull trying to kick a rider free. CLUNK. It was a hit and enough to startle the deer. Rooker watched their long legs kicking up, galloping farther and farther away. He pulled the bolt back and dumped the round, shoved the bolt back in, and got ready to fire. He moved the rifle slightly right for the two-hundred-yard target and squeezed. CLINK. Hit. He kept his vision downrange, shifting slightly left again for the target at three hundred yards. He centered it in his scope, breathed out, and fired. CLINK. Then the next target. CLUNK. He was no marksman, but he had gotten pretty good with the rifle. It was starting to feel familiar in his hands. Like the weight of a newborn.

He ejected the round smoothly. Once the five-hundred-yard target was in his scope, he exhaled and fired—nothing. Dirt and leaves soared feet in front of the target. He made the slightest adjustment and fired another round. The target convulsed. He started to get ready for the next one, and right as he peered down the sight, he heard the ringing.

The rooster-shaped timer he had taken from Evelyn's kitchen crowed, and he turned it till it shut off.

He reloaded the weapon and started over.

Just past nine o'clock, he called it a day. He was satisfied that he'd hit five of the targets in his minute window. Twice. Two loud cracks came from Rooker's knees as he stood up and gathered the bags. He headed back through the woods to the cottage, which was starting to look less like a "house of horrors," as Tess had called it, and more akin to a legitimate home. The front of the cottage had been severely damaged in the fire. Now there was new wood downstairs, along with a new window where Geralt—who was acting less and less like a stray these days—tended to sit. The upstairs had been built out with a modern addition that made him think of a partial face-lift. Gone were the old planks of wood nailed across the wall. Massive, paneled windows were now what Rooker peered out when his nightmares woke him. However, he'd been able to repurpose the boards to patch up the front steps, which now harbored a thick stack of letters secured with two thick rubber bands.

Evelyn's Volvo was there, beneath the weather-whitened blue tarp. It belonged to him now. Her daughter had come by to sort through her belongings after the funeral. Rooker paid her cash. It was well more than its Kelley Blue Book value but less than his guilt.

He groaned as he hunched over, lifted the stack, and hauled it inside. Leaning the rifle upright behind the door, Rooker tossed the sleeve beside it and shimmied and slipped the backpack the rest of the way off his shoulders to the floor. While he attempted to roll the rubber bands from the mail, they snapped. He tossed them into the pile metastasizing on the kitchen counter. He shuffled through the stack: literary agency, publishing house, agent, talent agency, agency, publicist, talk show, film production company, television network, agent, agent, agent, on and on and on. A small fortune awaited him from any envelope he plucked from the pile. Everyone wanted his story. Wanted to turn it into a hit television series or a blockbuster winter film or a bestselling novel. Rooker imagined grubby little hands shooting out for the rights or a slice of the pie. But there was none to go around. He tore most of the envelopes in half and dumped them in the trash bin.

There were only two offer letters that made his eyebrows raise. They were from the two most vaunted *Times*: Los Angeles and New York. He set those on the end of the table. Whether he intended to reach out or hoard them for safekeeping, he wasn't sure.

The answering machine flashed shot-clock red. He brooded toward it, shaking his head, his finger slamming down against the glowing button. "Hi, Rooker, it's Danny Ross again. I have some things in the works, some ideas for you. Give me a call back, thanks." Rooker waited for him to repeat his telephone number a second time, as if Rooker had dialed the wrong number after the first or second or third message Danny left. Rooker enjoyed hearing his former agent squirm. He was a worm—a slimy, disgusting night crawler of a man, a soil-dwelling piece of shit whom Rooker wanted to squash beneath his boot. Now Rooker had a story that was good enough for Danny. Marketable, but it wasn't for sale. He deleted the message. His cheeks had pinkened, flush from the numbing cold, his eyes a water-bleared mess. He dabbed at his eyes with the loose neckline of the sweater and went to the kitchen.

He tugged the duct-taped handle of the fridge and pulled out a carton of large eggs and a package of bacon. He swung open a cabinet and watched one of the hinges come loose. Unfazed, he bent down and yanked an old steel skillet free. He wriggled his hand between the wall and the stove, flipped the cobwebbed valve to the gas line, and turned the only dial on the range that still worked. The rest were either snapped or missing entirely. He pressed down on the button of the long lighter. With a click, the neon-blue flame hissed. He cracked a few whole eggs on the counter and dumped them into the warped pan. After he'd rinsed the yellow slime from his fingers, he dumped the finished scrambles on a plate and slapped five pieces of bacon sizzling into the pan. He had taken Evelyn's coffee maker after she died. He figured she'd want him to have it. He put on a pot of coffee, sat down not long after with a cup piping hot and his food steaming.

When he finished scraping every morsel and crumb onto his fork and into his mouth, he got up, tossed the plate in the sink, and went to the bathroom and undressed. Feeling an itch on his leg, he pulled down his pants and saw it there crawling up between the curly hairs on his thigh. It hadn't yet burrowed into his skin. He pinched the tick between the nail of his thumb and pointer finger, watched its tiny legs squirm to break free. He flicked it into the toilet, pissed on it, and flushed. After he wrestled with the shower nozzle, he let the water spray and then fall in a steady rain. He stepped inside and washed the cold chill from his body. The water beat down against his face, the peaks at the sides of his neck, his broad shoulders. The moment he heard a hiss, he turned the nozzle off. It meant that the water was about to turn icy. He dried his hair and wrapped the white towel around his waist.

Rooker had made a few other home improvements to the cottage. He had replaced two of the stairs going up to the bedroom, the two that would win the superlative of "most likely to kill him." Now two unstained cedar boards stood out awkwardly in their place. He had thrown out some of the things in Gunner's kill room. He contemplated auctioning them off or having a tag sale. But he didn't. Instead, he dumped the lot of it into a black heavy-duty garbage bag and that was that. He had plugged a few holes in the roof where water was coming in with a waterproof rubber sealant. Despite it, water still snuck its way in from a few other areas. In reality, the roof needed to be replaced, but a temporary fix was good enough for him.

◆　◆　◆

At seven o'clock at night, he collapsed in the chair and reclined. The second he picked up his laptop from the ground, the phone chirped beside him. His arm dangled, reaching for it while balancing his laptop. He saw the number and didn't answer. He knew who it was. He'd let it go to voice mail. Waiting out the beep, he wanted to press his fingers into his ears and act as a child would when they pretend not to listen.

"Rooker." Tess Harlow's voice pressed. "Pick up. I know you're there." He knew she was probably just calling about the other night, maybe to scold him for her having to bail him out of trouble again. He didn't care to hear it. He didn't care to hear from her. "Rooker, this is serious. I need you to pick up." He didn't budge. He thought he could hear electricity in the absence of words. He imagined it crackling on his skin, the way the silence buzzed all around him. Whatever she needed him for now, he didn't want to know. "Rooker, goddammit, turn on the news, then!"

He didn't want to. For her to be calling about something on the news, he wouldn't like it. It probably meant she needed him for something. Maybe Xander had shot a civilian. Who the hell knew? He grabbed the remote, pressed the red button, and watched his reflection in the murky dark glass disappear. Chief Jim Larsson stood behind a podium, an outcry of badged media personnel on the other side. Rooker watched the chief try to silence everyone with a shaky hand. It didn't take.

He looked even older than Rooker remembered. Windswept hairs stuck up and looked ready to blow away. The boxy suit jacket gave him the appearance of a cold skeleton. His face was as crinkled as a tissue someone had tried to unfold and smooth out, his forehead a topographical map of ridges and hills and flat earth. White bristles poked out from his flared nostrils.

Rooker picked up the phone, and before he could speak, Tess said flatly, "I told him not to." Rooker could hear voices buzzing on her end, though it didn't sound as though she were outside with Larsson.

Wearily, Rooker asked the first thing on his mind. "Did you find a body?"

She didn't answer. *That's a yes,* he thought.

Rooker turned up the volume.

"We retrieved a woman's body from Itasca State Park yesterday evening. Though we don't have a positive ID at this time, we believe the victim went missing quite some time ago. For that reason, we have delayed announcing anything because we wanted to let the family know, in the event that we can confirm that it's her. The last thing I want to do is worry our community, so just know that the fatality seems to have happened years ago and that our team is currently pooling all their resources and committing all their time to positively identify her. This is an ongoing investigation, so we can't release too much just yet on the nature of the investigation. I ask that the public please be patient at this time."

Whispers. The room seemed to have fallen ill and lost its voice.

"Chief Larsson, is the victim's death being ruled a homicide?" one of the voices yelled. But Jim Larsson either ignored it or didn't hear.

"Chief Larsson, my source says there was an envelope left on the victim's body. Is that true, and if so, can you say what was inside it?"

The old man waved the question off with a dismissive hand, as if a fly were buzzing around his face. "I can't disclose that at this time. The investigation is ongoing."

Jim Larsson raked the delicate wisps of hair with a flat palm and shuffled away.

Rooker turned off the TV and lifted the phone to his ear. Felt it snag on his beard. "What is all this?"

"Chaos. And the message the reporter mentioned? That's real. It was mailed to the station. But it was written to you."

"Nice of them."

"Look, I may need your help. And before you go on a tangent, I just pulled you out of a holding cell. You owe me."

Rooker sat up in his chair and let out a heavy sigh. "What do you need from me?"

"I need you to look into the disappearance of a girl. Her name is Malin Jakobsson. She vanished in September 2011. We think she might be our victim."

"You mean that you want me and *Millie* to look into it."

"Don't—"

"I'll see what *we* can find. But you need to stop pretending I stole her out from under your nose—Millie handed in her badge because you turned her into a glorified secretary. All this private detective stuff—it was her idea. If *we* help you, that's up to her."

She didn't respond.

"What did the message say? How do you know it isn't just some prank?"

"What, you think someone found a body and taped an envelope to their chest? I don't know that it isn't a prank. But it sure as hell doesn't feel like one."

"Was it addressed to the station or me?"

She hesitated just long enough that he knew the answer. "You." Warily, he leaned forward. Strange, though. Anyone in the world could have found the address to Lindström Manor with a few simple clicks. Was it odd that they hadn't just sent it in the mail? But he shook the dim-witted thought away with a smile. He knew that leaving the envelope on a dead woman's body definitely got the message across. And the killer knew it would. He tried his best to joke. "You went through my mail?"

"Will you help or not?"

He didn't want to. Every part of him wanted to say no. Especially the scar in his chest from a .270 Winchester rifle round and the scar left in his hand from being stabbed by a hunting knife. Every day that rain fell from the sky, the two spots throbbed and ached.

"What did the note say?" He pressed his phone hard into his ear. Waited.

"It says, 'Won't you come out and play?'"

A pit grew in his stomach. He sighed. "Okay, I want to see it. Text it to me. I'll look into the girl. And I'll do my best to get Millie on board."

He hung up.

A few minutes later, his cell phone dinged.

There were three photographs.

The first image was a black envelope. There was an odd wax seal no longer intact, its dark purple bled, that of a rotting grape.

The second was a photograph: a black-and-white eye, bleeding mascara or blood.

The third one was what gave him the willies. He read his name handwritten in cold, demonic letters. Below the bottom flap of the envelope, a card sat with the same ugly handwriting. He zoomed in on the illustration of a dead black bird with X's for eyes. Straight out of some sick how-to drawing book. Underneath the bird was the invitation: *Won't you come out and play?*

Rooker sighed again. "Thanks, but no thanks."

Chapter 4

He always carried three keys on him: one was the override for the safe, one to the basement, and one to the freezer.

Her first forty-eight hours had run cold thirty years ago. She was gone, dried up like the granule sands in an hourglass. They had long forgotten her, but he hadn't. He closed his beady eyes—in grade school, Marta Josephson had said he had marsupial eyes—and breathed in slowly, taking in the smell of her summery amber perfume while her flesh rotted. His head drooped down to where his jaw met his chest, and when his eyes flicked open, he looked down at her. There she was, the black-and-white photo of her, the newspaper headline dated thirty years ago today. September 19, 1989. He reveled in the article, as he'd done every year on her anniversary. Then he folded the paper crisply, matching the creases perfectly, and pulled the perfume out of the safe. It was hers, Chanel N°5. He spritzed the top and watched the mist shower against the crotch of his pants. Flicked himself hard on the penis. It was all part of the ritual. But tonight would be different from the others.

Tonight, he left a message. He invited someone into his den.

A yellow light from the lampshade on his desk cast an ugly glow against his face, one of two in the room. The other was an LED light inside the safe. First, there was a small, twelve-by-eight-by-eight black security box, nothing special; just four digits on the keypad opened it. But now he had a pry-resistant solid-steel locking safe more than double its size with a 500 DPI optical sensor biometric fingerprint reader. A certain number of incorrect PIN or unregistered fingerprint attempts would send the safe into a penalty timed lockout.

He sat down, kicked his feet up on the gray ottoman, and pressed the button on the remote. The flat screen flickered white; he surfed the channels until he found the news. Once he found it, he cracked a sly smile, pressed another button on the control, and a red circle popped up letting him know it was recording. On his plate, his food was cut up into tiny cubes of identical dimensions. He forked a square of meat and dabbed it in a dark sauce, bit it off the prongs, and started chewing.

He watched the old man saunter behind the podium. He stood hunched over, cadaver white. Chief Jim Larsson, the man responsible for the team who had caught Gregory Sadler, the killer dubbed the Man in the Lake.

He couldn't take his eyes off the television. Instead, he just stabbed around the plate blindly, gnawing on whatever it was that his fork found. For someone like him, it was like playing poker without seeing your own cards. For someone who measured everything out, made the slightest calculation for anything, had backup plans for everything he'd done since he could remember. He was diagnosed obsessive compulsive at a young age. Everything he did needed to be just right, and the doctors never really helped with it. Neither did the shrink. He didn't appreciate her mind games. He watched Chief Larsson peek down at his notes and recite the same old statements: "no positive ID," "ongoing investigation," and "I cannot comment on that at this time."

He wasn't sure what he'd expected. Did he really think Rooker Lindström was going to fly onto the stage in cape and tights to accept his invitation? His face soured. Then a sly smile cracked across it like a bird darting into glass. The game was just beginning. He had to give the police time to catch up. After all, they hadn't even identified her yet.

Malin Jakobsson. He looked down at the wallet-size photo of her, which he'd retrieved from the safe in anticipation of the press conference. He turned it just perfectly beside the newspaper and went about his routine. He closed his eyes and rubbed himself, picturing her all those years ago. Just as he was finishing, he looked up to see the nurse standing there in the doorway, pretending that she didn't know what it was that she had just walked in on.

"I, um, I gave her the pills," she said. "I'll be back tomorrow." The door shut quickly; the image of her shocked face embedded itself parasitically in his brain.

The next thought that consumed his mind was the image of her dead on the floor before him. But she was too close to him. She'd raise suspicion and lead the police to his door. Instead, he adjusted himself, zipped his pants, and put his mementos back where they went and locked the safe. His socks dampened against the semen-stained carpet. He sauntered out of his office into the blubbering snores and hacking coughs that filled the hallway, took the set of keys out, and unlocked the silver padlock to the basement door.

He opened the door slightly. Squeezed past the opening into the pitch-black, locking it from the inside. At the bottom of the creaking stairs, his finger found the switch, and a spot of the room flickered in semidarkness. He gave one look at the girl tied to the chair and smiled.

Chapter 5

Sleep had come to him only in five-minute intervals. He was restless. But when he thought he heard a bang downstairs that reminded him of one of the cupboards whipping shut, his head snapped forward. A cramp lodged in the side of his neck. He thought he'd heard the damsels of Deer Lake again. They screamed, their faces hanging ugly over his, like a baby mobile spinning with severed heads attached to wires and hooks and string. Under black briefs, one of his hands scratched his groin while the other massaged the spasm in his neck. The white elastic snapped against his stomach when he pulled his hand free. Then he put both hands behind the crook of his skull, trying to doze off again.

Sleep couldn't come sooner. And then, he knew, it wouldn't come at all.

The room was raven black. Although he hadn't taken a drink tonight, his body felt sluggish. His mind drowsy but sober, he couldn't fall into one of his deep drunken slumbers. He could swear that he heard the tick every minute the green digital numbers on his bedside alarm changed. He faced the lambent 12:15 a.m. With alcohol on his mind, he thought about drinking himself to sleep. For him it was the equivalent of warmed milk and a back scratch. He decided against it.

Instead, he pulled the blankets off him and slid his bare legs out over the edge of the bed. The cold floorboards mewled beneath him. Weather-bleached, ashen, and bright were his legs aside from his hair in the starlit sky. One wool sock was still on his left foot; the other was somewhere buried at the foot of the mattress. He threw a crew neck shirt on and walked down the groaning staircase. It was the time of night that any and every noise was all the more startling, the time of night that conjured memories—nightmares, really—of kicking up snow, running through the freezing night with a bullet in him, waiting out death. It was the time of night that the silence deafened him.

He peeked into the kitchen and saw that one of the cabinets was open, and he left it that way. He didn't want to upset any of the women living with him. It was a polyamorous household without any of the benefits. Fourteen women, but all they did was haunt him. He was about to sit when he caught a glimpse of something moving at a dead sprint outside. It was small.

Hunched?

But when he squinted and couldn't see it anymore, he wondered if it was just his mind playing tricks on him. He backed away to the cabinet and reached in until he gripped the cold steel. He turned the Glock 17 over, switched the safety off, and moved along the wall beside the window. It was dark, but he thought the moonlight cast a shadow somewhere out there. He peered outside and waited, his pulse thumping too powerfully in his wrist.

He held his breath and listened. Finally, he heard leaves crackling lightly. Someone was out there. He saw the figure move fast and low. The last step to the porch creaked. Then a lightning-fast *thud-thud-thud.*

Rooker moved silently to the door, then whipped it open, pistol aimed at the intruder.

The boy bolted. Four more boys waiting by the tree line all got up and took off running. They were gangly but fast, like a herd of frightened deer. Not the one sent to the door, though. He was the portly one of the bunch, by far the slowest. He did his best to catch up to them, his arms flailing. Rooker took aim and fired a stray shot into the top of the trees. The boy stumbled and crashed hard to the ground, losing his pants as he did. Two of the faster kids came back for him and snatched his arm and shirt, pulling him to his feet.

"Run, he's gonna kill us too!" The words echoed in the darkness. He listened to them scream on a loop.

Rooker switched the safety on and watched them scurry off until they disappeared. He was the urban legend now. His was the house that you didn't walk past, haunted by a woman who rose from the mist and the boy who drowned in the lake. Whatever bullshit they came up with, that was now him. The smell of sweat and fear and garlic lingered at the door, the smell of shit pungent too. He looked down for the little brown bag filled with it, but it wasn't there. The boy must have soiled himself. A cold draft of the night air slithered its way inside before Rooker slammed the door shut.

He put the Glock on the table next to the facedown photo of his boy.

He flopped into the recliner, pulled a blanket over his legs, and tucked his sockless foot underneath. Transfixed by the darkness outside, he groaned and muttered, "Fucking kids." The laptop was where it always was, on the floor beside him. He reached for it, lifted it, and opened it on his lap. While he waited for it to boot up, his gaze fell over the gift from Gregory Sadler, the painting by Henry Hult. It was an original; there was only one in the world, and it was Rooker's. He thought that it could definitely be worth something, unlike Gunner's photographs. Rooker wondered what had happened to them. He figured they were in some kind of evidentiary vault; he didn't really care. If they were ever given back to him, he surely didn't want them.

Rooker spent the next hours scouring everything he could find on Malin Jakobsson. He started from ground zero—NamUs, or the National Missing and Unidentified Persons System.

Missing Person #MP27431 was Malin Alice Jakobsson. She grew up in Grand Rapids. Age twenty-six at the time she went missing. Last contact: May 6, 2010. She was last seen by friends in the evening at Celebration Cinema Grand Rapids North. Her current age would be thirty-four Height: five foot four. Weight: 126 pounds. Caucasian. Hair and eye color both listed as brown. She owned a vehicle that went missing, a 2004 Jeep Grand Cherokee. Seeing her face gave him the chills. A face so full of conventional beauty: full lips, a dainty freckled nose, and perfectly plucked brows, with silky brown waves of hair parted in the middle. He imagined her face now, ruined. Rooker printed the profile along with a newspaper article about her disappearance.

A few hours later, he hadn't found much else of interest, aside from some documents relating to a court case with Soren Jakobsson, Malin's father, as the defendant. That it was underway only weeks after Malin went missing was interesting, though it was for a DUI. He stared at her photograph for a couple of minutes longer before closing it out.

A glimpse of marmalade in the sky made him picture a world on fire. In Rooker's mind, it appeared as though the world was crumbling to ash beneath flames. Even the horizon's cotton-candy blues and pinks couldn't shake the image. He saw ruin and death. He saw locust swarms and hissing yellowjackets, little white worms wriggling over the scraps of bodies. He didn't need to search deep down to know that it was what the loss of his boy had done to him.

The world had failed him. And now he saw it for what it was. It was a place where evil not only lived and breathed, it triumphed. It made him think of the note and how, yet again, evil was knocking at his door.

Chapter 6

The second-story bedroom still reeked of mothballs. Millie's grand-mother had left the farmhouse to her. It was built on a half-acre plot of land in 1876, with a wraparound front porch and white railings and thin square columns that nested a few swallows and house spiders.

She'd spent a lot of time here in her youth, a Minnesota girl through and through. At the age of ten, it was here that she'd picked off her first gopher and garter snake in the same day with a Win Action pellet gun. In spite of the redness that painted her cheeks and earlobes, the cold months in Itasca County hadn't fazed her. She'd stay outside until sup-per and come back filthier than the neighborhood boys. While everyone else treated her like a child prodigy, Nana let her be who she was. And when she was meant to be her class valedictorian, she let her grades slip just enough, because she was too afraid to make the graduation speech. Nana knew and never told.

Nana Mildred always wore one of a collection of wool coats, which were stored in the bedroom closet behind white bifold doors that opened outward. After she passed, Millie was the one who had opened the closet doors to find a pile of opaque white dust on the wood floor. Pungent, like cleaning acid and tobacco smoke. She had never seen the little crystals before.

That's when she saw something—shriveled little cocoons that she thought were dead maggots in the corner.

Moments after the doors creaked open, a hundred of them—wings fluttering, dirty shades of beige and brown—swarmed her.

She batted them out of the room, out through the open window with an old dustpan and broom.

The coats were classic. *Chic,* as her nana would have said. Mostly three-quarter length, with different colors and collars and buttons, that made Nana look and feel like Audrey Hepburn. They might've been worth something, had they not mildewed or been chewed through by larvae, holes the size of cigarette burns void of scorch rings.

Millie Langston stared past her reflection at the cardboard box collecting dust on her nightstand. She never thought the contents of her desk would fit so tidily, like *Tetris* pieces falling perfectly into place. There was something sad about the fact that there was still room inside the cardboard walls. Maybe it was a sign that leaving the department was the right move. That's what she told herself anyway.

But all sixteen weeks in Minneapolis at the academy now seemed to be a waste. The studying, fieldwork, polygraphs, firearms training, patrol procedures, crisis intervention, self-defense, criminal investigation, the list went on. Test after test after test. She had learned how to reload her service weapon under duress. She had learned what to use for cover and concealment against an active shooter. She had learned the easiest ways to incapacitate someone bigger than her.

Now it was all for nothing.

Of course her instructors had noticed she had a knack for cybercrimes. Minneapolis PD sent her to take all sorts of courses and ultimately tried to keep her on by offering her a spot on a task force for special crimes, either on their Electronic Crimes Task Force or Internet Crimes Against Children. She'd turned them down.

People kept telling her she could go work for the private sector. A computer forensics specialist wanted to refer her to a colleague responsible for protecting systems and confidential information at Homeland Security. Ultimately, she got a call that was different from the rest. It was a woman who told her she'd be an asset to her team. Millie chose a badass female lead investigator in Itasca County—where the grandmother she was named after lived.

She chose Tess Harlow.

And she'd chosen wrong.

Before the Sadler murders, Millie had hardly used any of what she learned. Instead, she hunkered down behind her desk every day and did research and paperwork and answered the phones. Took apart her service pistol and cleaned it while everyone else went out into danger. Perfecting the skill of barista art, she taught herself to make a heart in her coffee with milk. If anything, maybe she could work at a Starbucks. Then, briefly, she really was a part of something, first poring over files with Rooker late into the night, then poring over Rooker's life as Tess's suspicions grew. And there every step of the way those last few terrifying days. But after the dust settled, the boys closed ranks again, and Tess became distant—just her boss. The only person who seemed to remember she existed was Rooker.

In her eyes, she was as good as any one of them, maybe better. But she never got a chance to prove it.

Good job, Mill. You just helped track down a serial killer . . . why aren't you working for Homeland Security or working a cybersecurity task force at the Bureau?

Instead, you're here. Badge-less.

But she was ready to take her skills elsewhere, freelance. As a private investigator, she could be her own boss. She could pick and choose whatever cases she wanted and consult with Rooker.

She stared at her phone. Why wasn't it ringing off the hook?

She plopped down behind her desk. Leaned back into the cold leather, the black-and-white chair resembling the seat in a race car. There was a desktop PC setup that cost her a pretty penny. An Alienware 4K gaming monitor where she played *League of Legends* and *Counter-Strike: Global Offensive*. An Alienware Aurora R7 tower with two terabytes of storage and thirty-two gigabytes of memory. A top-of-the-line NVIDIA GeForce graphics card. A backlit Logitech G Pro Wireless mouse.

In front of the second monitor, a picture frame was facedown on the desk. It was a trick she'd learned from Rooker. If you wanted to avoid the truth, don't stare it in the face.

She picked it up and observed herself standing beside Tess Harlow. Martin Keene had an arm clasped around the necks of Xander Whitlock and Vic Sterling. She smiled. She glanced at the scissored cutout where she'd removed Elias Cole's head.

She missed the team. But not enough to go back with her tail between her legs. Not ever.

Half an hour later, Millie was ambling around the lower level of what she still referred to as Nana's home, mulling over what she'd eat for breakfast, when four knocks sent a chill up her spine.

No one ever came to Nana's. Not since she passed away.

She went to the door and pulled a sheer curtain from one of the glass panes that bordered it. It was a cop. One she wasn't supposed to have known.

The low voice penetrated the wooden door. "Millie Langston?"

In a single motion, her right hand unlatched the chain, and her left hand twisted the bolt lock above the knob. She swung open the door.

A waft of autumn wind and mint aftershave breathed in her face. It made her want to take a step back. But she didn't.

The man had a scraggly dirty-blond beard that reminded her of a bird nest and short, light hair barely long enough to spill out beneath the bill of his brown cap. He had the physique and demeanor of former military.

"And who might you be?"

"Detective John Riggs." He flashed an Itasca County sheriff's badge at her.

She inspected the shine of it longer than she should have, as if she were analyzing a counterfeit bill. His face was that of someone who'd consumed a stale bite while he put the badge away. "You mean Jonathan Francis Riggs Jr. Graduated the academy two years ago. Twenty-eight years old. Father was an army ranger. Mother a nurse at Fairview."

"Guess you're as good as they say, huh? Probably have my transcripts somewhere too?"

She smiled sarcastically. She did.

"Left me some tough shoes to fill, I'll be honest."

"Can't say I'm sorry about that," she said. "They give you my desk?"

"May I?" He nodded to the room past her.

She hesitated. "Shoes off. Nana would throw a fit if she saw you mark up her floor."

He slipped his heels out of his shoes one by one and placed them carefully next to the door. He stepped inside. She noticed him scan the room quickly before he spoke.

"To answer your question: no, actually. First time I walked into the station, I felt like the new kid at school, didn't feel like I belonged. Didn't know the first thing to say. Didn't know if I was meant to sit or stand. They gave me the dead guy's desk. Cole."

"Might be better off burning that one. See if they'll buy you a new one."

"Yeah, well, they left yours exactly how it was. It's like there's a ghost sitting in that chair. They're still hoping you'll come back."

"So, what is it you're doing here, Riggs?" She left the door open. Stared at the blue Ford Transit parked out front at the curb. "And who might be in the van with you?"

"I came alone."

"*Bullshit you did.* Xander or Vic?"

He said nothing. She took a step closer to him. Then another. Could smell the odor on his clothes. *"Bullshit."* She stepped out on the front porch and hollered at the unmarked Ford. "Get up here, Sterling!"

Just then, the passenger door opened a crack, and she watched Vic Sterling hop out of the seat in black boots, chewing what she assumed was the last bite of a sub—he was a regular at Matt & Mitch's Sandwiches on the corner of Seventh Ave—and crumple the wrapper in his fist. "Here's a tip: no matter how cold it is outside, if you drive with him, leave the window down."

Sterling jogged up the steps with his signature charming smirk and perfectly groomed stubble. He wore black pants and a matching quilted bomber jacket unzipped over a plain white T-shirt. The shirt didn't have a single wrinkle. While she contemplated how steep the jacket price tag was—Vic never dressed modestly—she watched as he wiped bread flakes from the corner of his mouth. "Millie," he said with a warm smile.

"Good to see you too, Vic."

The space between them was filled with nothing but unease. Silence crackled like wool on her skin. Still, as harmless as it was, the angst seemed as perilous as poisonous thorns. That was, until Sterling closed the gap, kissed her cheek, and wrapped her in a cold embrace. In spite of the bear hug he had her in, the zipper of his jacket digging into her skin and the smell of cold mayonnaise from his mouth, she hoped it wouldn't end as quickly as it did.

He started to slip his shoes off before she stopped him with a hand on his arm. "You sent the new guy to my door, Vic? Some balls on you."

"I'm sorry." He rolled up one of his ribbed sleeves and scratched at his arm. "I didn't wanna be the one to do it."

"Well, now we're finally getting to the matter at hand. What do you guys want?"

Sterling leered at John Riggs, whose eyes nearly fell out of his head onto the floor. "We have something. Did you see Larsson's press conference last night—about the girl in the water?"

"Yes," she said, trying to keep her voice disinterested.

"Well, the message that reporter mentioned, the one Larsson didn't want to discuss? It was left for Rooker. Really creepy stuff—a picture of a dead bird, asking him to come out and play. And the girl we found in the water—there's something really wrong about it too. About all of it. What was left of her—burn damage like you wouldn't believe but only to targeted areas of her body. It doesn't make sense."

"You think she was tortured. Killed."

"Yeah, I do. Tess isn't so sure, though."

"Why?"

"You know her, Mill. She's not one to wear her emotions on her sleeve. But if I had to guess, I think she's afraid of another case like the last one. Afraid of what it'll take from her. Afraid that if she makes one more slipup, Larsson will sideline her."

She shrugged. "What do you want from me?"

"We want to know what you think."

Her brow furrowed. The flesh at her cheeks burned. It was a cold, thudding, head-turning slap in the face. "I'm sorry. You thought you could just come here and ask me for help?"

"Millie, c'mon." He sighed. "Help us find out what the hell's going on here. Tess tried to talk to Rooker last night, but he—"

"Told her to go fuck herself?" Vic just stared at her. She heard Riggs clear his throat. "So did *she* put you up to this?"

"Who? *Tess?* No. I swear—"

"You're a piece of work, Vic. *Really.* Riggs, *great* to meet you," she said sarcastically. "But the two of you can leave now."

"Mill . . ."

"I don't owe you or her *anything*. Before you try, don't lecture me about ongoing investigations; I know how it works. I'll see you around, Vic."

She nudged Riggs toward his shoes and made him put them on out on the porch, after she'd already shut the door and locked it behind him.

She grabbed her phone and tried calling the cottage. Answering machine. Of course he wouldn't be awake yet. She left a message: "Rooker, what the hell is going on?"

Chapter 7

BANG! BANG! BANG!

Rooker's eyelids snapped open. Three booming thuds, the cadence of semiautomatic gunfire. He nearly leaped to his feet, but the blinding white light stopped him in his tracks. His chest raced. His mind wide awake before his body. When he looked to the door, there was no one. Odd.

It was noon. Just as he was prepared to recline even farther in the chair and do nothing with the rest of his afternoon, he heard tires spitting out gravel down the drive. His eyes nearly rolled back into his skull. He hoisted himself up and peered out the window at an unexpected sight: instead of Millie's vehicle or the usual police cruiser, he saw a gunmetal-gray Porsche SUV with a gleaming grill in the drive.

Out stepped a fifty-something woman in a pair of light, high-waisted jeans and a quilted coat over a black turtleneck sweater. She walked quickly toward him, fidgeting with a black Louis Vuitton purse swaying over her shoulder.

Rooker pulled the door open and stood on the porch, arms folded, observing her.

"Mr. Lindström?"

He winced. Looking into the trees and then back to her, he said: "This is private property."

The woman before him had an air of wealth and a face that matched. Her cheekbones sat high and unwrinkled. Her unblemished skin was stretched like wax, with a sheen of a wet apple. It could've been a skin-care routine, but Rooker guessed it was Botox.

"I'm sorry for intruding, Mr. Linds—"

"Rooker," he interrupted. "Rooker is fine."

She nodded. "My daughter is missing."

There was a long pause on his end before he said tersely, "I can't help you." He turned on his heel.

"She's been missing for five days," she said. Her voice climbed an octave higher as he neared the inside of the house. "I know the statistic; if someone isn't found in the first two . . ."

He turned his head toward her. "Miss?"

"Vandenberg."

"Ms. Vandenberg," he said as he looked down to meet her gaze. "I'll be honest with you. Statistics don't mean shit to me." He peered into the sadness in her eyes. Two sunken circles hung on him, clouded and dim blue. They were the eyes of a person who had cried so much, they probably couldn't shed a single tear. "I can reach out to the police, but that's about all I can do."

"The police can't help me," she said.

"Why is that?"

"I saw the news. The police are looking for a killer," she said. "Not a missing girl."

"Try the FBI, then. They have some of the best profilers in the world, people who can track her down. That isn't me."

"I drove all the way out here. I'm just asking for a few minutes of your time." When he didn't petition, she added: "May I?"

Rooker hesitated. He wanted to talk to Soren Jakobsson and had planned to track him down. Now that'd have to wait. He moved aside for her. Ms. Vandenberg stepped into the room. Her neck twisted as though it were made of rubber as she took in the dreary space probably noticing all its imperfections down to the different wood stains on the floor.

"Coffee?"

"Not much of a coffee person," she said. "Tea if you have it."

"Fresh out," he lied. "Afraid your options are water or vodka."

"I'm okay."

She moved toward Geralt, who perched plump as a pheasant on the back of Rooker's chair. The back was threadbare, rigid with loose stitching where he'd sharpened his claws. If you sat wrong, a spring would clang somewhere beneath the cushion, but it was comfortable. As she grew closer, his mouth turned to a snarl and he hissed low, his tail slowly whipping back and forth.

"He bites," Rooker said. That stopped her in her tracks. And then Rooker strolled over to Geralt, whose eyes unnarrowed as his fluffy white head rubbed into Rooker's scarred knuckles. He smiled once he heard the rumbling purr, but it dimmed when he remembered his guest. "Do you want to sit?" He was hoping that she wouldn't, that this would be a quick visit where he'd show her that she didn't want his help.

But she did. The cushion of the new sofa melted slowly beneath her. It was a buttery caramel leather, with two wide cushions and four silver peg legs. Millie had picked it, said it would look modern, good in the space. Rooker thought it belonged in a therapist's office. He pictured a patient lying flat with the crook of their neck rested on the arm, staring up while they paid an obscene rate for someone to scalpel their brain. Neither he nor Geralt had sat on it once.

She dug through her bag and pulled out her wallet; she slipped a small photograph of a young woman from a flimsy clear sleeve and handed it to Rooker.

"Nora," she said, and the somberness in her tone carried to the dull blue in her eyes. "My baby girl."

Rooker didn't know what to say. He nearly said nothing but instead forged a sad smile and said: "Pretty."

"Beautiful." The woman smiled and nodded. "Even through those awkward teen years, some of her friends were gangly with braces, but she was always beautiful . . . Please, I need to find her."

Rooker stared at her. "There's no guarantee that I could. And in my experience, some things are better left unfound."

"How much?"

"Excuse me?"

"Everyone has a price, don't they?"

He laughed. "Please, just go."

"What?"

Rooker pointed with his chin. "Do you see that answering machine blinking red? The calls are nonstop. Offers to write a book about Gregory Sadler, to get a television series or movie rights rolling. You see how I'm living—do you think I care about your money?"

"Then do it for my daughter."

"Your daughter probably went out partying or is staying with her boyfriend."

"That's not her," she said, "not my Nora." She started riffling through her pocketbook once more.

"Lady, I don't want a check. I don't want your money."

But she pulled out a cell phone in a thin violet case and unlocked it.

"It's Nora's phone. I found it in her bedroom. This is one of the last messages she received." She held it up for Rooker, and he saw a short exchange from a number with a blocked caller ID.

I SEE YOU.

Who is this?

Rooker's body went cold. For a moment, it reminded him of that night months ago, stumbling through the piercing cold, floundering through shin-deep crests of snowfall to escape the gunman. Not the fear but the cold.

Numbing.

"Did you show this to the police?"

"Only to one of them. They said they'd look into it, but there may be nothing they could do. It was run through some program; they said it was probably a prank. One of her friends."

Considering his next words carefully, Rooker stared laboriously at the message. "It wasn't one of her friends."

Suddenly, he felt Ms. Vandenberg's eyes on him. He looked down and met them. "What?" she asked.

"What can you tell me about her? Age, height, weight, hair, and eye color?"

He wrote it all down after scribbling her name.

Nora Vandenberg.

25 Y.O. 5'4"/Slim. 100–110 pounds. Long brown hair. Hazel eyes.

"Boyfriend? Occupation?"

No boyfriend. Paralegal.

"If you could get me a few recent photos of her, I'd appreciate it." He gave her one of his email addresses, and she started scrolling through her phone for pictures of Nora. Rooker scanned Nora's contacts and recent emails and text threads with her actual friends. Everything else looked ordinary to him, but he wasn't as good at spotting these things as Millie.

And as though he'd summoned her with that thought, he heard another car door slam and footsteps on the creaky porch. Millie walked in the door with an army-green backpack slung over one shoulder and unbuttoned her jacket. "A visitor?" She smiled quizzically from Rooker to the woman on the couch, then took her jacket off, threw it on the hook by the door.

"Ms. Vandenberg, this is my partner, former detective Millie Langston. She's brilliant, and she puts up with me." Millie smiled cheerfully at their guest. "Millie, Ms. Vandenberg is looking for her daughter,

Nora. She hasn't been seen in five days. The cops are moving slow, but I think there's good reason to expedite the search." He showed Millie the text message, and the cheer drained from her face.

"Yes, I understand." Millie directed one of her trademark determined looks at Rooker. "Let's see what we can do."

"Our fee, Ms. Vandenberg, is $180 per hour with a $5,000 retainer. I hope that isn't an issue?" When Ms. Vandenberg shook her head, Rooker continued. "My partner and I will get to work right away."

"Who do I make the check out to?"

It was a good question. Millie often quipped about them having a name, but he always shot it down. Now, as he looked at her, she walked over to him and whispered: "Lindström and Langston?"

He turned his face toward her ear. "Told you that one sounds like we're a Swedish superhero team."

"Blur Investigations," she said.

He shook his head no.

"Night Owl Investigations."

"Hmm."

"Manor Investigations."

He cracked a smile, then fought it off before he turned to Ms. Vandenberg. "Manor Investigations," he said to her.

Ms. Vandenberg scribbled hard enough that Rooker could hear the scratch of the pen. She stood. While she put the check into Rooker's hand, a wintry palm clasped over his wrist.

"Thank you."

He nodded and held the door open for her.

"Did you just find us a client?" Millie said once Ms. Vandenberg was pulling away from the cottage.

"No. I found *you* a client."

"Come on, Rooker. For the last three months, I've been looking for something worth *our* time. I know you. What that woman said in here—for you to say yes, you're curious."

"And what are we? Private investigators?"

"Let me worry about that." She paused. "What do we tell Tess? I had a visitor today. Sterling and the new guy. They want help with the body in the park. Oh, and something about a creepy message being sent to you? Thanks for letting me know about that last part, by the way."

He winced. He caught her up on the few scraps of info he'd dug up on Malin Jakobsson. But as he recounted them, they seemed more random than they had in the dead of night. And the kids who had pranked him earlier were late to the party: he'd been the target of so many bored locals and serial-killer obsessives in the past months, was there really anything special about the "play with me" note? Maybe Tess was losing it—jumping at every shadow, looking for any way to stick him in the middle. And the thought of Sterling bringing Millie's replacement to her door left a sour taste in his mouth.

"Screw them. They have nothing. Hasn't even been ruled a homicide yet," he said. "Also, let's face it—there's not much we can do for Malin Jakobsson at this point. Nora, on the other hand . . . if that text message isn't just a sick coincidence . . ."

He could tell by Millie's silence that she didn't agree, though she didn't fight him on it.

"Are you all right?" he asked her.

"Just peachy. So how does this work?" she said to him. "We've got a name now. Guess I'll file for an LLC and open a bank account. Do we get a sign?"

"Maybe it's best not to invite *all* the crazies to my door just yet. You know, I do live here."

He stood at the back door, touched a finger to the bullet-pocked doorframe, the paint-chipped holes from the gunfight with Gregory Sadler. The police pulled three 9mm Jacketed Hollow Points out of the wall. For a moment, he imagined the bullet expanding, tearing a larger hole through his soft tissue. Anyway, he thought they added character, history to a historical home, so he didn't patch over them.

While he looked out at the lake beneath a pleasant sun, he thought Deer Lake might really be magnificent. In the moments he wasn't submerged in conversation with Millie, he shut his eyes and listened to the gentle claps and gurgles of water, the breeze coming off it like tiny hands tugging on the hem of his shirt. The wind crackled. And when he opened his eyes, he watched the somersaulting yellows and oranges in freefall to the ground. For some odd reason, he pictured a skydiver hurtling from the clouds, tumbling over and backward, the parachute jammed.

Chapter 8

If anyone could talk Tess off the ledge, it was the large man sitting across the dinner table. In the moments of silence between bites or the sound of a knife scrape or conversation, she listened to the rain bat against the old windows and the shingle roof. It only made her think of the day of the fire and how it had rained. Water and mud slithering over bones.

"He helped us catch Sadler. Why are you still after him?" Martin asked.

It'd been a while since she accepted an offer to come over for dinner. Martin must've told Sheila that she was upset, because her favorite meal was sitting in front of her: medium-rare sirloin steak with garlic butter and crinkle-cut truffle fries.

"Why?" She peered up at him. "Because a body was found beneath the floorboards, and it doesn't match his father's MO. That's why."

"Is that really it?"

Sheila sat and listened. By now, Tess knew she'd become used to cop talk. The days of telling the two of them that this wasn't *dinner conversation* were long gone.

"What do you mean, is that 'it'? He helps us catch a killer and he's excused from what he's done himself?"

"Look—we don't know that Rooker killed her. Who's to say it wasn't Gunner? Maybe something in that moment changed for him. Maybe it was Sadler. I want to find out who killed her just as much as you do, believe me. But we may never know." Martin sighed. "You're upset. I'm not saying you shouldn't be. But Sadler was murdering women under our nose. Now he's dead. Xander was shot. Walter Erickson is dead. Evelyn Holmberg is dead. The victims are dead. Millie's gone. So no, I don't think it's just about Rooker."

Here we go again, she thought. Another person who couldn't just agree with her. Everyone was making her think she was crazy. "When Larsson brought Cole. Shit"—her fork clanged on her plate—"*Sadler* into the station, *I* thought he was a great fit. Funny, huh? When we couldn't catch a break with the murders, and after we cleared Rooker, *I* brought him on to help us, despite everyone who thought it was a bad idea. *I* am the one who keeps fucking up. Making these damn mistakes."

She looked at Sheila. "Sorry." She pulled her wallet out and dumped two folded bills into a glass jar. Another night the Keenes profited off her cursing. She figured it would just help buy dinner next time around, since Sheila never let her.

Martin sighed. "Tell me this: How were you supposed to know it was Sadler all along sitting at that desk? As for the latter, I think bringing Rooker in was the best decision you made. Without him connecting the dots to Gunner's case, who knows if we ever would have gotten Sadler."

She didn't answer.

She stared down at her plate. For a moment, she didn't realize what she was doing. The room went numb. And then she heard Martin's voice.

"Hon, can you grab another bottle of wine, please?"

"The cabernet or pinot noir?"

"Cabernet, please."

Sheila dropped her napkin by her plate and went into the kitchen. Suddenly, she felt Martin's hand close softly around her wrist. He pulled the steak knife away from her fingertips. "Hey," he said. She blinked hard. And then she saw the drop of red trickle away from her scar.

"Shit," she whispered. "Sorry."

Martin wiped the blood away with his napkin. "You need to talk to someone."

Looking up at him, she said, "What do you think I'm doing?"

Martin laughed. "I'm not a therapist—"

"Please," she interjected. "You've been my therapist for years. I just don't pay you."

"Well, I don't want you to come to dinner and use my best steak knife to slice your finger open."

Ashamed, she closed her eyes and raised her brow. It was a manner that said, *This is what I've come to.*

When Sheila came back and set a bottle of Chateau Montelena down on the table, Tess produced a cordial smile and sauntered to the restroom. She closed the door behind her. Staring into her reflection, she washed her finger off, then splashed a handful of cold water on her face. Patted her cheeks dry with a towel.

She pulled out her phone and scrolled through the images of the body found under the floor of Lindström Manor. She dialed Isaiah Hayes.

"Hayes, it's Tess." She paused. Looked over her shoulder as if a phantom moved through the wall. Watching her. Hayes made her flesh crawl, but he was one of the best at what he did. For a moment, Tess imagined him beneath harsh light, skin waxy and pale as one of his cadavers, his veins actually purple worms wriggling beneath translucent skin. "If you find anything on that body we recovered at Lindström Manor, call me ASAP. And do me a favor? Don't assume she's one of Gunner's."

She ended the call.

She went back to the table, determined to finish her dinner without further meltdowns or bloodshed.

After a few quiet bites, Martin leaned forward. "So what do you want to do?"

Jan Cullen and Clyde Miller appeared in her mind, faster than she could shake the thought of them away. "I want all these psychopaths behind bars. I want to figure out who killed that girl," she said. "And if it was Rooker, I want him to pay for it."

Chapter 9

After a bunch of dead ends and phone calls to Nora's contact list, Millie and Rooker had plenty of details on Nora's routine and no leads on who or what had disrupted it nearly a week ago. After Millie left, Rooker's mind kept spinning. Lindström Manor had an unnerving way about it. It did little to dampen the screams of the wind, or the shifting of weight inside that resembled the sound of someone's heels dragging, or the scraping rock of a wooden chair. When the home fell silent, it only made the demons in his head all the more present, as if they were lurking in the corners of his mind, watching. On the other hand, Tess's bitter words were buzzing loud in his brain.

Though he wasn't one for crowds anymore and hadn't gotten dressed up to go out in public in ages, he needed some background noise tonight. He put on the nicest clothes he had: a navy poplin shirt with white buttons, undone at the top; black jeans and black leather Chelsea boots; with a Bremont pilot's watch clasped around his wrist—a gift from his boy (through his wife) for his fortieth. And knowing full well that he'd be too drunk to drive himself home later, he called a cab to take him into Grand Rapids. A real cab. No Uber or Lyft—he was old-fashioned that way.

He asked the cab driver—a Bengali man named Devesh with a bald head circled with a crown of white hair—to take him to his favorite spot, wherever that may be, and after cruising past an A&W, a wholesale bait shop, and at least four auto parts stores, they'd ended up at the Moonshiner, a basement bar that was far nicer than its name would suggest.

Even though it was late, a crowd in their midthirties and early forties lingered on the barstools. Most of the men were dressed in oxford shirts, their collars unbuttoned after what Rooker assumed to be a long workday. The women had an array of half-full cocktail glasses before them, some dressed as if they just clocked out of work, and a few with necklines that accented their cleavage. Empty wine bottles with fairy lights inside dangled above booth seating, their glow dim against uneven walls of white stone. The back of the bar and the stools were a dark mahogany. The bar top and tables were wooden as well but much lighter, the shade of the lanes in a bowling alley. A man on the downside of thirty in a pristine-white tuxedo shirt and filthy black apron paced behind the bar. Ginger wisps of hair bounced from his man bun. Muttonchop whiskers ran the length of his jaw. For a moment, Rooker imagined him sporting the same look at sixty and pictured a slightly taller Mario Batali. He'd been hoping for more of a dive bar, one with mismatched stools and a jukebox no one bothered to plug in, but apparently he'd done too good of a job pulling himself together, and Devesh had overestimated him. But this would do.

Walking past not one empty seat at the bar, he kept his head down and settled into a booth in the far corner. A young blonde in a scoop neck white tee and striped apron appeared, and he ordered a screwdriver, since it was technically morning. *No fruit.*

A couple of minutes later, he came to his senses and ordered a vodka tonic. It was his father's drink of choice. He didn't necessarily enjoy the smell of it or the taste. The second the tall glass was put on the table in front of him, he conjured the image of it lingering on his father's hot breath. Gunner would hunch right in his face, salivating as a rabid dog, spittle foaming and flying out of his mouth. Rooker lifted it to his lips and downed half of it before wiping his mouth. In the farthest corner seat, he could see everything. He watched the other patrons, and they all seemed like animals: flapping their arms, clucking as they spoke with their hands. The croak of a heavyset man. Their lips as they squawked birdlike. He plucked one of the hushed conversations like a feather from the air. For a few minutes, he stared into his drink, dragged the water bubbles beneath his glass, eavesdropping on workplace-romance gossip.

He was growing bored when he saw her walk up to the bar. Auburn hair with hints of cabernet red shining beneath the soft bar lighting. She had the petite figure of a clothing designer's illustration, the mockup, the first draft of a garment before it was made. Her face was angular, lips the color of red velvet cake, eyes like two grayish-blue pools he wanted to drown in. She took a seat at the end of the bar close to his booth, said nothing, and the bartender slid a vodka cranberry her way. Rooker watched her twirl the drink on the bar top, the ice clinking against the glass, and take a hard gulp. She had small hands, thin and delicate and ringless, her nails the shade of pink lemonade. The image of them wrapped around his member burrowed its way into his brain like a tick. Moments later, he pictured her in a busty yet classy white dress and a silk veil walking down the aisle toward him. Funny how the male mind worked.

She took a sip that lingered, her eyes closed and the glass still lifted to her lips. Her backside shifted in her seat—he knew because he was looking at it, too long to notice she was now staring at him.

"To what do we owe the pleasure tonight?" she said. "A celebrity in our very midst." She put her glass down, and Rooker looked at the faint yet perfect outline of her bottom lip.

"It's actually morning," he said, ignoring the fact that she knew who he was.

"The famous Rooker Lindström."

Rooker peered off, diverting his eyes from hers to the white stone behind the bar. "Think you got the wrong guy," he said.

"Think you forgot the part where I said 'famous.'"

"That right? I'm famous now? And who might you be?"

"Caroline."

"Pretty name."

"Is that your best line?"

"You didn't let me finish. The rest of it was, *But not as pretty as your eyes.*" He raised his glass in a mock toast and took another gulp.

She smiled and sat down across from him.

"I thought you were a hermit, locked away in that cave of yours where your father did his work. Rumor is you only come out when there's a killer to be found."

Where your father did his work. He liked that. It made his father sound like a woodworker, a builder of something. But really, he did the opposite. He took women apart.

"Hmm . . . something like that. The last part is a little off."

He took a sip of his drink while he watched her.

"So you didn't come out to play?"

Now he watched her tilt his glass to her lips and take a sip of her own, her eyes hanging on him. He paused, smiled, and took another swallow. "Which station?"

She didn't answer.

"Must have a pretty good source. I don't believe the police have released what the note said."

"Oh, you *are* good. One of the anchors for WCCO. I'm a little disappointed you don't recognize me."

"So, what, you're following me? What do you want, a quote? An exclusive?"

"A drink."

"There's a look about a person who wants a drink, and then there's the look someone gives when they *need* one. Wouldn't say you have either."

"Are you an expert?"

"I fought the bottle harder than I ever fought my father, harder than I fought for my marriage."

"What do you think that says about you?"

"Says I'm a coward in more ways than one."

"Plenty of people lose that battle."

"Yeah, well. After . . . I used to hide it like an affair. It's how I've coped with . . . *things*."

"*A drink before the war* . . . you could say." She smiled.

He lifted his head, and a grin spread over his face. "You've read Dennis Lehane?"

"Looks and brains, I know. Most men can't accept it."

He raised his glass to her, smiled, and drank.

"Since we're on the topic, I hear you and that former detective Millie Langston teamed up. Rumor is she's a PI now. What's that make you?"

"Word travels fast around here, huh?"

"Like I said—whether you like it or not, you're a celebrity."

A drink wasn't all she wanted after all.

Twenty-five minutes later, Rooker took a cab with her, back to the home for one Caroline Lind, thirty-one years old, recently broken-off engagement. When he learned of it, he figured himself to be a one-night stand she'd get rid of by morning, but he didn't mind. Her head rested on his shoulder the entire ten-minute drive, her hand on his inner thigh. He tried to think about baseball, his grandmother, whatever it was that people tell you to think of. It was no use.

Rooker paid the cabdriver, held the door open, and closed it behind her. Looking up, he descried the two-story with a peaked roof and a window the shape of a half-moon on the second level, which he couldn't help but feel staring at him. In the dark, the white trim and pillars glowed over dark pavers like moonlit water. Crunching over leaves in the smothering black, she pulled him by a warm hand, laughing while she struggled to unlock the door in the dark and pulled him inside for a kiss.

He could tell instantly that it was no good-night kiss. "Maybe I should get going," he said.

But her face suddenly sobered. Her fingers found the front of his pants, pinched the tab of his zipper, and pulled it down while she kissed him. She twisted the button and slid his pants down, bit his bottom lip, and said, "Maybe you shouldn't." His face turned hot, some shade of pink or fire-engine red hopefully not noticeable in the dark. The door swung closed. Her set of keys rattled when she put them on the counter. She pulled him toward the staircase, where he kicked his pants the rest of the way off and followed her up to the bedroom.

The bed was made. She kissed him again on the lips and told him to turn around. His eyes wandered around the room, the six-drawer white dresser with some clothing and picture frames on top, the hamper overflowing in the corner. His eyes fell on the mirror, one nearly as tall as he was, just a few feet shy of standing nearly floor to ceiling. Until she saw her own reflection, saw him watching.

"No peeking."

He turned back around, his face flush with her having caught him. He stood there in his underwear until her arms startled him. She wrapped around him snakelike; one of her hands covered his eyes while the other pulled his underwear down. She pushed him back onto the bed. He inched up on his elbows, but she pushed him back down and straddled him.

When it was over, he breathed hard and fell forward on top of her. His hand waved around in the darkness beside the bed until his fingertips snagged against his underwear. He kissed her on the lips. He was about to get up from the bed, but she grabbed the back of his arm, pulled him to where he was behind her, his hand on her breast, and he drifted asleep to the rhythm of her breathing, a tidal ebb and flow.

Chapter 10

Her hands were steady.

There were only a handful of times in her past that she could remember them shaking. The first time she fired a rifle—a Mossberg Patriot bolt-action that her grandfather would take out when he hunted deer (but mostly brought home wild turkey). The only time she'd ever ridden a horse. That one always came to mind. His name was Gunsmoke. Dark gray with white hooves and black eyes she'd never forget. Still, she wasn't nervous until lightning struck. A white flash tore open the sky. Before she knew it, she was in the air, then flat against her back. Frozen. Wheezing. Afraid. From the ground, she stared through the haze of tears at a swarm of black. At first, she thought she was losing vision. But then far enough away, they took on the form of a single uneven black streak, soaring and cawing unpleasantly. Crows.

"Flash out," she said. Switching from her knife to her M4A1 assault rifle, she moved up along the cinder block wall. "Fall back off that!" She fired. The enemy in her crosshairs fell to the ground. "One down. Bomb's down long. Somebody rotate Cat." To those who play *Counter-Strike: Global Offensive*, in her mind one of the greatest team-based first-person-shooter games ever created, *Cat* was short for *Catwalk*.

She slow-peeked wide at the set of double doors. When she fired twice, she got the final kill and the round ended.

Games were always an escape for Millie Langston. An escape from reality. An escape from the pressure of maintaining perfect grades. An escape from the snobby girls throughout grade school who talked about their nails and their outfits and boys. An escape from the snobby girls throughout high school who talked about their nails and their outfits and sex with boys. Who had done it and who hadn't. What it was like. But ever since she could remember, she gravitated toward the boys. At first, they were intimidated by her. But she quickly became a friend. She had more in common with them.

The exception was her best friend, whom she'd met in the third grade. Barbara Collins. But Barb wasn't like the other girls either. The two of them built model rockets and re-created the Death Star out of Legos and played a version of night tag, which they'd helped invent, with the boys.

She'd never forget the first game she played. *Duck Hunt* on the old Nintendo NES. She'd sit and watch her uncle Lonnie play; he was pencil thin and chain-smoked Newports, but he was her fun uncle. There was a little gray-and-orange gun called the Zapper that came with the console. Within an hour of playing, she was better than he was. She'd been playing games ever since. She'd played in LAN tournaments with a team of friends. She'd earned a little cash when she placed in tournaments. But for her, games were just plain fun.

In her peripheral, she caught an email notification that came through on her second monitor. She turned her head. Her eyes narrowed. It was from Tess.

From: Tess Harlow
Date: September 21, 2019, 12:17 GMT
Subject: He's not who you think.

She sighed. "I'm going AFK." As much as she didn't want to put the game on hold, her team was ahead thirteen rounds to four. She pulled her microphone off her head, placed it on the table, and ran her fingers through her hair. Then she downed a few more gulps of her energy drink, ran the cursor over the email, and opened it.

The message area was blank. But there was a folder there at the bottom marked: LindströmManor.pdf.

She double-clicked on the file.

Up came a series of thirty-two images. She knew from the very first one what she was going to find. It was the aftermath of the fire.

Blackened two-by-four. Charred roof. Ash.

She even knew what Tess was insinuating: that Rooker had killed the girl beneath the floor. She did find it odd that Rooker never spoke about the girl they found. Not once. She couldn't help but be curious about the body. She wondered if he knew who she was, and if he knew she was there all along. She couldn't just ask. But she didn't believe he'd killed her. It was just a feeling she had. Anyway, in order to work with him, she couldn't believe he'd done it. Whether Tess was truly looking out for her or was attempting to drive a wedge between her and Rooker, she couldn't know for certain. Millie thought Tess was cracking; all the stress of the job was turning her paranoid and delusional. Hell, maybe it was just a ploy to get Millie back on the team. Maybe Tess wanted her back as a glorified IT person, conducting research and organizing files.

No chance in hell.

He's not who you think. The pot calling the kettle black. If anyone had ended up someone other than who she thought, it was Tess. Millie had found out her secret: the police report filed by Joe Harlow. Tess's father had put a search out on two men he believed assaulted his wife, Janice. Not long after Joe Harlow died, the same two men—Jan Cullen and Clyde Miller—were shot outside a nightclub. Cullen said it was a woman who did it. Millie knew it was Tess.

When she got to the bones of the victim's face, her palm hovered over the mouse. She froze. So what if the girl still had a head? That didn't mean Rooker was the killer. It didn't mean much of anything.

But for some reason, even after she closed out of it, her hands were shaking.

◆ ◆ ◆

In the morning, she drove out to the old rod and gun club just south of Grand Rapids. It wasn't so much a club as it was a trailer with a few guns on the wall, a tiny restroom with a couple of seconds' worth of hot water, and an open pavilion made of exposed brown wood. Her uncle Lonnie owned it. Eight makeshift lanes—some of them with white lattice fence dividers that could've been stolen from a home garden—sculpted a shoddy private range of dead grass and a variety of cheap targets. When she parked and got out, a tall, thin man with the heavy odor of cologne jogged her way. "Hey, Mill." He smiled.

She cocked her head in his direction. "Hey yourself."

She fell into her uncle Lonnie's embrace, a hug that made the bones in her shoulders pop. "Wanna give me a hand with something inside?"

"Sorry," she said. "I don't work for free."

"From what I hear, you don't work at all anymore." He smiled. "How do I get into that?"

"Funny. You think all that cologne is covering the cigarettes?"

"Maybe you weren't a bad detective after all. I tried the damn gum, y'know? It didn't take. Thought I was chewing paper." He scratched the hairs that were taken left and right by the wind. "You're not still bringing in that damn .357."

"It's a classic."

"*Exactly.* Firearms have evolved, niece. Say you get shot at with that thing, you fire six times. Open the cylinder. Unload it. Reload six shots.

64

You might as well just stand up and yell, *Wait! Time out! Let me reload!*" He laughed. "Retire that gun already."

She smiled. "I brought my .45. Don't worry, old man. I'll still outshoot you."

Uncle Lonnie was thin but a bit fatter now in the belly. The two of them set their cases and guns on a table in side-by-side booths. The other six stalls were empty.

With a blank stare, Millie peered down at the two guns and two boxes of ammunition.

The cigarette rasp in Uncle Lonnie's voice caught her attention like a hard punch in the arm. "What's goin' on in that big head of yours, girl?"

Without turning toward him, she closed her eyes and smiled. "Nothing."

"Bullshit. I may never be as smart as you—hell, maybe no one is—but I can tell when something's the matter with you. Spit it out."

"I'm about to be working on something. Something big."

"New job?"

She nodded. "Something like that." She paused for a long while. "A girl went missing. Her parents came to us. Rooker—"

"You're working with that Rooker Lindström?"

Suddenly she remembered the images on her PC monitor. She shook the thought away. "Unofficially . . . Maybe officially. Who knows—"

"Thought that guy doesn't come out of that cottage?"

"Uncle Lonnie," she said sternly. "People say a lot of things, but they don't know him. He's good at what he does. Anyway, I'd be a private investigator. It pays well. And I'd be doing something *good.*"

"Millie." He shook his head. "You think I don't know you? I don't know what this is all about? You've had that bug up your butt since you were a little girl. Since that girl Amy went missing. You would ask me and your mom about it all the time."

"You sound like you're telling me to give up before I even get started."

"Mill, I wouldn't tell you to give up even if I wanted you to. Hell, we both know you wouldn't listen anyway. Just be careful."

She stared down the range. At the woods all around them. But every time she blinked, in the milliseconds she was meant to see the black of eyelids, all she saw were bones.

Chapter 11

She was gone.

The next morning, Rooker woke up crust-eyed, cheek pressed into the drool-sodden top sheet. His neck was stiff. White light seeped through the blinds. He lifted his head. Caroline wasn't there. Her side of the bed was cold. He wiped his mouth with his shoulder and blinked himself awake. There was something clutched in his hand. When he opened it, he saw that it was her card with her telephone number, a pink imprint of her lips smudged against it. Maybe she wanted to see him again after all.

He rolled over onto his back, his underwear folded on the edge of the bed. He slid them on, went to the bathroom, and dressed himself in yesterday's clothes. He figured she had work, probably had to spend a little extra time in front of the mirror this morning, slap a little more makeup on to look awake.

But just then, he heard the door downstairs, the set of keys rattling as they did last night. He heard her coming up the stairs slowly, wondered if she'd want him again. And then once the steps turned into the doorway, Rooker was perplexed.

"Well, no shit," the stranger said, a what-else-is-new smirk across his face. Right—there were two dressers. Caroline's ex-fiancé was as polished as she was. Tucked into black dress pants was a white collared shirt with a blue windowpane pattern. He donned polished leather derby shoes that shined uniformly with his jet-black waves of hair. A strand or two fell out of place over the right side of his forehead, purposeful if Rooker had to guess. He walked to the far dresser and started rummaging through it, throwing clothes into a gym bag. He slammed the drawers shut, swung the closet door open, and pulled down a few garment bags and hangered suits. When he was just about gone from the room, he grabbed the television remote, turned it on, and tossed the remote onto the bed.

"It's been on all morning. Looks like she fucked you pretty good too."

And just like that, he was gone.

The newscast. It was her. Caroline. A snippet replayed from the 7:00 a.m. broadcast. It was playing on WCCO-TV, a CBS-owned news station in Minnesota. It was one of the primary news stations, along with KARE and KSTP TV in Minneapolis and Saint Paul. The numbers on the bottom right of the television told him the same. It was 8:25.

There she was, perfectly postured in her seat like there was a stick up her behind. Her hands folded on top of the desk, a white button-up blouse and gold pendant necklace. She dressed in standard but gorgeous anchorwoman attire—as if there were a catalog for such a thing. Her hair flowed slightly more cinnamon on the air. She looked nearly as lovely as she did last night, without the faint milky glow of moonlight caressing her curves just perfectly.

"I had the chance to sit down with the notorious catcher of killers himself, Rooker Lindström." A box in the bottom right appeared, the muted video of him behind the podium playing.

Rooker sat down on the sheet and cracked his back against the headboard, then leaned forward with his arms crossed, elbows on the bones of his knees.

"Rooker Lindström caught Tate Meachum after the tragic loss of his son. And just months ago, he drowned Gregory Sadler, serial-killer detective under the alias Elias Cole, in the frozen lake behind the infamous Lindström Manor, not far from where Sadler was thought to have drowned as a boy in the winter of 1992."

Two photos flashed on the screen side by side as though they were accomplices in a crime. It was them. Meachum and Sadler.

Then a photo of Rooker appeared in the upper right.

"When asked if he would come out and play, like the note said, Rooker told me: 'I'm not some expert like you people make me out to be. I caught two killers who were connected to me in some odd way. They wanted me to find them. Despite the note, this time around is different. And my answer is still no.'

"And what would you say to the victims? I asked next.

"He replied, 'I'm not a surgeon, or a doctor, or a detective for that matter. I didn't sign up to save lives. I'm a man who wants to be left alone.'

"So what do you say to the killer who clearly left a message for you?

"'Get in line. But find someone else to play your game.'"

She was good. She'd set him up, got the exclusive "interview" she wanted. Her career would catapult now, fake quotes and all. The story would make headlines on the *Star Tribune* and the *Pioneer Press*. He could see a newspaper editor in a frenzy, scrambling for a caption-worthy quote. It was probably undergoing copyediting for tomorrow's paper. Good for her. He wasn't upset by it.

He pressed the red button on the remote. The screen went out like a flame. Rooker sat there wondering if he was just a moth to hers. He could still smell sex on the sheets as though it were spritzed from a bottled fragrance. He could still picture her naked body in the dark, how her skin felt soft and smooth beneath his calloused touch.

He called a cab, made his way downstairs and out the door.

Chapter 12

As a boy, he dug graves. He'd dig up the wet earth in the backyard and bury his mother's belongings. He'd hide his cousin's toys in the ground. Let the red worms wriggle over his filthy hands. He'd have intense dreams of digging up coffins six feet deep, just to see what was still inside. But it wasn't until high school that he'd shoveled a hole so wide—into the middle of the night until the muscles in his back and neck screamed—that he fell to his knees and cried tears of joy.

It was the first living creature he'd ever covered with dirt and soil and clumps of grass.

In the darkness, he stood. For him, it was a hollow space between two worlds. Limbo. Calm. Quiet. It made him feel like he was floating. Whenever he hid from his mother, it was always someplace dark. Back then, the pitch-black injected him with fear—not of the absence of light—but of the lurking, soundlessly still, waiting for her to find him. Hiding on the cold floor of the closet behind hangered jackets and spare quilts and empty shoeboxes. Those days were beyond them now. He didn't have to hide from her anymore.

◆ ◆ ◆

Five days ago, he took her. He'd waited for the girl to leave the office. He wore a white dress shirt with black trousers and leather loafers. A dark-brown wig that concealed his black hair as well as his balding crown and receding temples. When she came out, he'd pretended to be on an important phone call. It was almost 7:00 p.m., and she walked at a quick pace through the parking garage, a half-empty lot enclosed with a metal roof but open to the gentle breeze and misty rain. He knew her vehicle. He'd made sure to park close enough to her driver-side door that she'd have to squeeze through the narrow space to cram herself inside. He stood thirty feet away next to a different vehicle. There she was. In a dark pencil skirt and white top. He sent the text. She looked down at the phone in her hand, at the message from an unknown number. Her head whipped around.

There was no one.

Not behind you. I'm right here.

She was parked in B18. Another minute and she'd be inside her car. Home free. She walked faster. He could hear her heels now—black and glossy—clicking loud. Faster and faster. She was at a near jog when he pressed the phone into his ear and one of her heels snapped off. She lifted her foot and removed it and hobbled with the one shoe still on. When she got close to the car, that's when he pretended to end the call and play the role of the innocent passerby.

"Miss?" he asked in earnest. Producing a scene of slipping the phone into his pocket. "Is everything okay?"

Startled, she peered up at him. Shook her head. "No. I think someone may be following me."

He looked past her. His eyes narrowed. "I don't see anyone."

She turned fast, the heel of her shoe dangling in her hand. Then she looked back at him.

He walked toward her. "Do you want me to wait with you?"

"No—" she shot back. He froze. She said it too fast. Insulting. Then she raised her keys in her hand. They were shaking. "I'm sorry." She winced. "I'm parked here; I'll be fine—"

That's when, for the first time, she noticed how close the vehicle was to her car. She started to squeeze through. She bumped into the Jeep beside her new luxury sedan.

Daddy's money.

And then she felt him there. Just as close. Behind her. Close enough to feel his breath.

"It's okay," he told her. And then he recited the text message he'd sent to her phone. *"I see you."*

In the span of seconds, she felt the point of the needle and her body numbed. A few seconds later, unconscious. He'd injected her with midazolam. When she began to fall, he caught her and put her in the back of the Jeep. Her broken heel tossed in with her.

With a gloved hand, he grabbed her cell phone and stuffed it in his pocket.

◆ ◆ ◆

Down the basement stairs was a world where he could become his true self. Down there in the musty silence, the damp smell he loved, the soothing whimpers from the chair. It was a place of truth. But up in the light, he pretended. He'd hide his rage behind a mask.

"Did you know that witches weren't burned at the stake?" He walked slowly, each methodical step as he'd memorized, his eyes closed. His words echoed. "Not in America anyway. They were simply exe-cuted. Strangled to death. Hanged. Still, people believe what they want to believe, don't they?"

He reached the bottom step. Skulked in silence to the desk and found the mask beside a hangman's noose he'd tied. He slipped the mask over his head and wrapped himself in a black cloak that hung over a hook.

A metal string dangled not far from her. He sauntered to it. Pulled the chain. Her eyes were still too heavy to open. Not that she would have even if she could.

He stood in front of her. The mask inches from her face: his third victim.

"Hmm!" She mumbled softly. A string of mucus fell from her nostril, down over the silver tape that trapped her voice. Exhaustion, he knew. He'd given her nothing to eat since he'd brought her home.

He spoke again. "They *should have* burned them. Stoned them. Drowned them. If I remove the tape from your lips, you'd only spill lies. *Just like them.* Just like *her*. You'd do anything—*say anything*—to be free."

She didn't move.

He whispered, "Do you want to know what it sounds like when your flesh burns? The smell of it? No? It sizzles like a fine steak. Your skin blisters—bubbles like boiling water. Peeling. Blackening. Putrefying. The stench—to the uninitiated—*sickening*. Like charcoal and singed hair. No worse than that *perfume* . . .

"You'll try to kick. Fight. Scream. The restraints, I promise you, will hold. Your body will go into shock. You'll convulse; then your body will give out. But that is only the beginning of what awaits you."

He'd considered digging her a grave; he hadn't dug one for the last one. Ultimately, he decided he had bigger plans for them both. His fingers fell over the metal string, cold to the touch. He yanked it and stood still, watching her from behind the mask. Watching her from the darkness.

Chapter 13

"Rooker," Millie hollered to him from the doorway.

"Shit," he hissed. He'd called the number listed for Soren Jakobsson. The phone line was disconnected.

He bounced one last pebble in the center of his palm, gripped it, and launched it as far as he could into the air. While his eyes followed it, the sudden splash as it plunged into the water, he saw a shadow. Then a hand. *No. Not again.*

From the edge of the water, another hand reached for him. Rotting flesh. A black hole in the center of it. Gunshot. What was left was bone for two of the fingers, the other three pruned, sagging purple and white. He squeezed his eyes shut, felt a shudder behind them. Took a deep breath. He could still see it behind his eyelids.

Darkness. The deathly pale hand. The preserved grave: the water broken apart. It clawed at the frozen hill of earth just out of the lake. The biting cold choked him. The lake breathed down his neck. And at the same time, his skin grew hot, as though fire spat against his pores and sweat trickled down his forehead. He opened his eyes. It was gone.

He heard Millie say his name again, this time in a soothing tone. He turned to her.

"Yeah," he half hollered as he surveyed his surroundings. Crows squawked in the trees. He lumbered back to her, watching her cradle the laptop in one arm. Her neck twitched to keep the windswept hairs out of her face. He took one last look at the lake before he trudged up the stairs. Millie had settled on the therapist couch and was staring intently at the screen.

"Find something?"

"Does the name Warrel Haney ring a bell?"

Rooker shook his head.

"Haney is a conspiracy theorist. He believes the US government is running a child-trafficking ring, backed by the White House—thinks the government is using the children to lure and control politicians. Suffice it to say, he has a few screws loose. But he runs a site called PHENOMENA that has a disturbingly large following. He lives near Minneapolis."

"Where's this going, Millie?"

"The police have had him on their radar for a few years, and they keep tabs as best they can. Usually what he posts is bullshit. But he posted this last week." She faced the laptop to him. "He knows about the women."

Rooker squinted at the headline.

THE HEX OVER ITASCA COUNTY

Three women are believed to have gone missing according to my sources in blue, and the police are doing little to find them. Not only that, but is it really too far-fetched to expect that at least one of them is involved?

In recent events, a cold-blooded killer of women posed as a detective in the Itasca County Sheriff's Office. In the disappearances of three women: M.J., C.H., and N.V., who's to say it hasn't happened again?

The female victim found in Itasca State Park is believed to be a decade's old missing person's case. Police believe they know who she is. And let me tell you, the torture inflicted on the body is straight out of a horror flick. Black contusions all over her and burns deep enough to expose bone.

That isn't the worst of it. A black envelope was left on the body, addressed to someone *connected* to the police. Yes, I said "connected." My source tells me that the person the message was for is not a cop.

N.V. Haney knew about Nora Vandenberg even though her family had not yet made a public appeal. That plus the detail about Malin— someone at the station was talking out of school, but that was Tess's problem. He turned his head to Millie. "C.H.?"

"I haven't been able to find a single person who's gone missing in Itasca County with those initials. Maybe they relocated before they went missing. I'll keep digging."

Rooker clicked on the About link. Over a rambling "bio" was a picture of Haney clearly taken with the desktop's camera.

Loose strands of black hair fell away from their part, and a greasy black clump spilled over the right side of his forehead. He had the features of a rodent. Behind thin rectangle frames were two large brown eyes, one droopier with a dark mole over the eye fold. A bulbous nose and a cleft chin only made his face squarer, his cheeks chunky, and his skin ashy and rigid aside from the five-o'clock shadow coming in.

Under the bio was an email address. "Let's see if I really am a celebrity."

To: phenomena@wh.com
From: Rooker Lindström
Date: September 22, 2019, 12:08 GMT

Subject: IT'S ROOKER LINDSTRÖM

I'm investigating the disappearance of N.V.

Who is C.H.? Willing to trade information.

Rooker Lindström

It was only a matter of minutes before he got a response.

What do you have?

W.H.

Rooker contemplated how much he should really give to a guy like this. But Haney clearly had a source within the station.

Nora Vandenberg received a text message from a blocked number before she disappeared.

He paced back and forth. Waiting.

Did it say: I SEE YOU.

Yes.

C.H. is Camile Hedström. Mother: Aurora. She reached out to me, saying the police never found her. Seemed a bit odd but confirmed her daughter Camile went missing in 2014.

Did Camile get the same text?

Not sure. But Malin Jakobsson did.

Chapter 14

September 22, 2019

Haney had an address for the Hedströms in the nearby town of Warba. With no luck in locating the Jakobssons, Rooker and Millie decided to try the low-hanging fruit first.

Half an hour later, they pulled up to an old single-story ranch house. The white paneled siding resembled crooked teeth. It sat on a half-acre lot, but judging by the marsh behind it—the rotten-egg odor embedded in his nose—Rooker assumed it was a flood risk. He didn't understand how someone could get used to the smell and figured that's why all the windows looked sealed shut. Dark trim surrounded the blurry windows. Brown paint peeled from the front door. Wet leaves covered the grass and spilled out of the blackened gutters.

A woman of about sixty-five opened the door, the chain still latched. "Mrs. Hedström?"

"Yes." Her cracked mouth quivered. Her lips were thin as baby worms. When she pressed them together, it only made them look like they were caught on a fishing hook.

He looked to Millie, who stared back. Her face spoke volumes—that something here was wrong.

"Aurora Hedström? We were hoping to speak to you about your daughter Camile."

"Camile." A smile spread across her mouth, but her eyes remained still, vacant.

"May we come in, ma'am?" Millie asked.

"Where are my manners? Please . . ." She gestured for them to come inside. Millie stepped in gingerly as though she were trying not to kick up dust, and Rooker shut the door behind him. Aurora Hedström was a plump woman with silvering hair and large hips.

They followed her down a dimly lit hallway past a den with an old oak rocker facing a fireplace, into the kitchen.

Cupboards hung open and bare. Laminate countertops with a metal edge wrapped around the horseshoe kitchen. Warped white squares of linoleum retreated beneath his weight.

While she stood frozen, she started batting at her hair. "I'm so sorry. Had I known I'd have company, I would have done my hair." Rooker stared at white flakes where a spot had thinned enough that he could see her scalp.

"No worries, ma'am." Millie smiled pleasantly.

"I think it looks great." Rooker grinned and looked away.

His gaze fell over a vintage stainless-steel pot on the gas range, where red speckles like blood spatter pockmarked the aged tile behind it. Sauce.

She walked the two of them into the next room, where a small dining room table sat awkwardly beside a lopsided hutch filled with a white-and-blue china set.

"Please," she said and motioned for the two of them to take a seat, which they did. Rooker sat down beside Millie, while Aurora Hedström muddled around in the kitchen. Millie stared at Rooker while they listened to the pop of the refrigerator door, then the bang as it slammed shut. From the force, the cabinets ricocheted closed too.

The place reminded Rooker of his own living situation, with about as much charm as a musty dark cellar collecting rainwater.

Rooker was left wondering: Why did this woman let them in without asking a single question?

They hadn't mentioned Warrel Haney. They didn't present badges. All they had mentioned was her missing daughter.

It almost seemed as if she was expecting them or she knew who they were. Or maybe that wasn't quite it either.

A couple of long minutes later, Aurora Hedström returned, donning a blue apron with a brown leather string tied across the front, below a chest pocket. Two larger pockets bulged from her left and right waist.

"I hope you don't mind," she said as she sat down. "I was going to start dinner soon."

Rooker looked at the clock on the wall that hadn't moved since he sat. Then he checked his lap for the third time, where he hid the bold white glowing numbers on his cell phone lock screen. It was only 1:38 p.m.

"No worries, Mrs. Hedström," Millie said pleasantly. "Do you mind if we ask you about Warrel Haney?"

At the name, she flinched. Her face grew cold and serious. "Warrel Haney?"

Millie folded her hands on the table. "Yes, he runs a well-known conspiracy website and YouTube channel. He wrote a story about two missing women, possibly connected to the recent discovery of the body of another missing woman in Itasca County. When we followed up with him, he said that your daughter Camile may be connected to these cases."

"Yes, we spoke."

"Can you tell me how he contacted you?" Millie asked.

Rooker knew it was bait.

She hesitated, watching Millie. "Through my husband," she said.

Lie number one. Warrel Haney had said Aurora Hedström contacted him.

"Your husband," Millie said.

"He reached out to Warrel. I didn't want the media staked out on our front lawn. I asked Don not to."

"You didn't want police looking for Camile?"

"My daughter is dead."

"Where is your husband now, Mrs. Hedström?" Millie asked. But again, her face was dark.

"Gone."

"Can you elaborate?"

"He left us—*me*."

As much as he didn't want to leave Millie in a room alone with this woman, he needed to look around. "Do you mind if I use the restroom?" Rooker asked her.

She stared at Rooker. And so did Millie, with eyes that revealed how uncomfortable she'd be without him there.

"Down the hall on the right. If you smell something, it's the plumbing in the other bathroom. I'm working on getting someone out to fix it."

"Thank you," he said. And then to Millie, "I'll be quick."

Rooker got up from the table and forced a painful smile at Mrs. Hedström. Walking down the hall, he pulled out his cell phone to use the flashlight feature. The beam shined over an old maroon-and-gold floral wallpaper. Then back to the floor in front of him. He found a small powder room on his right. He stepped inside and flipped the light switch. Nothing. He kept moving and turned a corner into another hallway.

It had the best lighting in the house. Through the grime-coated windows, a dim light that looked anything but natural floated coldly over his shoelaces. A few old sconces buzzed. He appraised a door at the end of the hall on the right. As he peered at the wall lined with picture frames, he realized every single one was still wrapped in plastic. Each one of a mother and daughter. The price sticker carefully removed. But they all hung there from the wall. All different women. None of them, not one, was Aurora Hedström.

When he got to the farthest frame on the wall, the smell hit him. Something awful. But it wasn't sewage, or shit, or rotten eggs. It was worse. Far worse.

He stared up at the oldest photo on the wall, shining his light on the little face.

This one, he was sure, was Aurora Hedström. With tired, sad eyes. Lying in bed in a hospital gown. She cradled a baby who did not appear to be alive.

He made his way farther down the hall, closer to the door on the end, and fought back the urge to vomit. He choked and coughed. Tried to do so silently. He jiggled the handle of the door. It didn't budge.

He started back toward the dining room. When he reached the bathroom he was meant to use, he flipped the light switch, forgetting it didn't work, then flushed the toilet and walked out. Millie and Aurora were still chatting, but Rooker didn't rejoin them. He stood stone-still in the doorway.

"Find it okay?" Aurora asked him.

"Yeah," he answered. He stared at Millie. He wanted her to get up from the table. With his teeth gritted, he did his best to communicate telepathically to her.

Get up, Mill. Come on.

"Come sit," Aurora told him.

"Actually, Mrs. Hedström," Rooker spoke kindly, "we need to be leaving."

"Oh, nonsense. We were just talking about Camile."

He stared at Millie, who started to fidget in her seat but didn't get up. "Was Camile an only child?" Millie asked. Aurora turned back to her.

"Yes, she was. Never thought to have another one after her."

Fighting the adrenaline that was making his hands shake, Rooker took the opportunity and typed a four-word message to Millie: Daughter died at birth.

He heard a faint buzzing sound, but Millie didn't reach for her phone.

He went back to the table, pulled his chair in close to Millie's. "This is a lovely home," he said to Aurora, nodding back toward the kitchen. As the woman turned, he swatted Millie on the leg. "The kitchen reminds me of the house I grew up in."

Millie looked at her phone, and he felt her stiffen. And then he lifted the hem of her shirt and felt the black steel on her hip. She was no longer a detective, but she continued to carry. He remembered what she'd told him about the Heckler & Koch. The pistol held ten .45 ACP rounds, plus one in the chamber. He didn't think they would need it, but it sure as hell made him feel less like he was living in a nightmare. There was clearly something wrong with Mrs. Hedström's mind, but she didn't really pose a threat. Still, there was an odd feeling, tiny but thundering in his mind, telling him to be glad Millie had brought the gun along.

"Thank you."

Slowly, Millie slid the gun out and rested it sideways on her thigh. "Mrs. Hedström, do you mind if I ask what happened with your husband?"

In a flash, it was like a sheet had been pulled over her face. Ghost white. She said: "He wanted another child. I couldn't . . . He cheated. He came home one night, *drunk*. And he told me. And he smiled while he did."

"I'm so sorry. How long ago did this happen?"

If his suspicions were right, based on the foul stench leaking through the door, he assumed it was quite some time ago.

But she said nothing.

She only peered down into her lap. Rooker watched the woman crane forward. Her back hunched. Two teardrops dribbled down the creases of her face and fell. And then her hand raised, just enough where he could see the silver above the tabletop, the little revolver convulsing in her wrinkled palm.

She rocked back and forth.

"Aurora," Millie tried. But it was no use.

They'd come to a home where a woman wanted to die. And she'd rather die with company than wait until someone came to the smell of her corpse.

Hell, he should've known. Should've known there was something wrong about someone reaching out to a conspiracy theorist.

Swiftly, the barrel of the gun pressed into the fleshy spot beneath her chin. Rooker watched the tremor in the old hand, and he hollered, "Camile." He called her name out as though she was about to come walking down the hall and make some sort of grand entrance. But it was enough to make the woman freeze, and the pistol began to fall away from her face. Tears ran like faucet water from Mrs. Hedström's red eyes. Millie was out of her seat, knocking the gun from her hand. As it rattled across the tile, Aurora Hedström crashed to the ground, and Millie had her arms knotted behind her back.

"I thought you might have to shoot her in the leg," Rooker said to her, just as she made a face at him, and he dialed Tess Harlow.

When he decided Millie had the situation under control, he made his way back down the hall, took a step back from the door, and launched his boot beneath the brass knob. It took only the one shot. The door whipped open. Out came the putrefying smell. Like a kick to a hornet's nest, all at once the odor swarmed him. It clogged his nostrils, even felt as if it clogged his pores. He winced, but he was able to see a man about sixty years of age dressed in a ruined blue shirt, charcoal paisley tie, and gray pleated pants. Don was sprawled out in the tub with a dark hole in the center of his chest. Chin pressed to his collarbone, hand in his lap, he appeared to be asleep, aside from the blackened gooey mass. But then Rooker stepped closer. Maggots as white as his hair crawled over him. Splattered streaks of dark red ran down the wall behind him. The bottom of the shower curtain was stained black. And as Rooker backed away, he jumped when his shoulder grazed Millie's, and as he turned to her, it gave him just enough time to grab the waste bin. Slime flew from her mouth, and Rooker ushered her away from the door.

In the next ten minutes, the first squad car and the county medical examiner arrived. Out of a white Ford Taurus bustled a man with a shaved head and trimmed salt-and-pepper beard, donning wayfarer sunglasses and a beige-and-brown uniform. The other was a woman, wearing black trousers, white running sneakers, and a nondescript navy-blue windbreaker. Rooker watched her from the window, tucking collar-length brown hair behind her ear, then putting on a pair of gloves. When she entered the house, she asked if the man had just been killed. When Rooker said it looked as though he'd been dead quite some time, she turned on the coffee machine. "For the smell," she said.

A few minutes later, Detectives Tess Harlow and Vic Sterling rolled through the door. Vic knocked knuckles with Rooker. Tess ignored him.

The coffee had just finished gurgling, and Aurora Hedström was already in the back seat of the cruiser. Tess looked to the beat cop, a guy near forty named Sutton, and asked: "What do we have?"

"Homicide, it looks like. Woman in the car"—he nodded toward it as though she could see through the wall—"killed the husband. Tried to shoot herself, according to—"

"Yeah, I know them. Thanks, Sutton." Tess looked past Rooker to Millie and said, "You want back in yet?"

Without turning to her, Millie answered, "I'm good, thanks."

It made Rooker smile.

"What is this? You two are out here playing cops?"

"More like Sherlock Holmes and John Watson," Rooker said. "Haven't decided who's who yet."

"You think this is funny? Some woman about to shoot herself in the face? And a dead guy in the bathroom?"

Rooker couldn't resist. "That's Don."

"So you stumble upon a crime scene. Bathroom door kicked in clean off the hinges. You expect me to believe she did that? And you just found it that way?"

"Yeah, we found it like that."

"And if I check the knob for prints and run the boot print on the door, it won't lead me to you?"

"No, ma'am," he said.

"Want to tell me what it is you're doing here?"

Millie spoke up. "A client came to us, wants us to look into her missing daughter. The search led us here."

"*A client?*" She shook her head.

"That's right," Millie answered.

"Tell you what." Tess put her hands on her hips. "I don't want to find another dead guy in a bathroom or some woman blowing her brains out and you two standing in the kitchen. If you have information, you bring it to *the police*. You bring it to *me*. If I find you two interfering with an investigation, I'll bring you both in for obstruction of justice. Are we clear?"

"Crystal," Rooker said.

Rooker walked out alongside Millie. They sat in the Volvo and stared at the front of the house.

"When were you going to tell me about Caroline Lind? I had to see it on the news."

"You think Tess is jealous? Maybe that's why she's so mad at us."

He felt Millie's cold stare on his cheek. Rooker scratched his forehead and gave a somewhat embarrassed smile. "Sorry. Didn't think it worth mentioning . . . Not my finest moment."

"You men, always thinking with what's in your pants."

"It's not that. I went out for a drink. She set me up."

"So she caught you with your pants down?"

"They were on at first."

Millie keyed the ignition and the engine buzzed. "Did you fall in love?"

While she shifted the car out of park, he found himself staring at the shape of Tess Harlow through a murky bay window. "A lesser man would have."

Chapter 15

"Well, at least we can cross C.H. off the list of Itasca's missing women. *Christ.*" Rooker shook his head and sank into the blue recliner, evicting Geralt. He watched Millie pull a bunch of cables and gadgets out of her bag and line them up on the couch.

"Mm-hmm," she said distractedly as she started connecting everything to her laptop.

"What is all of this?"

"SSD storage, extra RAM, the usual . . . I'm running Tails. It's an amnesic OS . . ."

"Millie . . ."

"The Amnesic Incognito Live System," she said while she typed. "Get it? *Tails.* T-A-I . . ." She stopped. "It's an operating system run from a disk or an external drive. Basically, it's designed to allow anonymous communication on the dark web and protect sensitive data on your computer. It leaves no trace of anything after shutdown."

"And what is all of this supposed to do?"

"It might help us trace those I SEE YOU texts. Someone was watching Nora—but they also had to have other info, like her cell phone number—and they had to get that information somewhere. And if Haney isn't full of shit about Malin getting the same text, maybe the phrase itself will yield something."

"What makes you so sure we'll find something there?"

"I'm not. I may not find anything, but it's worth a shot. Think of it as a community. These people . . . they talk to each other. Maybe there's something—*someone*—who can help us."

"Do me a favor? Find me Haney's address before you get too deep into all of this."

She smiled and pulled a folded yellow Post-it note from her pocket. "Already got it."

◆ ◆ ◆

Rooker let the car idle at the curb of Colfax Avenue and looked up at a secluded home with dark sage-green siding and darker seaweed trim. He didn't really know what to expect, so he left the engine running.

The brown garage door was closed. He could see a screened-in porch out back. As he stared at the house, he noticed every window had the shades pulled. It looked like no one was living there. Hedges and shrubs had overgrown wildly in the front yard. He looked for the faintest light throughout the house. But there wasn't one.

Rooker rapped his knuckles against the door and turned his face away from the peephole and toward the street. He heard the sound of footsteps on the other side. Then the voice. "Who is it?"

"Delivery for Mr. Haney," Rooker said and looked down as if he had a box in his hands. The door opened enough for him to recognize the face he'd seen on the site.

Warrel Haney touched a finger to the birthmark above his eyelid, just beneath his arched brow. They looked like two thin, bushy millipedes.

"Rooker Lindström?"

"Warrel, how are you, buddy?" Rooker gripped the edge of the door and pushed it into Haney's gut.

"Hey! What the hell? I'll call the police!"

"Go ahead, Warrel. You think I give a shit? We'll see what shape you're in by the time they get here."

"Is that a threat?"

"Maybe that source you have in the station will come out and have a chat. You sent us on a wild goose chase. Aurora Hedström? A woman with an only child who died at birth. Her husband is dead in the tub, and the old woman tries to blow her own head off with a snub-nosed .38 Special in front of us. She hid the damn thing in her kitchen apron."

"What, you think I knew?"

"You sure as hell didn't think she was 'credible,' right?"

Haney paused. "What do you want?"

"I want what you have on Malin Jakobsson. I want to know how *you*"—Rooker jammed his index finger into Haney's sternum—"know that she got the same text as Nora Vandenberg."

"You were a journalist. You can't just expect me to—"

"Warrel." Rooker shook his head. "Do not fuck with me. I've had this pounding headache. I can't get any sleep. I'm trying to find a girl—"

"Don't kid yourself. You're looking for a killer."

Rooker glared at the unattractive face, closed his eyes for a moment to calm down, and opened them. "That may be true. But Nora hasn't been missing long. If you know something that could help us find her alive . . ."

Haney extended an upturned hand. "Give me your phone."

"Why?"

"Do you want what I have or not?"

Rooker slipped his hand into his pocket, caught hold of the cell, and handed it over.

Warrel checked it for a moment. Then he went to the fridge, put it on the top shelf next to a carton of milk, and closed the door. When he looked back at Rooker, he said, "They listen."

With a snicker, Rooker shook his head and grimaced. *"Yeah,"* he mocked Haney. *"They listen all right."*

Haney limped into what Rooker imagined to be the dining room, closed a pocket door behind him. The only light came from a station where three curved monitors were mounted on a monstrous desk. The blinds were drawn tight. The keyboard glowed green. All three monitors moved in unison, an image of what he imagined to be the cosmos: floating celestial purples and oranges.

Haney swiped the mouse, and when he started opening files, he turned over his shoulder and told Rooker not to look. When he heard him say, "Okay," he turned and saw an image of two mirrors facing one another at the foot of a bed.

Rooker craned forward. "What am I looking at?"

"A crime scene photo. Believe it or not, I have friends in the police force too."

"What crime? There's nothing here."

"Malin Jakobsson, age twenty-six. She disappeared in September of 2011. Presumed dead. You see the two mirrors? One of them is from her living room."

"So what? She could have moved the mirror herself."

"She didn't. Look at how bulky that mirror is. It would've weighed more than her. Her father had to move it back afterward, and even he struggled with it. You think a woman as petite as Malin could've carried it, let alone dragged it, without help? Her father said it wasn't how she kept her room." Haney paused. "You see, some believe that two mirrors facing each other affects the calmness of an individual. Some believe it creates a portal where spirits can pass through to the living world. Some correlate mirrors with witchcraft.

But some . . . believe that by facing two mirrors at one another, you can summon the devil."

"You're telling me this guy is trying to summon the devil?"

"That or he thinks he *is the devil.*"

"*Christ* . . . No sign of a struggle? No DNA other than hers?"

"Correct. Nothing missing, aside from this spot in the medicine cabinet. A perfume bottle."

"So, what? Someone abducts her? Faces two mirrors together and steals a perfume bottle?"

"It's a centuries-old tale that women who wore perfume were believed to be witches. It was said to have magical properties. It could cast evil spells or it could protect against disease."

Rooker un-pocketed a ballpoint pen and started writing on his skin. "Or you could be a sick fuck who collects trophies from your victims."

Perfume thief. Protecting himself? Collecting trophies? Target based on perfume or something else? Mirrors faced together—thinks he's the devil?

There was something else bothering him. The layout of Malin Jakobsson's bedroom. Why would someone go through the trouble to move things around?

"There's more." Haney spoke as he clicked back on the file. He opened another image. "The phone was on her nightstand. Look at the text." Behind the crack in the smartphone screen was the exact same text sent to Nora Vandenberg. Haney opened another image. "This was found in the floorboard beneath her bed."

Rooker stared at the symbol carved into wood. The ground was lighter there where a sharp instrument dug about a quarter inch into the oak. It looked like a flower with six petals bordered by a circle.

"Haney—"

"It's a hexafoil. Also called a daisy wheel. It can mean good luck, and it can also be a symbol of protection against evil."

Rooker's head was beginning to hurt even more than it already was. "Why would someone—" He stopped himself. And when he saw Haney's understanding smirk, Rooker uttered, "It's not for her. It's for him. He thinks he's protecting himself from her."

Chapter 16

Rooker slumped into the cracked leather of the driver's seat, shut the door, and pressed a finger to the cold screen of his phone. First, he dialed Christine Vandenberg. She answered after a ring.

"Ms. Vandenberg, it's Rooker Lindström. I need the key to Nora's home—can you meet me there? I need a look inside."

She gave him an address in Cohasset and told him she'd meet him there shortly. He wrote in neat black ink on a blank spot on his hand. Next, he dialed Millie and switched over to speakerphone.

"Yeah," she said.

"You busy?"

"Just surfing the web." He could hear the jokey quip in her tone. "What's up?"

"I just saw Warrel Haney. We need to make a trip."

Every angle of Nora Vandenberg's two-story home had a panoramic view of Pokegama Lake. The three-car garage appeared brand-new, as did every detail of the house, even the grand window arched above the front door. Christine Vandenberg's Porsche was parked in the circular drive.

Ms. Vandenberg walked them into the foyer where the ceilings were vaulted high enough for a deadly fall. She shepherded the two of them up grand stairs. A chandelier glistened overhead.

Rooker thought about his question for a moment before asking it, then changed his first word from *was*. "Is Nora single?"

"As far as I know, yes. If there were someone worth bringing around, she would have."

"If you don't mind my asking, why so much house for a single woman?"

"Because she's a Vandenberg."

On the lower level, there was a sauna, exercise room, and entertainment room. She led them into the bedroom upstairs. The four-poster bed was made, and nothing looked out of place.

"Ms. Vandenberg, have you touched anything—moved anything in this room?"

"There were two mirrors at the foot of her bed. On the floor there and there." She pointed to the edges of the bed. "Facing each other. This one used to be here." She pointed to the corner of the room where she had put it back. "The other was from the bedroom down the hall."

Rooker's pulse climbed. "I'm going to need to put both of them back *exactly* how they were. Just as you remember them."

When Christine Vandenberg left to retrieve the mirror down the hall, Millie turned to him. "What are you thinking?"

Rooker shook his head.

The pounding . . . behind his left eye . . . as if someone were tapping away with the face of a hammer. And when he thought of a hammer, there was only one face that came to mind.

He drove away the thought. "I don't know."

"You think there's something *here. Something* the killer left."

Rooker said nothing. The room, all of a sudden, felt like it had ignited.

A few moments later, Millie was moving the one mirror while Christine Vandenberg was struggling with the other through the doorway. She placed it just beyond the bedpost, where Millie placed hers across from it.

Rooker stood back, as far away from it all as he could, and stared.

Suddenly, he had a thought. "Aside from the mirrors, Ms. Vandenberg, is the room how you remember it?"

"Well, now that you ask, it does look like she's moved things around a bit."

"How was the room the last time you saw it?"

"Well, the last time I saw it, the bed was on that wall." She pointed to the western wall. "And the nightstand was there." She pointed to the right side of where the bed was positioned.

Rooker walked over to the bed, hunched down, and peered into the darkness.

And that's when he saw it—a hand . . . what was left of one. Blackened bone, putrefying pared flesh, an awful, nauseating stench of rotting earth. A white-gold and diamond bracelet, with a silver pendant that read C.L.

It grabbed him.

And he leaped back.

"Rooker?"

His chest jackhammered. He blinked hard. When he opened his eyes, he squinted, then stared into the dark space before him.

Nothing.

"Sorry," he said to Millie. He hadn't thought about the Tiffany bracelet in years . . . It had been an anniversary gift for Laura. His ex-wife. "This person—they rearrange the rooms. I don't think the mirrors are the only thing they move. Mill, give me a hand with this."

Rooker began to strip the bed, first chucking the pillows into the corner of the room, until he met Millie's gaze. She didn't move. And when he turned to see an expression of shock and sorrow on Ms. Vandenberg's face, he understood.

"I'm sorry, Ms. Vandenberg. You might not want to be here for this. But you paid us a lot of money to look into the disappearance of your daughter, and I think there's something in this room . . . something that will help us. I—*we*—just need to find it."

"Do what you must. Please bring my baby back."

"And Ms. Vandenberg," Rooker said. "Was there anything missing?"

She stared blankly at the bathroom door. "I got her perfume for Christmas. A bottle of Santal 33. She always wore it. If she traveled, she took it with her. She kept it in the bathroom. It's not there."

With that, Christine Vandenberg was gone from the room. The sadness evident even in the slow creak of her gait down the staircase.

"When are you going to start taking those pills?"

"I'm fine," he snapped.

I'm fine.

He could sense her doubt. While she helped him remove the sheets and the mattress, he wondered if she was rethinking taking her old desk back at the station.

Then again, maybe he was being tough on her. She'd stuck by his side so far. That was more than he could say for most.

"If there's nothing here," he said to Millie, "we might lose our first client."

"Our *only* client," she said.

"We check everything, then."

The two of them reconfigured the room. The bed needed to be moved so they could check the floor beneath a massive white-and-gray Oriental rug. When they each lifted an end and rolled the rug over to check beneath, that's where they found it. A tiny marking, carved with precision into the floorboard beneath the bed.

Unlike the hexafoil, Rooker was familiar with the circled star.

"Pentacle," Millie said. "I guess it tracks with the mirrors and the perfume. Magic."

It was skillfully done. The lines. The circle. Whoever carved it had taken their time. They were after someone with patience: the disappearances of the women spanned years. Rearranging the room. The carving.

"Yeah," Rooker agreed. "Now what do we tell her mother? That we can say with certainty her daughter was taken? That all these bizarre details match the case of a dead woman the cops just fished out of a lake?"

"Well, at least we've got *something*. The texts, the symbols, the perfume—it all means a lot to someone. I think the next question is: Why?"

Chapter 17

Her hands and legs were bound to the chair.

She was still groggy. Spittle coated the edge of her lip. A stringy web of it dripped down to her thigh. The damp must, something like mold or mildew, wet earth, clogged her nose.

The room was stark black. Invoked terror.

Where am I?

"Nora," he whispered.

The soft tone echoed. There was a calm coldness to it, something abnormal—something eerie—a voice in the wind that you tell yourself you didn't really hear. It was more unpleasant than a human scream. Though it startled her, she couldn't move.

Her blindfold was gone. But the weight of it, the tightness of the knot at the crook/base of her skull, remained.

Her head drooped. Bobbed around. Her neck swiveled as if it were loose on its axis.

As her eyes began to adjust to the darkness, she thought she could see symbols on the walls . . . concrete walls . . . Were they runes?

What is this place?

There were mirrors placed all over the room. She could see a dim light bleeding beneath a doorway. And that's when she began to panic.

No. No. Please, God. No.

She hyperventilated. Tried to scream through the gag in her throat. A dark figure cloudily came into view.

"Shh . . . ," it whispered.

Just do what they say, Nora.

That's when she saw him. A dark, tattered robe. A cowl-like hood draped over his head. And a mask . . . his finger pressed to the lips of it. For a moment, he left her there in the chair to stare at himself in the mirror. When he was finished, he looked past his reflection. He looked at her. Glided toward her. His feet didn't make a sound, as though they weren't even touching the floor. He bent down in front of her.

Her eyes bulged. She thought she could see two different masks pieced together: a black-and-silver masquerade disguise, the middle resembling a Halloween mask, an old witch hag made of latex. She stared at two almond-shaped cutouts, behind which were vacant black eyes that reminded her of empty vessels. There was a long, hooked nose and wrinkled skin and boils. She found thin black lines . . . where it must have been cut and stitched with thread.

"EEEZ," she let out. She went to try the word *please* again, but the finger pressed against her lips now.

"Quiet, child." He wiped his finger off on her pants leg. She could feel the spit from his mouth, the damp sliminess of his breath. He squeezed her trembling face in hands that weren't so big but powerful. "The devil is down here."

Chapter 18

Rooker and Millie had been waiting for Soren Jakobsson to arrive at the post office. Jakobsson's day typically began around 6:45 a.m.

They'd been waiting since six, but Rooker had been up for hours. Staring at the backs of his eyelids or the wood boards above him. Listening to the hum of silence. Around 5:30 a.m., he'd stirred Millie awake from the couch.

His filthy boots left a dusty pattern on Millie's dash until she slapped him hard on the arm and he brushed it away.

The post-office building was brown brick with a big silver door. In the early-morning sun, it had the radioactive glimmer of an atomic bomb. All four parking spots out front were taken. Millie drove through the intersection, past a loan company, appliance showroom, and drug-store, and parked in the much larger lot in back, where a stream of white mail trucks looked like they'd been abandoned.

At 6:38 a.m., a man parked between two faded white strips of paint in an early-2000s Honda sedan. A circle of rust painted the dull silver hood. A dark ring stained the asphalt beneath it. He guessed it was where Jakobsson parked every day and that his vehicle was leaking oil. Judging by the whisking sound coming from it, he thought maybe the catalytic converter had been stolen for the metals inside it or there was something very wrong with the muffler. Trailing the car was a violent chemical smell. The engine ticked and died. When the driver door screeched, out came a thin man with a light-blue shirt unbuttoned and a wrinkled white crew neck tee beneath it. The collar stretched. Rooker put him near sixty. Though he was tall, his pants were baggy and cuffed at the bottom. With sunken eyes and a sleepless face, he limped toward the post-office doors.

He had the look of a drunk; Rooker had viewed it plenty in the mirror. A stagger in his stride not entirely caused by the injury to his leg.

Despite a long concrete ramp, he opted for the two sets of stairs, hobbling while he planted both feet on each step.

"Mr. Jakobsson," Millie said.

Like his car, a strong odor trailed him. A pungent body spray that Rooker felt he was choking on. The man's neck twisted to peer over his shoulder at Millie. It gave his anatomy the stiff look of something that had once broken and never mended properly. His head was perfectly straight, as if it were braced by invisible pins and needles. "I know you?" He spat the words venomously. His eyes milky and red with cracks.

"No, sir, I—"

He waved his hand in a gesture that signaled he didn't have time for them. "Not one for talking to people I don't know." He turned and sauntered in a gait that favored his left leg.

"We just want to ask you a few questions," Millie called to him.

He stopped. Without looking at them, he said, "Questions?"

"That's right," she answered.

"What kind of questions?" His throat whistled. The man had a breathing problem. A faint wheeze like something was clogging his airway. He was trying to hide it.

She hesitated. "It's about Malin, sir."

He turned to her. With pain and anger in his eyes and hostility in his voice, he spoke. "You knew my daughter?"

"No."

103

"Then what gives you the right t' come round here speaking her name?"

"I'm sorry. We think we have some information on her case. We thought you might be able to help us."

"*Help you?* My baby's gone, miss. She ain't coming back. Not here anyway."

Rooker took note of that. *Not here anyway.* He wondered what he meant by it. "Five minutes," Rooker spoke. "Five. You'll never see us again."

Millie gestured a hand at the building. "Is there someplace we can talk?"

The man sighed. He shifted most of his weight onto his left leg and shook his head. "You got five minutes." He looked down at his watch. Rooker noticed it didn't have the right time. The dials weren't working either. "Ask your questions."

"Were there ever any suspects?"

"Sure. Until alibis cleared them."

"Could you get us those names? They might still be worth checking out."

"Not worth it, miss. When I say cleared, I mean it. Anyway, one of 'em's dead. Other one in prison for violating parole. Junkie."

"They have a name?"

He smirked. "Karl Jakobsson. My brother. And he didn't take Malin. He's just a glutton for punishment. And drugs."

"Was there anyone you suspected?"

"Can't say so. No."

"This image—" Rooker unfolded the paper from his pocket. It was the image he'd gotten from Warrel Haney of Malin Jakobsson's bedroom. The symbol carved in the floor. "Have you ever seen this?"

"The police showed it to me back then, when they found it in her room. Still don't know anything about it."

"Mind if I ask what happened to your leg?" Rooker jutted his chin at Soren's leg. "Couldn't help but notice."

"It happened a few nights after she went missing. I was walking home after putting signs up. You know, posters. Telephone poles, storefronts, you name it. I printed hundreds of 'em. Anyway, it gets dark, and I'm walking back home alone. I see this figure. Staring at me. Some kind of mask on. I thought it was a few kids pulling a prank. Trying to be funny. When the guy ran off, I followed. Turned a corner at the back of a house and took a heavy hit to the head. I could feel warm blood sticking between my fingers. Can still feel it to this day." He pressed a hand to the edge of his forehead, where he pulled his hair back and revealed a long scar. "Next thing I know, I'm looking up and see him lifting something high over his head. Damn thing swings down like a wrecking ball at my leg. You ever hear your own bones break? I woke up a day later in the ER. As you can see, my leg never healed quite right."

"Do you remember anything about him?"

"Nothing that'll help. Dark clothes. Tall and lean. Skinnier than he was muscular. That's about it. At least my court date was more than a week earlier, so I didn't have to show up looking like a damn fool. Butterfly bandages on my head and my whole leg in a cast. That would have been something for a jury to see."

Rooker looked at Millie. Then back to Jakobsson. "Court for what?"

"*Bullshit*, that's what. Bogus charges."

"What charges?" Millie asked.

"DUI. A week before Malin went missing, I was drinking. After, I was drinking way more. But that night, I felt good to drive. Still, one of my damn tires caught the curb, and a cop saw it. Next thing I know, I got the sirens flashing behind me. Pull over and do the damn Breathalyzer. Blew a .10: .02 over the limit. Had to go to court for it. Malin went with me."

Chapter 19

"Anything?" he asked Millie for the fourth time.

With the slow swivel of her neck and the furrow of her brow before her head snapped back into place, he got his answer.

"Believe me," she said without so much as a glance up at him from the laptop. "When I find *something*, I'll tell you."

Now that they'd found the symbol on her bedroom floor, Nora Vandenberg was the second confirmed victim. Victims of serial murder in almost every case were not random. Knowing that, he decided to go at it a different way. He typed Vandenberg Enterprises into the search bar. Not to his surprise, there were pages upon pages of hits. He opened the first three in separate tabs. The first one listed Thomas Vandenberg as the director. The company had three subsidiaries, listed as:

- Vandenberg Construction
- Vandenberg Electric & Energy
- Vandenberg Securities

"They have to be worth millions," Rooker said. "The Vandenbergs. No ransom? No extortion? Whoever is doing this doesn't seem to want or need the money."

"Doesn't look like it, does it?" Millie said.

"So why are Malin Jakobsson and Nora Vandenberg targeted? What would make the same person take them both? They're in completely different income classes. We can't say he's punishing the rich because he went after Malin. Soren doesn't have money."

Leaning back, he scratched his forehead and sighed. "But still," he insisted. "There's something here. Something in how he *chooses* them."

"The two of them are nearly identical in description," Millie said. "Malin was twenty-six when she was taken. Nora is twenty-five. They're both five feet four. Malin was one hundred twenty-six pounds; Nora was between one hundred and one hundred and ten. Both brown hair. Malin, brown eyes. Nora, hazel."

He stared at the screen. Reading up on Vandenberg Enterprises. *There's nothing here.*

But then he began reading up on Thomas Vandenberg.

Rooker skipped past his Wikipedia page, which listed him as the forty-nine-year-old chief executive of Vandenberg Enterprises. He found an article written in the *Pioneer Press.* Thomas Vandenberg had been sued in 2016 for granting stock options to employees rather than providing salary increases and benefits and attempted to erase the evidence.

A photo showed Thomas Vandenberg walking up the courthouse steps, fastening the top button of a fitted charcoal suit.

His eyes grew heavy. The next thing he knew, he was dozing off in a twitchy sleep. "Rooker." His body jump-started.

"Hmm," he muttered.

"I've got something. Take a look at this."

His face scrunched. As his nose wrinkled and his eye unlatched to a squint, he acknowledged the pulsing pain behind his brow.

The migraine blur in his eyes—shimmering speckles and waves—strayed from Millie to the black world outside. "What is it?" He cleared the rasp from his throat and twisted a bony knuckle into the corner of his eye.

"It's a web page." She turned the monitor to him. "Look familiar?"

It was the same photo of the eye—black and white, bleeding—on the back of the note left for him on the victim. He was suddenly awake.

Staring back at him was the black-and-white eye of a woman. It was evident in the length of the lashes and the dark mascara brushed over them. But then where it ran below the eye . . . it wasn't *only* below the eye . . . it was above too. *Blood.* The circle around it . . .

"How did you find this?"

"A good Samaritan." She smiled. "I've been going from one chat room to the next pretending to be a creep. Someone sent me the page. Anyway, I think whoever runs it wanted the page to be found."

"Creepy."

"Yeah." She turned to him. "Creepy, all right."

"How do we know if it's even the killer?"

"One way to find out."

He sat up, closed the bottom of the chair, and sat beside her on the sofa.

"This couch sucks."

He studied the page as Millie scanned it, and when the cursor hovered over the eye, a pentacle turned.

"What the . . ."

The circle around the eye unlocked as if a key had opened it. And then the page transformed. Flashes of images appeared on the screen. They were women. But they were gone too fast to tell if they were the victims.

When the images stopped, a dialogue box opened.

Rooker looked at Millie, who only stared back, just as bewildered.

Three dots appeared below the box.

Is someone typing?

And then the message appeared.

WICCAN: Hello.

Hello. Such a simple greeting was all it took to pimple his skin with gooseflesh and lift the hairs on the nape of his neck. In an instant, his body temperature dropped.

Rooker watched the hesitation in Millie. She froze. "Millie?"

He watched her type into the chat.

Did they deserve it?

Three dots.

WICCAN: They always do, Rooker.

The screen turned red. And three black words appeared on the screen.

I SEE YOU.

"Shit!" Millie said. "My computer—" She tried all sorts of keys. "I can't—" She yanked her external drive from the computer's USB port.

Then the screen went black.

"Did you see that?" she said.

"Did you get any of that?" Rooker asked frantically.

"Yeah . . . ," she said. "I should've gotten all of it recorded on here." She held the black portable hard drive in her hand. "I think my computer is toast."

◆　◆　◆

Millie ran over beside Rooker's chair and lifted his laptop from the ground. He knew it was no use saying anything to her right now. The next thing he knew, she was hitting keys and opening programs before she connected her portable drive to the computer.

"Give me a sec," she said.

He hovered over her shoulder, watching her play back the images that just flashed across her screen. She slowed it down to 0.5x. Then hit "Play."

The first image they saw looked like a flash went off in a dark cellar. Millie paused the video on a pale white face and bare skin. She was tied up to some kind of strange chair. Despite the harsh light and exposure from a camera flash, he knew the face. It was Malin Jakobsson.

When Millie pressed "Play" and froze the image on the next girl, Rooker felt as though he'd sunken into the floor. Nora. Nora Vandenberg was in the very same seat.

Millie pressed "Play" again and froze on the third woman. The photo looked much older. The picture quality not quite as good. The image didn't look to be taken in the same room or even the same darkness. But his view of the girl was suddenly blocked by Millie's pointer finger. Her face much closer to the screen now.

"It's her," Millie said in shock. "It *has* to be her."

Chapter 20

Millie paced back and forth. Ignored the hair-raising creak of wood beneath her steps. Felt the tremor take control of her hands. She'd stopped breathing.

She could feel his eyes following her around the room. "Who was she?"

"*Who was she?*" Millie repeated. "She's a legend around here. You really don't know?"

He didn't answer.

"She was the 'it' girl. Popular. Beautiful. Smart. All the boys wanted her, and all the girls wanted to be her. Valedictorian of her class, she was Ivy League bound, off to Princeton with a full ride. She disappeared the year I was born. Thirty years ago. *Shit.*" She raked her hair. "It's been *thirty* years? When she disappeared, the whole world knew about it. It was on *World News Tonight.* Everybody knew Amy."

Clearly, he didn't.

She'd spent years wondering what happened to her. She'd studied the case through high school. Even into her years at the academy. She'd have dreams of being the one to find her alive. When she became a detective, she was able to get her hands on case files. She'd read transcripts of conversations between police and Amy's family and friends. But there was never a shred of physical evidence discovered—she'd just vanished. Everyone knew Amy was dead, and she became a cautionary tale.

"You don't get it. Even years later, all our parents warned us to stick together and not to stay out late. They warned us we'd be the next Amy." She paused. "There are two reasons I wanted to be a detective. One was Clarice Starling in *Silence of the Lambs*. The other was Amy Berglund."

"*Clarice Starling?* You've gotta be kidding."

She shrugged. Shook her head. "She's the reason I got a .357 Magnum revolver. It mostly just sits in a drawer, but it's the same Smith & Wesson Model 13 that she carried. And who wouldn't want to go tit for tat with the doctor."

"Yeah, and have the guy in the next cell throw his semen on you."

She rolled her eyes. "All I wanted was to do something meaningful. Whether that meant locking up bad guys or catching someone like Buffalo Bill or protecting people like Amy Berglund." She thought about the way her mother would lecture her. On a school night when she wanted to stay over at her friend Barb's house. Her mother told her not to go out at night or she'd end up like Amy Berglund. Or she'd warn her about what she could and couldn't wear, as if Amy Berglund dressed like a skank and some guy couldn't resist snatching her. "I wanted to make sure nothing ever happened to a girl like that again. Or if it did, I'd find her before it was too late."

"But listen to what you're saying. You mean to tell me this person killed her? *Thirty years ago?* If Malin was killed soon after she was taken, that puts eight years between her death and Nora's disappearance. It doesn't make any sense."

"I'm not saying any of this makes sense. *What I'm telling you* is that the woman in this photograph is Amy Berglund."

Chapter 21

On the outside, Mrs. Caldwell's Victorian home was a quaint two-story dwelling with a double-peaked roof, a fresh coat of white-painted trim, and charming dark shutters. A front porch bordered by shrubs with a wide white railing, a balcony—one that fairy tales are made of—off the main bedroom toward the back of the home with a screened-in porch below, and potted plants beneath a few of the windows. She found it as pretty as a dollhouse.

But not on the inside.

The entrails of the home were grim and bleak. She imagined a deer sleeping on its side on the highway shoulder—only when you turned it over, the innards were seeping from the carcass, as was blood and stool and maggots.

Dim lighting did little to counter the dreary thought in her mind. She pulled the curtains, and dust flew into her face. The powdered filth choked her. Hazed her vision of the water damage that stained part of the walls a murky gray or rust brown. Sometimes she saw faces in them, like ink blotches in a Rorschach test.

There were rules.

Rule number 1: Never give her anything sharp. No knives, pens, anything with a point. *She's a danger to herself and others.*

Rule number 2: Never disturb Mr. C while he was working.

She was lying flat in a full electric hospital bed. The footboard and headboard were faux walnut wood, some sort of laminate look-alike except where it peeled. A pair of heavy-duty steel side rails on either side of her. Pinch resistant. It was designed for patients to be at a low risk of injury. Visible screws in the side of the bed frame reminded her of Frankenstein's monster. A control dial could raise and lower the bed and adjust the head or legs of it. Casters locked the bed in place.

Without the mattress, it resembled a torture device.

She could never tell if Mrs. Caldwell was asleep. She pressed her thumb into the button, and Mrs. Caldwell arched forward. She tended to Mrs. Caldwell the way she did every time she visited. She got her out of bed and placed her into a folding transport chair, then replaced the linens. She changed her systematically, limbs flailing around but without fight. The same few nightgowns—crisply folded, floral patterned, shin length—in rotation after a wash. She fed her by soft plastic spoon, always. Because of rule number 1.

She winced at the floor of Mrs. Caldwell's mouth, a hollow space of pink flesh. Her tongue was missing.

She watched with pity as a beef, potato, and corn purée mashed around in Mrs. Caldwell's open mouth. Anytime she missed the mark, runny chunks of mush coated her lip, usually a color resembling throw-up.

She brushed her hair. The whites and grays tangling in the soft bristles of the paddle brush. Oftentimes, it matted and detached from her scalp in sad wiry clumps.

And then she watched a tear fall down the old face.

"Mrs. Caldwell? It's okay."

But then like a cobra, Mrs. Caldwell's hand latched around her arm. Cold. For a bedridden old woman, her strength was startling. She tried to break free. But she couldn't. "No . . . it's just me, Mrs. Caldwell. *Cynthia*. Let . . . go . . ." She struggled.

And just then, one of the nail edges dug into her skin. "Ouch!" As she fought to get the cold claw of a hand off her, she saw the mark on her, and the nail found a new spot of flesh on her arm to dig into.

"Please!" she mustered through gritted teeth. And finally, she broke free. But as she looked down at her arm and saw the red seeping from the cut . . . the same from the second one . . . the hand snatched her by the shirt.

She yanked her body backward. Once. Twice. Then a third time. And the woman nearly collapsed out of the bed. But as she fell onto her back, her arms jutted out to break her fall.

What the hell?

Just then, she thought she could hear the swivel of the chair . . . the shift in weight on the wood floor on the second level.

As she watched the silent sobs of the woman in bed, the snot and tears stringing into webs from her nose, she stood up. And as she looked down at her arm, turned it in the harsh yellow light, she made out the letter *K* . . .

Is it a K*? And is that . . . an* I*? Or an* L*? Maybe the number 1?*

For the first time since working for Mr. C, she disobeyed rule number 1.

She skulked to the cabinet as quietly as she could. Pulled a pad and a black pen from the drawer. As she crept toward Mrs. Caldwell, she spoke in the softest voice she could.

"I'm going to give you a pen and paper," she whispered to her. "If you try to hurt yourself, I'll scream."

She put the pad in front of the woman and let her clutch it in her hand. And once the pen closed in the woman's palm, she started writing furiously. Hard.

As she watched the letters *K* through *I* again, she knew she was right. But when the rest of the ink smudged beneath her hand, letters falling blindly, unevenly on the page, she looked down in horror as she read them.

KILL ME.

"I can't do that."

She wrote again. Low clicking. *Wisp.* The edge of her hand dragged across the surface. First there was some kind of symbol, a star? She scratched over it again. Then again. There was something else. Letters digging through the paper.

THEN KILL HIM. OR RUN!

"Okay. That's enough, Mrs. Caldwell." And as she tried to take the pen out of the hand, it shook, and the whole of her fist turned white. She wouldn't let go. And then her arm wrenched back, and she jabbed it with all her force at the wrinkles, the purple vein of her own wrist. Cynthia did all she could to stop it. And as she pried the pen loose, the pad fell to the ground, the pen soaring beneath the cabinets, and the old woman toppled halfway over the bed rail.

And that's when she heard him.

While he stared mindlessly at the Milton briefing, he pictured Gerry McAntis, the slicked-back dark hair, the puffed chest, and that smug face above the dipshit bow tie. The suits rarely matched; they were separates purchased off the rack at Macy's. Clashing plaids and stripes and solids, tweed and corduroy, cotton and wool. How this man had graduated from Northwestern Pritzker School of Law, he couldn't fathom. He must have cheated his way through school. He could only picture Gerry upside down doing a keg stand, scarfing down deep-dish Chicago pizza, or drunkenly slamming a buddy through a flimsy table designated for drinking games. They called Gerry the Jury, short for Juryman. More than once, he had tried to sleep with one of the female jurors on his cases. More than once, he was successful.

In his eyes, though, Gerry was a loudmouth oaf who talked out of his ass. If it hadn't been for *his* work on the Anders case a few years ago, no one would know who the hell Gerry was.

He loathed Gerry. Detested him. Still, he was occupationally forced to tolerate him.

It was Gerry who'd hired him. Now, *because of him*, clients paid Gerry a premium to go to bat for them. Now, because he was too close, he could never kill Gerry. Not that he fit his type.

Roger Milton, the seven-figure acting CFO of J&L Co., was a ball of dough where the top had been flattened. He had a blocky head and a crew cut and barely what one could call a neck. Even in his lifted Tom Ford derby shoes, he had to stretch to be five foot eight. Even beneath a black beard, his cheeks were perpetually red from anger. Gerry called him a bull.

"You know why they castrate those sons of bitches?" *Squeak.* Gerry was always squeezing that damn hand gripper, lips tight, cheeks and arm shaking like a buffoon. "To make them less aggressive and stop their male hormones. You know the saying *fuck like a bull*? How horny those fuckers must be? Just picture that little guy Milton go!"

He pictured Gerry again, thrusting his hips over the edge of his desk while ogling a photograph of Milton's latest fling.

He didn't think quite as highly of Milton as Gerry did. Milton was an idiot.

Milton had faced embezzlement charges in 2017 for wiring transactional funds from a corporate account to three offshore subsidiary accounts in the Cayman Islands: $4.5 million. Gone. When financial statements couldn't account for the missing funds, Milton, being the chief financial officer, claimed they had never been collected. Imagine the person responsible for tracking and analyzing the company's finances saying the funds weren't there. The investigation eventually caught Roger Milton in a lie: initially, he stated that he was unaware they went missing. But he was. They found proof.

An email, Roger? How could you be so stupid. A fucking email? He could still hear Gerry's voice. *Just because you delete the fucking thing doesn't mean it's gone for good.*

The investigation also found that Roger Milton was involved in an affair with a Colombian swimsuit model, Ximena Hernandez. The two had been sleeping together for about a year. Lucky for Milton and his money, he wasn't married. Ximena was. She had three children—Dario, Isabella, and Luisa Fernanda—whom he'd never met, claimed he didn't know about.

Milton said it was love. He said he'd "buried his bone in enough dirt to know which hole felt like love." Class act. When the company came after him for the money, he did what he knew best. Run.

When that didn't work, he turned against her. Not only was he filing blackmail charges, but he'd set her up. The three subsidiary companies that each received a lump sum of $1.5 million were listed as Dario Oil and Gas, I&A Ltd.—the letter *I* short for Isabella—and LF&Co, the *L* and *F* short for Luisa Fernanda. On the board for each company named after one of her children was Ximena Hernandez.

If Gerry—meaning, he—did his job right, Roger Milton wouldn't be found guilty of wire fraud by a jury. Though it wouldn't save his job, Milton wouldn't face prison time, which could be anywhere up to twenty years. If he did his job right, Gerry would receive all the glory, hymns sung in his honor, and maybe another woman out of the jury box and into his bed.

He could picture Gerry now, as he was after every win in the courtroom. In the office, with two old-fashioned glasses that he referred to as a Tender Nob: two tall pours of cognac brandy over rocks, rye, and splashes of different orgeats. Gerry would down one, then pour another for himself before handing the other glass over. Gerry drank like a fish. He, on the other hand, hated the taste. Still, he sipped it fast, so Gerry wouldn't harass him.

He stared long at the financial records, the sixteen pages' worth of allegations—not so much slandering as discrediting, all carefully selected and curated—Gerry would throw like rocks at a wincing

Ximena Hernandez before a courtroom, before the numbers and letters started to jumble and dance around and his eyes blurred.

His head lifted from his work. Leaning back in his chair, he scratched hard at his thinning crown. Fingernails digging until he felt like he'd pried up a round speck of scalp.

It was the ultimate test of will, to keep the safe only feet from him. When he worked from his home office, knowing his trophies were so close to him, the urge to open it and the will not to kept him on his toes.

Just then, there was a bang downstairs. He craned forward, laced his fingers together, and knocked his skull against his knuckles again and again.

That girl again . . .

Fair-skinned and spectacled, frizzy curls of long dark hair spilled just short of her slender chest, a birthmark above her glossed lip not remotely as appealing as Marilyn Monroe's.

The girl was studying to be a nurse. He told her that by working for him and tending to his mother, she'd get real job experience and good pay. He could pull some strings and get her a job in one of the nicer hospitals or private practices.

She had a gummy smile. One that reminded him of fish bait. Night crawlers—pink and ugly creatures—wriggling above her upper teeth. Ready to be impaled by a metal hook and fishing line.

He hated her smile.

He slid the chair out from under him, the wheels rolling silently against the plush carpet. Arching back, he pinched the bridge of his nose, walked to the door, and pulled it open.

Moving down the creaking stairs, he came around the corner and down the dark hall to his mother's bedroom. When he poked his head in, his mother was there, lying flat in the bed.

Where was the girl?

He flicked the switch on the wall, and his mother came into view. A damp shimmer coated her upper lip. Her chest was climbing and falling fast. As he walked beside her, he reached down and snatched her by the wrist.

He whispered, his words a hiss, hot on his breath. "Don't pretend to sleep, Mother."

He tried to unlatch her hand. The fingers that curled tightly. She whimpered. And when he forced it open, he stared down at the black smudge on her palm and index finger. He licked his finger and rubbed at it.

"Bitch."

Her hand shot out at him. He fell backward to the ground, his elbow banging into the floor. That's when he saw the pad beneath the bed, scanned the floor and found the pen under the cabinet. He pulled the pad out and scrambled back to his feet.

Despite the uneven tilt to the words, the jagged ink marks, he knew his mother's handwriting. For a moment, he smiled at the spottiness of it—the fear of *him* that had caused her hand to tremble. But then he was angry again.

Even after he'd done what he did, she was alive. And what a gift it was to be allowed to live at his mercy.

"When she dies, this one's on you."

Tilting his head back, he sighed. His mother let out one last whimper before he rushed out of the room.

Just then, the grinding tick, like a banshee at the curb out front. He hurried to the front door and watched the girl in the front seat. He popped the door open. The metallic sound echoed again, as though the car were crying. He walked outside. Felt the chill of the wind down his back. He looked left. Then right. There was no one else on the road. Then, as his steps fell closer and closer to the passenger door, the engine rumbled and squealed.

Rapping his knuckles delicately on the glass, he gave his most sincere face and held a hand up. Not to his surprise, the window rolled down.

"Is everything okay, Cynthia?"

"Yes, Mr. C." Her voice quivered. Her hands trembled on the steering wheel. "I'm sorry. I just felt a little sick."

"That's okay. Take the rest of the night off."

"Thanks, Mr. C."

"Of course. But you haven't gotten your pay for this week yet. Do you want to come inside and I'll give it to you?"

He watched the hesitation in the girl, as if it were seeping from her pores. "No . . . I'll get it next time I'm here if that's okay. I don't want to get you sick."

"Absolutely. No worries, Cynthia. See you next week?"

"See you then, Mr. C."

The window rolled back up. He fought the urge to jam his hand inside before it reached the top. As the low grumble disappeared down the road, he looked up to the window across the street at Mrs. Adams. He gave a smile and waved as pleasantly as he could, and the old bitch did the same.

Chapter 22

Rooker found the videocassette marked "Fresno '93." The handwriting was sloppy. The marker faded.

He blew a layer of dust from it, the grime floating a filthy snow into the air. It choked him.

Fresno was a tasteless memory to Rooker. Like toast.

It was a drive. About four hours north of the old house, spent mostly in silence with his father gripping the wheel of a 1990 BMW 535i. He could still taste the tobacco in the car. Tan upholstery marked up by cigarette embers. Gunner never let him touch the radio. It left him to think for four hours, about how no matter the outcome, the drive home would be spent in the same deafening silence as the drive there.

There was no pleasing Gunner. There was a lesser chance of making him proud than to walk on the moon without a space suit.

While he rummaged through the boxes, he muttered to himself.

It has to be here . . . somewhere . . .

When he reached the bottom of a box, his fingers closed around something cold and damp. When he lifted it, along with his arm from the box, his hooded sweatshirt sleeve was covered in cold grime and webs.

But there it was. The VHS player.

Rooker carried it under his arm into the living room where he plugged it into the outlet, then the back of the television.

Come on. Work.

To his surprise, it did. The power was on. He fed the tape to it, listened to the churning, like it was chewing it and ready to spit it back out.

Clunk.

Waves. Like heat shimmer on burning asphalt, only white and gray. And then the picture came through.

It was grainy. The kind of picture that would make you give the TV a good open-handed smack, only he knew it wasn't the television at fault.

He could see through the ropes. Two lanky boys in headgear and gloves, circling each other like sharks. One afraid to throw the first punch but the other more than happy to oblige. It was him.

He was much smaller then. Lean, with muscle thin as rope and wire.

He watched his left jab probe at his opponent's face and snap back to defend just as fast. There weren't many tapes of him as a boy in existence. To his surprise, he discovered the dimpled smile and grin in his eyes and attempted to fight both off.

He remembered that from the outside, the boxing gym appeared to be a garage. Two massive roll-up doors. Tiled brick exterior. Flags quivering from the roof ledge. Across the street, rusted chain-link fencing, plastered with signs that read BEWARE OF THE DOG, with spiraled barbed wire at the top. The dog, he couldn't remember ever seeing. Or hearing, for that matter. A moat of dirt stretched behind the fence. The curb was lined with beater cars coated in dust. But outside the gym, there was always the same 1980 Mercedes-Benz S-Class. Pristine white. Not a ding or scuff anywhere. Rims glistening like polished cutlery.

Next door to the gym was a fenced lot called Mike's Garage. Boats and cars—really there were just a few old twenty-five-foot Bayliners and Cobalts, surrounded by sedans—Saturn, Toyota, Mazda, Cadillac—up on blocks or wrapped in weathered tarp that reminded him of a cold blue sky. A few cars had rust spots that looked like old puke. It looked more like a police impound or a scrapyard.

On more than one occasion, Mike, all six feet and three hundred pounds of him, limped over in a flannel shirt and jeans to try to sell him his first car. He had thin strands of black hair, a white goatee like dog fur, squinty eyes, and a big smile. But after the one time he tried to shake Gunner's hand, he never spoke another word to Rooker.

On the inside of the gym, there were a few old heavy bags and speed bags, tall marine-blue lockers with built-in combination locks, and steel silver folding chairs.

Rooker watched himself circle to his opponent's left to stay clear of the counter right. Jabbing his way in and then throwing quick shots to the body and his opponent's headgear. One of the punches lifted the padding off his chin, and Rooker moved in and started throwing heavier blows until the referee stopped him.

The camera never moved. Even when the referee held his arm up to present him as the winner. He never once heard his father's voice on the tape. That, alone, was enough to unnerve him.

"Home movie?"

He gave a start and then laughed. "Didn't even know you were still here. But yeah, I guess you could call it that. How's your computer?" Rooker asked.

"I don't know," she said. "Fried, I think."

He studied her as she did what she would do anytime she was deep in thought: twirl the ends of her hair. "There must have been something on the page, maybe when I clicked on the chat box . . . Take a look at this," she said while walking his way, with his laptop in tow just below her chest. "Your old pal Warrel." She smiled at him and turned the screen to him. "Can't say I've ever seen him make the tabloids, but I have to say, it's a pretty good story. You'll get a kick out of the title."

He analyzed today's date, then the tabloid logo, just above a headline that made him feel like he could hear his blood tick.

THE NOT-SO-WITCH HUNT FOR A KILLER'S KILLER SON

BY WARREL HANEY

MINNEAPOLIS, Minn. — The apple doesn't fall far from the murderous psychopathic tree, does it? Not for Rooker Lindström.

It isn't a trail of Granny Smiths or Golden Delicious so much as it is the cold corpses of those who come in close contact with him.

Not for the man who trespassed into my home and not only threatened me and put his hands on me but forced me to give up sensitive information.

How many felonies is that?

But noooo. Rooker Lindström is protected by the police, despite the trail of bodies that follows the once-acclaimed ace reporter. All because he aided in—get this—not the capture, but MURDER, of an Itasca County detective by the name of Elias Cole.

Guilty until proven innocent, right?

Fleeing from a tragic past, the prodigal son returned to the murder home of his serial-killer father, where too many women to count died, including his next-door neighbor.

In an attempt to take the cowardly way out, he lit the home on fire. SERV PRO employees indicate that the body of a woman was excavated beneath, to no one's shock, Lindström Manor. So why hasn't the body been identified yet? Is Rooker the killer? I'd sooner believe so than not.

The killer of Rooker Lindström's son, the infamous Madman, Tate Meachum, is in solitary confinement at Pelican Bay State Prison in Crescent City, California. I think Rooker Lindström should be sent home, back to California, right there in a cell next to him.

An anonymous source within the supermax facility left me with this chilling photograph, which shows six tally marks carved into the concrete wall of what was formerly Meachum's solitary-confinement cell prior to his relocation. Only, we all know, there were five confirmed victims.

Police suspected Meachum might have had an accomplice during his murder spree; who's to say it wasn't the prodigal son?

"Breaking and entering? When were you going to tell me?"
He raised his index finger. "Technically, I didn't break anything. He opened the door, and I just gave it a little nudge open."
"You don't have a badge, Rooker. Neither do I—not anymore."

He handed the laptop back. "I'm aware I didn't graduate from the academy. Thanks, Millie."

"Yeah, well. This guy has a hard-on for you. He has a platform; maybe don't poke the bear for a while."

"Don't say hard-on. It's unbecoming."

"Maybe it's time you give *your girlfriend* a call." She pronounced it *gurrrl-friennd*. "I'm sure Caroline Lind is just dying to get another exclusive or maybe a little hanky-panky—the famous Rooker Lindström back in her bed."

"Don't call me famous. Or say *hanky-panky* . . . ever again. Add those to the list."

"Look, all I'm saying is—"

"Yeah, Millie. I got it."

"Don't do that. Don't try to shut me out like I'm everyone else."

He sighed. "I'm sorry. I won't."

"I mean it. Caroline Lind can help us. After what she did, she owes you."

He grumbled, "Maybe." As much as he didn't want to admit it, Millie was right. As she oftentimes was. But he knew that Caroline Lind could be of value to them. "Anything on Amy Berglund?"

"Well, I have to get a new laptop now. But so far, no luck. I haven't been able to find a current address for her family."

"Did you try the old one?"

"They moved away after everything. When Amy never came back, they left."

◆ ◆ ◆

It was another hour of Millie's jokes before Rooker relented and drove the Volvo over to Caroline Lind's town house. The leather seat crinkled as he settled into it. It smelled the way you'd imagine an old car would, and the new air freshener swinging from the rearview mirror did little to help. But the car was starting to grow on him.

He pulled over at the curb, where the gearshift fought a bit before it locked into the parked position. He vaguely remembered the brick steps and the glass that looked like rain behind swirling wrought iron. He pressed his forehead against the cold steering wheel. He shut his eyes and thought about how much he didn't want to go inside. He spent a few more moments taking deep breaths—there was a faint musty odor mixed with tobacco that was actually quite pleasant to him—and then got out and walked up the stairs, where he remembered watching Caroline fumbling in the dark for her keys.

Ignoring the doorbell, he rapped three times on the solid wood. The door opened, and Caroline stood there in an oversize charcoal Penn crew neck sweatshirt with her hair in a messy bun. While she smiled at Rooker, who tried not to glance down at her bare legs, she said, "Didn't expect to see you so soon."

He snuck a glance at the four light-gray letters on her chest and stopped himself. "And I didn't know you were Ivy League."

"Go Quakers."

The first floor of Caroline Lind's home was foreign to him in the daylight. Even though he'd left abruptly the previous morning, his awkward exit put blinders over his eyes.

Dark hardwood floors ran throughout. Past her, he could see the tall staircase to the left of the hallway and what he thought was a dining room on the right.

"I was hoping I could ask you a few questions," he said.

She smiled again. "Are you a reporter?"

"Not exactly. Can I come in?"

"Do you have credentials?"

"I have this?" He pulled out her card with her lipstick smudge. "Does this get me in the door?"

She let him in. As she led him down the hall, he watched the backs of her legs.

"No apology?"

She turned at the end of the hall and stopped in the kitchen. "Is that your first question?"

"How many networks came running?"

"A couple. *Star Tribune* and KSTP-TV. FOX News reached out about giving me my own segment."

"Congratulations."

She smiled. "Thanks. And for the record, I am sorry. It was just business."

"What happened upstairs didn't seem like 'just business.'"

She smiled again. "That it wasn't . . . So can I guess why you're here?"

Rooker plopped down into one of the bar seats behind the kitchen island. "You aren't going to ask my drink of choice first?"

She opened the refrigerator door. "Warrel Haney. I read the article this morning. Can't say I've ever seen a conspiracy theorist get a column in the tabloids before. It's everywhere."

"Ratings must be down."

She laughed. "Not anymore. Word of advice?"

"Sure."

"Steer clear of Haney. He has a strange following. Probably the QAnon crowd. The kind of people who will leave a dead animal at your door. Maybe stalk you, leave a handmade bomb under your car."

"Noted. I was actually hoping we could help each other out."

"How so?"

"I have information—"

"Which you'd like to exchange for . . ."

"A favor. When the time comes."

"Pretty broad."

"And if you find out anything you think is relevant to missing women—some wackjob who phones in to your station, a message, anything—you bring it to me."

"Sounds like a one-sided deal."

"Believe me, the information I have . . . this is far from one-sided."

"Deal. Should we make a toast?"

"Next time."

Rooker recounted the last twenty-four hours while Caroline speed-typed notes on her phone.

When he was finished, he said, "Don't screw me over again."

"You don't want to come upstairs?"

Now he was the one who smiled. "Next time."

Stay away from me was what he wanted to say, even if he didn't truly mean it. The people around him had a funny way of turning up dead. Maybe it was best to stay far, far away from Caroline Lind.

As he turned away, he took one last look up and down at her, like a grabby airport pat down. She smirked and curtsied. Maybe he did want that drink . . . Then in his mind he heard Millie teasing him about thinking with his dick, and he headed back to the car. Caroline had every reason to help, if only for her next scoop, but as he left her standing there, he wondered how much he could really trust her. At this moment in time, he figured very little.

Nearly the entire winding drive home, every agonizing moment spent beneath every cherry-red traffic light, he'd thought about how stupid he was for not going upstairs with Caroline. But it was too late. It would look too desperate to turn back now.

While he slowed past the gate, the squealing churn of the engine reverberating off the rusted black bars, he thought he could make out the door to the cottage hanging wide open just past Millie's SUV. And no sign of Millie.

Rooker let the car crawl forward. The engine no longer ticked. All he could hear was his own breathing and the gravel snapping beneath the tires. He slowed to a stop. Put the car in park and shut the engine off. From a distance, the addition to the front of the house looked like a wall of black glass. While he stared at it and the open doorway, he dialed Millie and listened to the repeated ring. When it sent him to her voice mail, he pulled the latch to the glove box, which snapped open and rattled. Beneath a filthy old hand rag, he grabbed the Glock 17 that he didn't technically own. Nor was he permitted to have it.

It would classify as a gross misdemeanor if he ever got caught. He knew he wouldn't.

Federal 9x19mm rounds. Jacketed hollow points. Ever since his showdown with Gregory Sadler, his paranoia was at an all-time high. He found the exits in a room once he'd strutted inside. He found the shadows just the same. He'd analyze the level of malice in the faces around him. Rarely would he go anywhere unless he'd stashed a weapon in close proximity. There was an eight-inch chef's knife in the bedside nightstand. Sadler's rifle leaned up against the wall at arm's length from the back door. Peter Sundgren's Glock 17, which he kept in a drawer behind his recliner. And at least if he drove, he knew he might have a chance to get to the glove box, to the newer-generation model Glock 17 he'd gotten from Millie.

He checked the slide, pushed his door open slowly, and left it ajar. He crept the rest of the way. Skulked up the front stairs. Peeked his head inside. With the gun held down at his side warily, he stepped inside and called out to her. "Mill?"

He turned from the living room and moved silently into the kitchen. He found Geralt with wet paws, his white fur dirty, lapping water from the dripping faucet. Rooker scratched the feathery fluff behind his head and turned the faucet off. She wasn't there.

"Millie?"

That's when he heard the step behind him. He turned on a dime. Luckily, he didn't bring the pistol up, because Millie was standing there, hair in a bun, with a new laptop in her hands.

"What the hell are you thinking?" he said to her.

"What?"

"The killer knows we're looking for them, Millie. And here you are, just leaving the front door wide open?"

"*Please.* It's the middle of the day. I could hear anyone coming up the driveway."

"Yeah? Like you just heard me?" He went to the fridge. The door jangled; loose condiments clinked and clanged while they slid around and knocked into each other on the top shelf. He pulled out a fresh carton of milk, went to the cupboard, and pulled down a bowl, wiped the inside of it with the hem of his shirt, and poured a heavy serving. "And what if they don't come from the driveway? Sadler didn't." He set the bowl down beside the sink and listened to Geralt purr.

"I get it. Where were you anyway? Figured you might have left for LA or New York."

"What are you talking about?"

"I saw the mail on the table. Were you going to tell me?"

"Just like Tess. Snooping through my stuff." He watched her stiffen. That one, he knew, was a bit of a low blow. "And tell you *what*, exactly? It's just more people who want me for a story."

"But it isn't."

"It isn't *what*?"

"*The same.* It's the *Times.* You know, and I know, that was your dream. That's why it's not in the same pile with everything else you rip to shreds."

"*Dream?*" He scoffed. "I don't *have* a dream anymore, only nightmares . . . God forbid I don't put it in the same pile. Everything means something to you . . ."

"To you what?"

"Women. You all make nothing out to be something. Evelyn did it. My ex-wife did it. Tess did it. Now you're doing it."

"Well, we for damn sure aren't sleeping together."

"No shit. Your loss."

There was a hint of a smile on her face.

"So are you going to tell me where you were or are we keeping secrets?"

"I was taking your advice. I went to see Caroline."

"And?"

"*And* she's going to help."

"Until she isn't."

"Correct. But thanks to me, she got a brand-new segment with FOX News. So I give her some information—"

"And what? She blows you?"

"*Christ.*" He scratched his head. He thought of his next words carefully. "She owes us one. So when it comes time we need a favor, we call her. And if she hears anything that seems relevant to what we're looking into, she comes to us first."

"Not bad."

"Not bad at all. And I didn't even have to sleep with her."

Chapter 23

"Audio check," a voice said beside her.

Massive lights dazzled as bright as diamond chandeliers overhead. An enormous wall of monitors played her segment logo behind her. And she knew the faces that would cover it soon enough.

Off camera to her right was a step-up platform with two chairs and a table positioned between them. It was for her very first guest.

The IFB earpiece was already secure in her ear. Eddie was fastening the microphone box to her back. Janet was doing a last-minute touch-up on her makeup.

"Two minutes out," she heard a voice call out somewhere behind a dozen monitors someone had referred to as the "cockpit."

Caroline was loving every second of it.

They were eating out of her palm. Scurrying around like chickens, feeding on the scraps she gave them.

She was finally getting her moment. This segment would make her career—maybe even get her out of Minnesota for good. She pictured herself in a new place in a fast-paced city and pondered if that's the life she still wanted. She wasn't so sure anymore. Despite their conversation and the pit in her stomach, she was about to screw Rooker over again.

As much as she'd liked him, she told herself it was part of the job. She'd make it up to him.

Afraid she might blow it, she skimmed the scripts on the table in front of her. Flipped through the pages with a snap as she flung to the next paper in the stapled heap. She'd already read it countless times. But you could never be too prepared.

"It's almost showtime, Ms. Lind."

She smiled. "Thank you, Eddie," she said politely. Looking up at the clock, she read the time. 6:59 p.m. Less than a minute to go. She read the first words on the teleprompter, though they'd practically been tattooed to her eyelids at this point.

They played the intro.

From FOX News, this is Late Night News *with Caroline Lind.*

June, the pale and pink-faced woman beside the teleprompter in a hideous sweater and peacock-print scarf, held a firm hand up to Caroline, then jabbed one finger in her direction.

"Good evening, everyone. I'm Caroline Lind. In tonight's top story, a chilling connection emerges between the murder of a local woman and a thirty-year-old missing persons case that rocked the nation . . ."

Rooker sat in his recliner. Millie returned from the kitchen with a steaming bag of popcorn and shoved it in Rooker's face. He took a handful, felt his knuckles dampen, and without looking away from the television piled it into his mouth. "Did you just pour butter all over this?"

He watched her flop onto the awful couch. "That I did. Are you nervous?"

"Maybe about a heart attack from how much butter—"

"I thought maybe you'd be nervous for her."

"Why would I be?"

"Are you?"

He smiled. "I'm not," he declared. "She strikes me as someone who doesn't get nervous anyway."

"Think she'll burn you again?"

He'd already thought about that. He didn't think she would so soon. Maybe it was more that he hoped she wouldn't. "With her, you never know."

"Nora Vandenberg, the daughter of Thomas Vandenberg, CEO of Vandenberg Enterprises, was reported missing on September 17, a complaint the police have been slow to take seriously. But according to a source close to the case, the search for Ms. Vandenberg reached a new level of urgency yesterday when they discovered a link between her disappearance and the 2011 disappearance of Malin Jakobsson, whose disfigured body was found in Itasca State Park the day before Vandenberg was reported missing. Evidence of occult practices have been found in both cases.

"Even more shocking, this investigation has uncovered new insight into the 1989 disappearance of Amy Berglund. Does Itasca County have a new serial killer in its midst? Stay with us . . ."

Chapter 24

Tess hadn't slept. It was no longer the shadows on the walls, or the gurgle of the toilet valve, or the usual sleepwalking of Mrs. Crawford upstairs. There were plenty of reasons now not to sleep.

She stared at the mess of her desk—her dual-way radio beside two of her dad's old mugs that smelled of stale coffee, a depleted stack of sticky notes, the ME report on Malin Jakobsson, printouts on the Vandenberg family, the article by that nut Warrel Haney that almost made Tess feel the littlest bit sorry for Rooker. And underneath it all, of course, the file on the body at Lindström Manor.

"You gotta see this, boss." The voice called out from the other side of the glass. She instinctively looked out at Millie's desk. It was empty. She could picture her in a sweater, typing in a frenzy while doing two or three different tasks at once. Oftentimes, the thought of Millie gone made her want to both smile and cry. She pushed the thought away as she heard Vic say, "Boss," again, this time more urgently.

She got up and walked out into the bullpen. She walked past Riggs, his hatless head down, dirty-blond hair flattened and visibly thinning. Vic was staring intently at his computer.

"What is it, Sterling?"

He pushed his chair to the side so Tess could see his screen and reloaded the previous night's news clip on the local FOX affiliate's website.

Caroline Lind sitting to the right of a gigantic monitor, on which was a famous photo of a girl. Tess was much younger when it first was on every news channel, but the girl was legend around here. The beautiful blonde hair, a few perfectly windblown strands like spider silk. The radiant smile . . . "That's—"

"Exactly." Vic slumped back down into his seat. "Amy *fuckin'* Berglund."

"Can you pause it?" The picture froze, and Tess stared at the woman sitting behind the desk. She'd only ever encountered Caroline Lind once in her career. Two years ago, Lind had questioned her about a homicide: foul play suspected where a twenty-seven-year-old female washed up on a muddy bank on Gunn Lake. The victim was stabbed eleven times, and her boyfriend was later charged and confessed to killing her. But that one time was enough to tell her that if there were a fire, Caroline Lind would step over anyone in her way to save herself.

"This is surreal. Let it play, Sterling."

"According to a confidential source, evidence from all three scenes, including the use of sinister occult symbols, suggests that the same person is responsible for the recent disappearance of Nora Vandenberg, the disappearance and possible murder of Malin Jakobsson, and the disappearance of Amy Berglund . . ."

"Confidential source my ass," Vic said.

"Shh!" Tess hissed.

"The disappearance of Amy Berglund received national media coverage in October 1989 and the following year. Not only did the investigation spark an outrage, but a mandated curfew was put into effect. Thousands of residents volunteered for search parties. But nothing was ever found . . ."

Tess felt her face redden. There was a fierceness, a fire she felt in her bones. The only word she could think of burned off her tongue. *"Fuck."*

Goddamn Rooker Lindström.

Riggs, who had been hovering behind her, said, "There's no way. You mean to tell me . . . Rooker and Millie went to this two-bit anchor before coming to us?"

Vic popped a shiny doughnut hole into his mouth and slurped down some coffee. The black mug in his hand read: CAUTION: HOT DETECTIVE. "It has to be them"—he waved a second doughnut hole at Tess—"you saw the clip of her in the bar with him. Maybe the hot anchor lady agreed not to divulge how she *came* by her information."

Tess gritted her teeth. "I warned them." She bit down hard enough that she thought she might break through enamel. A sharp pain was forming behind her eyes. She unclenched her jaw, tried to tell herself to relax, but her anger forced two thoughts into her mind: the scar on her fingertip and the woman beneath the floor. "Rather than coming to me, they let this *clown* tell the world about a link among three victims."

She escaped to her office and slammed the door behind her. She heard the scrape of the picture frame as it dragged down the nail. She flumped into the chair and leered at the black-and-gray article framed on the wall, now at a tilt to the left. It was a gift from Chief Larsson— not a surprise to her that the old bastard scrapbooked. She read the headline, then turned away in disgust.

DETECTIVES IDENTIFY SERIAL KILLER AS ONE OF THEIR OWN

She wanted to rip it off the wall. Smash the frame to bits until there were thousands of invisible pieces of glass. Thousands of tiny new scars.

With a judgmental stare at her dark reflection in the computer monitor, she rubbed at the bags beneath her eyes. The makeup she'd applied to hide her insomnia was no longer working. The color was there, but the dark spots sprouted up like weeds. As her hand fell over the mouse, she winced, and her face recoiled against the screen's brightness. She appraised the scene again. She'd looked at it more times than she could count, remembered each photo. The damage from the fire. She clicked the next button. A new photo of scorched earth emerged. *Click.* The charred front left portion of the home. Rubble from part of the roof. *Click.* The blackened doorframe. *Click.* The ruined floorboards. Dust particles like soot and ash. *Click.* A view of something beneath the floor level. Something wrapped up in an old sheet in a crawl space invaded by webs. *Click.* The same thing, covered but closer up. *Click.* The figure uncovered. Bone. *Click.* The skeleton.

Her body went cold. A strange feeling consumed her; it was as though someone was following her. The feeling that someone was there and you should run. Her skin crawled. It whispered to her.

The bastard wanted you to find her. He wanted you to know he did it all along. He wanted you to know and not be able to do a damn thing about it.

She dug her fingernail into the snowflake. Looked down and watched a pinprick of red blotch from it. As her hand trembled, she thought the same thought she had been thinking for months: Gunner wouldn't have left her head. She grabbed her phone.

After a few rings, he answered. He always answered.

"Did you find anything?"

She listened to maybe a quarter of the exact same spiel he'd given her the last time she phoned him before cutting him off. "I don't care how long she's been dead, Isaiah. Find me something. *Now.*"

She ended the call.

At this point, she didn't even care who the woman was. If Rooker was going to interfere with her investigation, and make a fool out of her by doing it, she would take him down with her.

Now she couldn't fight the darkness that crept into her mind. She tried to suppress it. Tried to reel it back onto land, steady the tremor in her hand. It was no use. Like soil-squirming worms, the impulse, the hunger, her thoughts fed on her. It was as bad as it had been that night.

She could see them in her mind's eye.

The two of them and their matching limp, side by side. Dressed in the latest club fashion: some kind of patterned button-down or a blazer or leather jacket with skinny black pants. Chummy smiles on their faces while they boyishly shoved one another, hooting and hollering at female passersby. Reeking of cheap spirits, nicotine, and weed—and enough cologne to put on a rag as a substitute for chloroform. Jan Cullen. Clyde Miller. Maybe tonight was the night. Not only could she see the change of clothes inside the duffel bag in the back seat, she could hear her mother's words, but right now, they didn't make her want to curl into a fetal ball and cry.

"WHAT HAVE YOU DONE?"

WHAT HAD TO BE DONE.

Chapter 25

"Rooker . . . hey." He felt a bony finger jab the front of his shoulder.

He pretended not to hear her until she repeated the same process and pressed harder. "Ouch, Millie."

"Get up already."

He unfurled one eyelid, felt his nose scrunch while he looked at her. "I figured you'd go away."

"Yeah, well. We have work to do. Remember Christine Vandenberg, *our client*?"

"What about her?" He felt a sharp slap on his arm that echoed louder than it hurt. "Christ!"

"Up!"

Rooker groaned and sighed while he rolled onto his side. Twisting his knuckles into the edges of his eyes, he said, "Shit! The segment."

"Correct. She saw it."

"What did you tell her?"

"That we *are* the anonymous source. And then I lied. I told her it was a tactic that we were using to flush out whoever may have taken Nora."

"Did she buy it?"

"I think so. She said they were willing to offer a reward and go on the news if we thought it might help."

He yawned. "What time is it?"

"Ten. I found a number listed for Charles and Eva Berglund: Amy's parents. I phoned them an hour ago. The father answered."

"What did he say?"

"He asked me how it's possible to move on when the media keeps digging up the past. Guess he has a point. The wife is really torn up over seeing Amy on Caroline's segment. Charles said she won't talk to us, but he will. Seems like he still has some lingering hope that he'll find out what happened to his girl. Don't worry, I didn't make any promises."

"Good. We aren't doctors." He made a face.

"What is it?"

"I'm not really sure. I think a few things just aren't sitting right."

"Like what?"

"Well, when we went to talk to Selma Sadler, she said she stayed in the same house all that time just in case Gregory ever came back. So why didn't the Berglunds stick around longer? Amy went missing. She wasn't declared dead."

"I think you're forgetting the magnitude of that case. Gregory Sadler's disappearance was overshadowed by your father's arrest. But Amy Berglund was way more than the talk of the town. She was on the front page all over the country. She was on *World News Tonight* when it was Peter Jennings."

Rooker thought for a moment. "But what about this 'witch hunt' theory of Haney's? Were there symbols near the Berglunds' house or on any of Amy's belongings? And should we even be going through all this effort to see them? Their daughter disappeared three decades ago. What could they possibly tell us that the police didn't already get from them? It should all be in the file."

"But we're the ones who found the photo. A photo that isn't even in her file—"

"But why go to their house? Why not go to the old house? The one they lived in when she went missing."

"What's gotten into you?"

"I don't know. We aren't wanted there. Maybe it's just best to leave these people alone."

"And what about Nora Vandenberg?" She paused. "Maybe back then, with Amy, they found something and didn't know what they were looking at. Maybe they didn't know what they were looking for."

"Who's to say we know what we're looking for?"

"We have to try. I don't know that it will be enough, but it will be enough for me. They live out in Holyoke. We may need to stay overnight somewhere. You should probably bring a clean change of clothes—assuming you have one."

He sighed and groaned dramatically and hoisted himself out of the chair.

◆ ◆ ◆

Rooker locked the door behind him. He carried his duffel bag to the Volvo, where he pried open the glove box and grabbed the pistol beneath the old rag. He shoved it to the bottom of the duffel bag beneath his change of clothes and pulled the zipper tight. He placed the duffel bag in the back seat of Millie's SUV and hopped in the passenger side.

The drive out to the Berglunds' was just over two hours. Rooker never enjoyed car rides. They made him think. Mostly of the past, of sitting in silence in the passenger seat while Gunner floored the gas pedal.

With his feet kicked up on the dash and his laptop on his thighs, he inserted a wireless card into the USB port. He pulled up a YouTube clip of the *World News Tonight* segment on Amy Berglund. The iconic photo of Amy was beside Peter Jennings. His hair was parted, and he wore a russet blazer over a light-blue dress shirt and striped tie. Rooker analyzed the thin upper lip and the lines that creased his forehead as he spoke. The deepness of his voice, and the genuine tone in it, Rooker thought, were made for television.

The picture changed to a full-screen view of a prayer vigil. A river of people gathering. Crying faces and heads hanging low. Tall candles lit, cradled like dead birds in their hands.

He stared at the handmade signs: BRING AMY HOME.

The picture changed to the search parties going out, grabbing supplies and backpacks and flashlights from the beds of trucks and car trunks. Groups waded cautiously through woods, stepping over broken tree limbs and brush. "Wow," he said. "It's like everyone in Itasca County was looking for her."

"And I would bet you that one of the people there knew where she was."

He froze. It was a thought that shamefully hadn't occurred to him, but now the thought was ice-cold liquid pouring down his spine. His leg twitched. He turned to her, watching her attentive face on the road. "You think so?"

She glanced over and said, "Wouldn't you?" Her head turned back to the road. "Let's say you take someone, and it makes headlines all over the country. They send search parties out deep into the woods, and these prayer vigils pop up like herpes sores; you wouldn't want to be a part of that, knowing all along you're the one who has her? A chameleon. A wolf in sheep's clothing."

She had a good point. Rooker stared at the images awhile longer, wondering if he should be paying attention to anyone in the background. Then he let out a yawn, reclined his seat, and folded his arms across his chest.

"You just woke up. There's no way you're going back to sleep."

He closed his eyes. "No. Of course not."

"Remind me to never go on a road trip with you again."

◆ ◆ ◆

His head bobbed with the splash of tires against a gravel road. He opened his eyes. Wiped his mouth with the veiny back of his hand to the crunch and crackle of rock being spit out beneath the wheels. The suspension swayed against the clumped dirt. He looked up at the two-story farmhouse that had old brick pillars and a chimney that matched. Patches of grass out front reminded him of egg yolk, with a brown tinge that looked scorched. From where he stood, the house looked crooked.

"We made it."

"What was your first clue? Look, I do most of the questioning. We probably get one shot at a guy like this, and I won't be happy if I drove all the way here just to be sent away."

"You got it."

They walked toward the front porch, where a chocolate-and-white border collie snarled at them, perched at the bottom of the steps. Rooker stood still, watching the wrinkle of the dog's nose, the guttural, clicking growl behind the sharp white teeth. In that split second, it transformed from peaceful pooch to rabid wolf.

The porch door whined as it swung open. An old man hobbled sideways down the few stairs, and the rickety clatter blasted as the door shut wildly behind him. Rooker recognized him immediately from the newspapers and the *World News Tonight* segment.

Charles Berglund was now eighty-one years of age and living in the middle of nowhere on three acres of land with his wife. His daughter would be forty-eight years old now, yet he hadn't seen her since she was eighteen. Rooker stared into the man's face, wondering if this was what he was meant to become.

"Sorry, he doesn't much like company."

If the remoteness of the home wasn't enough to go on, judging by the face of Charles Berglund, he wasn't one for company either. Rooker ambled a few steps in front of Millie to shake the man's hand, and the dog barked from beside him. He sat on the ground, held his hand out, and when the dog walked cautiously toward him, Rooker scratched behind his ear. "Me either."

"He doesn't let many people that close to him. 'Specially strangers."

"Sounds like we have some things in common."

The old man patted the dog on the head a few times and smiled. "Not much of a guard dog anymore, huh, Red?"

Rooker stood.

"Mr. Berglund, I'm Millie Langston. This is my partner, Rooker Lindström."

Rooker watched the old man appraise him up and down, then turn back to Millie. "Charles is just fine, ma'am. My wife doesn't want you in the house. Hope you don't mind. When the law couldn't find our girl, Eva took on a real hatred for 'em."

"No problem at all."

Mr. Berglund asked matter-of-factly, "I hope you don't mind my asking, miss, but what is it you think I can do for you exactly?"

"I was hoping to ask you some questions."

"Thirty years ago, they asked all the same questions you're about to ask me now. I don't think the same answers are going to do us any good."

"I'm willing to find out."

"All right, then. Come this way. Stay, Red."

Rooker and Millie followed behind as the man limped toward a garage port detached from the home. An old Ford F-100 was parked outside it. The white-and-beige paint was weathered and chipped, corroding below the driver door. To the left of the garage was a taxi-yellow turn mower; deep-green clippings and residue coated the wheels.

Charles Berglund unlatched the door to the garage and pulled it open.

Rooker saw enough tools to fill a garage three times the size. A worktable in the center of the chaos. Charles pulled up three chairs that may have even been handmade and sat down last.

"You made these?" Rooker asked.

"I do some woodworking in my spare time. Which happens to be every day now."

"I'll let my partner do most of the questioning, but I do have one. Why didn't you stay in the old house?"

"Because we had to move on."

"But your daughter went missing." Rooker hesitated. "I'm sure you heard about Gregory Sadler. When I spoke to his mother, she said that every morning since he fell through the ice on the lake, she'd drink her coffee and stare at the door. She said she stayed all those years because she wanted to be there in case he ever came back. What if Amy came back to you?"

"It's far too late for 'what ifs,' wouldn't you say? There were never any *real* clues. My daughter is gone. And by gone, you damn well know I don't mean *missing*."

Rooker felt the warmth of sunlight drained from the room. The chair stiffened beneath him. Every square inch of the old man's face darkened.

The color of spring on Rooker's face whitened. He started to feel woozy. A tremor seized control of his legs, and a nauseous bubble metastasized in the pit of his stomach.

Suddenly, a black curdled slime oozed from the cracks of the old man's nails. It gushed down his crooked fingers. Webbed like black snot between them. Rooker squeezed his eyes shut.

No. Stop it.

148

He clasped a hand over his wrist, where his pulse sharpened to a stabbing pain.

Millie sat up straighter. "Were there ever any suspects in the case?"

"None that they ever told us about. And no, Amy wasn't dating anyone."

"Were there ever any volunteers in the search parties, any people at the vigils, anyone at all who you were suspicious of?"

"To be honest, miss, we're talking thirty years ago. There were a lot of our friends—good people. People who truly wanted nothing more than to find Amy. I'm sure there were some weirdos who just wanted to play a part in the investigation. Maybe get lucky and find a body. Maybe some kids horsing around. But I can't say I remember anyone."

"Rooker?" Millie said.

He felt her eyes on him as he teetered shakily toward the door. "Yeah, just need to get some air." He attempted a convincing smile as best he could. It fell short, abrupt and blank.

After he staggered out of the garage, he felt the sweat bead on the back of his head while he hurried toward a lone elm tree on the front end of the property. Nearly tripping over a root that reached out for him from the earth, he slowed to a stop. He pressed his back to the tree, felt the old bark flake against his back. Staring down at the tremble in his hands, he hyperventilated. He felt his knees weaken, and just as they buckled, a volcanic eruption of watery yellow and beady chunks with a pinkish tinge landed before his feet.

The sound muffled in the breeze. All he could hear was the splash against the ground and the pounding of his chest.

He shut his eyes and wiped his mouth. Swallowed hard. Inhaled deep, cool breaths of autumn air. And when he looked up from the shine spots spattered on his shoe, he thought he could see a woman, a judgmental face on him from behind the gray veil of the screen door.

He stared for a few moments before the figure disappeared. He dragged his shoe across the tall grass until the bile was gone.

He walked the way back toward the garage but stopped short, sitting down in the crabgrass. Red came over and lay down beside him. For a couple of minutes, he felt okay. But he knew where he had to go, so he stood, petted Red one last time, and went back in through the open door.

"Told you," Rooker listened to the old man say. "Wasting your time here. All these questions, it's the same as back then. It won't do any good."

"I just have a few left, Charles. Then we'll be out of your hair."

Charles was losing that too.

"Can you tell us if anything in these photos looks familiar to you?" She slid the printed photos out of her pocket. They were images of both Nora Vandenberg's and Malin Jakobsson's bedrooms.

Charles shuffled slowly through the photographs, taking his time with each. Then, after he raked his fingernails across the aged lines of his forehead, he covered his mouth with his hand. "The rooms look just like hers did. Amy's." He handed them back to her. "It's been thirty years . . . but that's how I remember it. The mirrors." He paused. "There were mirrors at the foot of Amy's bed when she went missing. Two of 'em."

Millie hesitated. "Was Amy involved in any sort of group?"

"She was in the honors program since I can remember. And the high school's debate team."

Rooker followed up. "She was going to Princeton, right? What was she going to study?"

"Law." He smiled. "She was incredible on the debate team. Even in our house, she could outsmart my wife and me in conversations. Play the two of us against each other. She would have been a great lawyer."

"I'm sorry, I meant, was she—"

Rooker cut her off. "Sorry. Do you happen to still have her high school yearbook?"

"Uh. Yeah. We do. I can get it from the house for you."

Millie continued. "What I meant to say was, was Amy in any groups outside of school?"

"I'm sorry, miss. But I don't have a clue what—"

"This may sound strange. But did Amy believe in magic? Did she study anything medieval? Supernatural? Did she perform any sort of witchcraft?"

Rooker imagined this was where the man would tell the two of them, in much uglier language, to leave and never come back. They'd asked him if his all-American, dead teenage daughter was a freak.

Charles Berglund's face blanched. Stiffened as though he'd braced for impact. "Witchcraft? You think my girl—"

"No, that's not what I'm saying." She pulled out her phone and unlocked it. As she scrolled through the images, she faced the screen to Charles Berglund. "I'm asking if you've seen any symbols like this," she said. She slid her finger across the screen. Photo after photo. Until she watched Charles's eyebrows furl, not in anger but in recognition.

"That," he said to her. "That one there."

Rooker stood behind her and watched as she turned the screen so she could view the image. It was the symbol found on the floor in Malin Jakobsson's bedroom.

"You're sure you've seen this?"

For a moment, the old man stared with a peculiar interest at them both.

He knows something, Rooker thought.

Charles pushed off the table for balance and limped to a locked drawer beneath a set of wrenches. There was a massive organizer at face height, maybe eighty different plastic trays all filled with different-size screws, nuts, bolts, washers, caps, you name it. He slid one open and pulled out a key. He pressed it into the locked drawer and twisted until it came loose and he pulled it open.

Charles pulled out a tall stack of old papers and what appeared to be old black envelopes. "I kept everything, miss." He placed the pile on top of the table. "These were never reported in the newspapers. We've received four of these since Amy went missing. One on the night she disappeared. Five total. We moved in '92. The night Amy went missing, we found this one in the mailbox." He pressed a warped finger shakily into the envelope. "I know what you're thinking. Don't bother—they've all been dusted for fingerprints. I have a friend on the force; the newer technology they use can't pick anything up either. So no need for gloves. Anyway, two years later on the anniversary of her death, we found the flag up on the mailbox before bed. There was another one. These three—" He paused, placed each of them with care, evenly, on the table. "Even after we moved, they were postmarked and addressed to the old house. This one"—he jabbed his talon into the freshest of the five envelopes—"came two weeks ago."

Rooker stared down in disbelief at the envelopes. Each one with the same purplish-black symbol, like a sickly bruise, an old wax seal.

"Was there ever anything inside of them?"

"Same thing," he said as he went back to the drawer and plucked a silver tin from the inside. "All sent into a forensics lab. Nothing." He opened the tin and placed each item warily with an aged tremor on top of an envelope, except for the last.

A pebble. A stopper filled with clear liquid. A thin piece of rope. A match.

Rooker thought of one thing. Witch trials. All ways they had killed them.

Stoning. Drowning. Hanging. Burning.

Rooker plucked a ballpoint pen from his pocket, uncapped it, and wrote two things on the inside of his hand.

Princeton Law. Witches.

Millie went on. "What about the last one?"

"There was nothing inside it. We don't get a ton of mail here, so when I saw the flag up from the front window, I could feel it. Over the years, on the anniversary of the day she disappeared, I wait with a rifle and stare at that mailbox. I don't sleep. I don't take my eyes off it for a second. My wife has given up trying to tell me to stop because she knows I won't. So, the entire day, we just sit in silence. This time, he didn't come on the anniversary of her disappearance. He sent it on her birthday. If I ever see the bastard who took her . . ." A tear streamed down his cheek, and the sadness lodged in his throat. He turned his head to wipe his face, cleared his voice, but the sorrowful rasp remained. "I'll be the last thing the fucker ever sees."

Chapter 26

The two of them decided not to stay the night anywhere. While they drove back, Rooker flipped through the dusty pages of Amy Berglund's high school yearbook.

"Her yearbook? Why?"

"I just wanted to take a look. She died shortly after graduation. Maybe there's a connection somewhere in here. Maybe someone else who was going off to Princeton. Maybe there's something in here about Amy that will make sense to me. Maybe there's someone who wrote something odd in it." The entire way, Rooker thought about the last gaze he took at the crooked house and the shape of the woman who watched him from behind the screen door.

He didn't quite know what he was looking for. He started with the senior class of '89 and looked through every page. Stared at face after face. Flipped through the damp smell to find Amy's photo. She was there again, in the back, seated with the rest of the Debate Club. Again, he stared at each face and the name of each person below the photograph. He scanned the front and back where people typically wrote something like, "Have a great summer." Promises to keep in touch that almost never were kept. At least in his experience.

After scouring the yearbook, he found only one note that stood out to him. Swirling letters and neatly written—a girl. It read:

Secrets, secrets . . . sure are FUN. If only the trees could talk, am I right?

Have an amazing summer.

V.R.

He flipped through the senior class to the *R* section of last names, but there was no one who matched those initials. Strange. He did the same thing with the junior class but found nothing. It wasn't until he started with the sophomores that he found Victoria Reynolds, with dark straight hair, a look of menace, and a shiny hoop piercing in the right nostril of her pug nose.

He shimmied in the seat and plucked a pen from his pocket and wrote on his hand.

Victoria Reynolds.

"Listen to this," he said to Millie without turning to her. He recited the yearbook message for her. "She was only a sophomore when Amy was a senior. What do you think?"

"An inside joke?"

"I wonder if that's all it is, though."

"You can't be serious, Rooker?"

"Why not? When you were a senior in high school, how many sophomores wrote in your yearbook? Amy Berglund, the girl *everyone* knew, had an inside joke with this girl?" He flashed her image in front of Millie's face.

Aside from shoving the yearbook out of her view, Millie didn't answer.

"Look, I'm not saying she killed Amy. But maybe she knows something. It's worth checking out."

When the two of them got back to the cottage, Millie did a search on Victoria Reynolds and found hit after hit, but only one when she refined the search to Itasca County. There was no home address listed. Only an article published online that listed Victoria Reynolds as a server at a café called Betsy's Diner. **World-Famous Blueberry Pie!**

Rooker called the diner, and after four rings, a woman said, "Betsy's!" By the noise in the background, he could tell they were busy.

"Hi, is Victoria Reynolds in tonight?"

"Erm, no one here by that—wait, you mean Vicky? Hey, Vick!" He listened to her yell out with the phone not so courteously still in her face. "Some guy's calling for you. Called you Victoria!" He listened to her cackling before he hung up.

Thirty minutes later, Rooker pulled the Volvo into a parking lot that resembled a broken chocolate bar and looked up at the red neon letters that spelled out DINER. They were shut off or defective. The *R* leaned slightly to the right. While the engine ticked, he stared at the front that was mostly dark windows bordered with dull chrome trim. White-and-black tiles resembled a checkered flag, along with ruby-red tile above it and faded blue paint behind the neon sign. Two bloodred newspaper boxes stood outside. Utility poles and telephone wires served as an odd backdrop and made it look like the diner was a toy being manipulated by marionet strings.

He killed the engine. Pocketing his keys, he pulled on a dark cap, got out, and walked up the ramp through the glass door. A bell rang, and a woman with sagging skin and a walking cane in the shape of a question mark with a worn rubber base beside her perked up from behind the cash register.

"Good afternoon," she said to him, and pressed the cane so hard into the floor that her hand trembled, as if she were digging up wet earth. For a moment Rooker imagined little red worms and ugly black beetles crusty with dirt squirming to the surface. Lethargic, she began to rise to a standing position the way a toddler would.

"Afternoon." He smiled. "Don't get up. I'll find an empty seat."

She beamed at him and slowly, as if time stopped, plopped back down into the seat.

Rooker found an empty booth and slid into it. They were the color of pumpkin pie. Rooker appraised the framed memorabilia on the walls and the line of spinning barstools, each topped with a threadbare red cushion. When a woman came over and dumped a menu in front of him, he scratched his arm and read the thin silver name across her T-shirt.

PATTY.

"Need a minute?"

"I think I'm good."

"What can I get you, hon?"

"I'll do a cup of coffee and a slice of pecan pie," he told her without looking up. "And can I get a bacon, egg, and cheese sandwich to go?"

There was something about a good diner breakfast sandwich, regardless of what time of day it was.

"How do you want your eggs?"

"Scrambled but runny, please."

"You got it, darling." He could hear the phony smile beaming in her voice. He handed her his menu and turned his head to see a much older Victoria Reynolds—same dark hair but with a few purple highlights— transferring coffee from a pot to a patron's cup. She was wider than she was thirty years ago, her face chunkier and timeworn, with the glimmer of a stud nose ring in her right nostril rather than a hoop.

The feeling he was being watched suddenly tingled down his spine. For a split second, he could feel her eyes on him, but he turned his head out toward the US-169 freeway past the glass window. When Patty came back to the table with a warm plate of pie and a steaming cup of coffee, Rooker stopped her. "Patty, would you mind sending Vicky over?"

Patty paused. "You know Vicky?"

"Guess you could call us old acquaintances." He gave her his signature charming smile.

Rooker watched Patty go around to the kitchen and whisper something to Vicky, who glared his way. Sure enough, she came over to the table, with a curious hostility painted on her face.

"Sorry, do I know you?"

"Not exactly. Sorry, I lied. I was hoping you'd sit and talk to me."

"Look, buddy, I don't—"

Rooker slipped President Grant's folded face from beneath his hand and into Vicky's palm. "I just want to ask you some questions about an old friend of yours," he implored. "It'll take a few minutes. I'll give you another fifty dollars if you do."

She paused for a moment. Then she turned to Patty and said, "Taking a quick break, Pat." Sliding into the booth across from him, she dipped her head down to peer beneath the bill of his cap. "I've seen you on television. Rooker? Rooker Lindström?"

He smiled. "Unfortunately, yes. Do you mind if I ask you a few questions?"

"What is this about?"

"An old friend of yours. Amy Berglund."

"Amy Berglund?"

"That's right."

She scoffed. "Dunno if I'd call her an old friend. That girl's been deader than a doornail for thirty years. What's there to ask?"

"I found you in her yearbook. V.R. You knew her." He took a bite out of the pie and sipped the coffee without taking his eyes off her.

"Yeah, I knew her. And I'll tell you this: Amy Berglund ain't what everyone thought she was."

Maybe he'd come to the right place after all. "How so?"

She leaned forward. "They made her out to be Miss Goody Two-shoes. Like she was Jesus Christ reincarnated or something. You'd think she could walk on water. That wasn't Amy. Maybe to everyone else."

He nodded at her. "But not to you?"

Her face twisted into a smile. "Sure as hell not. We'd be out in the woods smoking joints, talking about boys we wanted to blow, dancing to Ozzy Osbourne and Van Halen."

"The woods?" He remembered what she'd written about the trees and about secrets. "Where?"

"It was only a quarter mile away from the back entrance to the school. Overgrown trails mostly. On the ground, littered with shattered bottles and crushed cans of Coors. That's what they were drinking back then. Some kids went into those woods to do drugs or hook up."

"Was there ever anyone else with you two?"

"No. It was just me and Amy."

"Police never questioned you?"

"Nope."

His eyes narrowed. "Why's that?"

"*Why?* She was the popular senior, and I was a sophomore. That's why. I was no one. She pretended not to know me at school."

"You wrote in her yearbook how secrets sure are fun. Care to elaborate?"

"Man, she's dead. *Been* dead a long, *long* time."

"I got that. What secrets?"

Vicky rolled her eyes and sighed. "The Princeton-bound golden child, out in the woods taking hits off a bong and hanging around some sophomore loser. That was it. The big secret."

"Was she dating anyone?"

"Amy? No. That girl was a prude."

"Was there anyone you can think of who wanted to hurt her?"

"Hurt her? No."

"What did you think when she went missing?"

"I guess I figured she was dead. She wasn't the type to run away."

He scribbled down the number for his cell and told her to give him a call if she could think of anything else. Then he tossed the fifty-dollar bill in front of her and took his paper-wrapped breakfast sandwich to go.

◆ ◆ ◆

Rooker planned to spend his evening washing whatever dishes were piled in the sink, then searching for more commonalities among the three victims. Were Malin and Nora living some kind of secret life, like Amy?

Those plans went out the window when he saw the two vehicles parked out front of the cottage. A gray Ford Interceptor. And a white Ford Taurus.

He ran up the front steps and opened the door cautiously. Millie was sitting on the couch glaring up at Martin Keene, Vic Sterling, and Tess Harlow.

"Wow. How nice of you," he said to Tess. "You brought the whole cavalry, minus one. Where's Xander?"

She ignored his query. "Either of you care to guess who I just got a call from? Carlton Sheriff's Department. Apparently, Eva Berglund received a visit from two people, harassing her husband about their dead daughter. So not only have you continued to interfere with my investigation, but you're harassing the parents of a dead child."

"Isn't that what you did when you came to my door?"

She said nothing.

"I thought so."

"Book them," she told Sterling and Keene, who only stared at each other in bewilderment. "I said book them!" When Rooker shrugged in their direction, he put his hands together and suddenly read the words again.

Princeton Law. Witch trials.

It had been bothering him. But now something—well, maybe not something, but something worth looking into—dawned on him, like a knapsack had been pulled off his head.

Law. Amy Berglund was going to study law at Princeton. Nora Vandenberg. Thomas Vandenberg, CEO of Vandenberg Enterprises, was facing a lawsuit. Soren Jakobsson, Malin's father, also had legal troubles. Was there a connection there? Who was the defense representing them? Who was prosecuting them? Who was the judge on the case? The bailiff? Hell, the stenographer. Were there other missing women?

Does it make sense?

And then he had one more thought.

Meachum?

But just then, Tess's voice cut through the barely blossoming thoughts like garden shears. "Both of you are under arrest for obstruction of justice. You have the right to remain silent. Anything you say can and will be used against you in a court of law. You have the right to an attorney. If you cannot afford an attorney, one will be appointed for you. Do you understand the rights I have just read to you?"

Both of them were silent now, with their hands cuffed behind their backs.

Rooker and Millie sat in the back of Vic and Keene's squad car. As they pulled out of the drive behind Tess, Rooker noticed that Vic kept staring in the mirror, turning around to check on them.

"Something you want to say, Vic?" Millie said.

He shook his head in a sad, frustrated way. "I never imagined it would come to this. That's all."

"Yeah, well. You have your boss to thank for that."

"Can you blame her? You two have been interfering with this investigation since the beginning."

Millie shifted in her seat. "Yeah? Ask her about Jan Cullen and Clyde Miller. See what she says about interfering with an investigation then."

With that, Rooker noticed Martin stare into the rearview mirror.

"Who?" Rooker asked.

Keene intervened. "Tess could've brought you two in earlier than she did. You think she wanted to?"

"Once again, you guys wouldn't know much of anything if it weren't for me." Rooker added: "And Millie. No offense."

"No offense taken." Vic craned his head toward them and smiled.

"Come on, Rooker," Martin said. "The first time around was personal for you. You were the one who was meant to have all the information. The queen on the board, let's say. You saw all the moves, and we were there to protect you. This time around, you're a pawn, just like us. I think it's time to stop acting so high and mighty and time we start working together and stop all of this."

Rooker thought for a moment, again, of Tate Meachum. *The Madman.* He was getting a feeling that this time might be personal too.

"We are contractually obligated to our client to investigate what we have been," Millie declared. "And we won't be stopping."

Martin Keene sighed. "Fine, Millie."

◆ ◆ ◆

Once inside the building, Martin and Vic led them down the hall past the sad fake plant toward the desks. "Have a seat."

Before Rooker could sit down, he heard Tess's voice from her office. "Martin, can you bring Rooker in, please?"

"I know the way." He smiled at Keene. He strutted into Tess's office and plopped down into the empty seat across from her desk.

She stared at him. "I want things to go back to the way they used to be, Rooker. Do you think I want you in handcuffs?"

"I think you want me to take the fall for the woman they found under the cottage. That's what I think."

She shook her head. "Why do you have to be such a stubborn jackass?"

"Lawyer."

"Goddammit, Rooker! You're interfering with my investigation."

"Jan Cullen and Clyde Miller," he said. "Those names ring a bell? Because Millie knows about them. And judging by your past, I like to think I know just who they are."

"Rooker."

"Lawyer."

"Do you even have a lawyer? You gave confidential information to that bimbo on FOX."

"What are you, jealous?"

She snickered. Glared into his eyes. "That you're fucking her? What I care about is you giving sensitive information to a reporter. Now look at how much is public. And a connection among Nora Vandenberg, the Jakobsson girl, and *Amy Berglund*? Are you kidding me?"

"Look, it's true."

"Amy Berglund disappeared thirty years ago."

"And someone operating on a dark net under the alias WICCAN has a photograph of her that has never seen the light of day. Not until now. Along with a photograph of Malin and Nora Vandenberg."

"Where're the photos?"

He paused.

"Rooker."

"You'll have to make peace with Millie if you want those."

"And when are you going to tell me what else you have?"

"I'm currently in handcuffs. If you think I'm helping you anytime soon—"

"Then you'll stay in handcuffs."

"Okay then."

"Okay then."

◆　◆　◆

Rooker had a pretty good feeling he wouldn't be seeing the inside of a cell. Not only would it take manpower and time—booking, arraignment, trial—but he knew how it would look for her. Detective Tess Harlow, the person responsible for bringing a civilian in to consult on an investigation. That person helping solve it, only to later be detained for investigating a different crime. Although Chief Jim Larsson may have been a deadbeat, Rooker knew it would raise questions. And if Larsson still had Tess's head on the chopping block, this might give it to him.

An hour later, Rooker was sitting beside Martin Keene's desk, hands steepled behind the crook of his skull. Keene had been nice enough to remove the handcuffs. He hadn't asked permission from Tess.

With a vacant stare at the ceiling, entrenched in his thoughts, the sound of the phone made Rooker turn his head to Tess's office.

It was only a matter of minutes before she stepped out of her doorway shaking her head. Whoever called, it couldn't have been good. "Your pal Charles Berglund. Seems he and his wife want you released. You're free to go."

◆　◆　◆

"I think I've got something," Rooker said to Millie once they were back at the cottage.

"Like what?"

"It may sound far-fetched; just hear me out. Amy Berglund: going off to study law at Princeton. Nora Vandenberg: the heir to Vandenberg Enterprises. Now, Vandenberg Enterprises was involved in a lawsuit. Is that just dumb luck? Or are there other victims out there who are related to similar court cases, and that's how he preys on them? Is that his MO—his version of a witch trial?

"Now, the other thing, I thought of it for a split second: Meachum. And then I thought it again, when Keene was talking. He said the first time around—Meachum—was personal. He said that this time, I'm merely a pawn, just like everybody else. But maybe I'm not."

"What are you saying?"

"Well, you remember the note. Someone asked me to come out and play. But the other thought I had in mind is, who smuggled the cell phone into Pelican Bay for Tate Meachum? It's a supermax. Someone, somehow, had access to the prison. Somehow, even though there are no visitors logged, they had access to him. Now, wouldn't a lawyer have access?"

"Interesting," Millie said. For a moment, she looked robotic. A neutral expression on her face, computing the information she'd just received. "The problem with your theory is the prison. If no one was ever logged to visit Meachum, there's still no way of ever knowing who gave him the phone."

"But maybe it's someone who picked up a new client around the time the Sadler murders started. Maybe they chose someone in the prison, and they were able to get it to Meachum."

"It's good. Worth checking out."

"How fast can you find the attorney for Vandenberg Enterprises?"

"I'll see what I can find."

Rooker leaned back in his chair, scanning the floor of the cottage where the old wood planks clashed with the new. He imagined Thomas Vandenberg kept a prolific lawyer on retainer, some hotshot attorney out of New York, flaunting Brooks Brothers suits and luxurious watches. A prestigious alma mater like Harvard or Yale.

When Millie hung up her phone, she frowned. "You were right. Harvard. Vandenberg Enterprises used their corporate lawyer. Jacob Wyndham." She typed the name into her laptop and spun it around. Rooker watched a tan, pineapple-shaped face come into view. Wyndham's black hair was parted neatly, and he was wearing an expensive-looking navy pinstriped suit. Weirdly, the combination of indentations around his mouth and narrow lips resembled an imperial TIE fighter out of Star Wars. Rooker looked up from the sunken folds like shadows beneath dark irises and wondered what they'd seen.

Millie skimmed the page. "He was named partner to a law firm on Park Avenue in Midtown Manhattan. Mercali, Kane and Wyndham Law. Forty-second floor of a high-rise. He was admitted to the New York State Bar in 1991. Fifty-three years old. Married to his wife, Adrienne. They have a son and a daughter."

"Is there any history of him living in Minnesota?"

"None that I see. It says he grew up on the Upper West Side, a couple of blocks away from Lincoln Center."

"It could still be him."

She sighed in disagreement. "Because he's in his fifties?"

"Look, Amy would be forty-eight. Whoever killed her has to be up there in age. Plus, he's connected to the Vandenbergs."

"So what? He killed Amy thirty years ago, becomes the corporate lawyer for Vandenberg Enterprises, and takes Thomas Vandenberg's daughter?"

"Maybe he couldn't help himself."

"But that's assuming that whoever took Amy, and whoever took Malin and Nora, are one and the same."

"Well, that's what I'm thinking."

"And you keep saying 'killed' Amy. We don't know that yet."

"Come on, Millie. Stop playing devil's advocate. You can't tell me you don't agree with Charles? Amy is dead. Whoever took her killed her. Buried or burned the body. Dumped her at the bottom of a lake somewhere. We may never find out where she is. Or what happened to her."

She said nothing.

"I'm going to Warden Hastings," Rooker said. "See if he can find me a lawyer."

Rooker dialed the number he'd saved in his phone. It was the private line for Lamonte Hastings, warden of one of the most dangerous supermax prisons in the world. Pelican Bay State Prison. He and Rooker had something in common: their children's names had been etched into the monster's wall. That was before they'd given him a new box, slightly larger than an elevator, to call home.

The other line chirped five times before it stopped.

"Hastings."

"Warden. It's Rooker Lindström."

"*Christ*. It's late, man. You're like the bearer of bad news. Anytime you call, I know some shit's about to be dropped in my lap."

"Good to hear from you too. Have a minute?"

"You want me to hold the phone up to Meachum's ear? Toss his cell? Kick him in the sack?"

"Not today."

"Want me to send you his fan mail? Since we've blocked his mail, we've got quite the collection. Might be worth something."

"You done, Warden?"

"Yeah, yeah. A minute for you? Sure. Why the hell not?"

"So, you never found out who got the phone to Meachum, right?"

"You calling to remind me?"

"No. But I do have a theory. And I need your help."

"I'm listening."

"I'm looking for someone in SHU who found themself a shiny new lawyer around the time the Sadler murders began."

SHU was Pelican Bay's Security Housing Unit, or solitary confinement. Some called it "the hole." Rooker imagined it was because it was like tossing someone in a black hole and throwing away the key. A dark, dreary place, where the most dangerous of the inmates went insane, if they weren't already. Although some people would argue with that, Rooker knew. If Tate Meachum was put there, that's where they put the worst of the worst.

"If you're looking for what was said in conversation, I can't—"

"No, no. I don't need anything that was said. I just need to know if someone got a new lawyer right around the time the Sadler murders began. It can be anywhere from before the murders—if they're as clever as I think, maybe even a year before—up to December third. That's the first night Meachum called me. I think a lawyer may have gotten the phone inside to an inmate or a guard, maybe a cleaner. But I think that's how it got into Meachum's cell."

"*A year before?* What aren't you telling me?"

Rooker hesitated. Though he'd met the warden only once, he had it on good authority that Lamonte Hastings was a good enough man. He was a churchgoer. Even coached the church basketball team, which his son played on. Still, the media was known to keep tabs on the prison and had made numerous attempts to interview their most notorious inmate, Tate Meachum. The Madman. If the media caught wind of anything, they'd pay Hastings handsomely to run a story.

"I'm working on a new case. Well, I guess you could call it an old case too. But I think whoever got Meachum that phone is a lawyer. I believe an inmate inside the prison got a new lawyer, and that's the person who somehow got access to a guard or to Meachum."

"This is going to take me a little while, so don't expect a quick call back. I've gotta get someone to go through the logs, pretty far back. Just know you'll owe me one."

"You got it."

"And, Rooker," he said.

"Yeah?"

"I think you left out a key part. If what you're saying is true, you're saying whoever it is you're looking for knew the boy in the lake."

Chapter 27

Millie stayed the night. Rooker watched her toss and turn, curled up in a ball on that awful couch. Judging by the freight-train snores that sent a rumble through the floor, she had to be overtired.

Before he'd shuffled, yawning, upstairs to bed, he'd double-checked the locks and draped a second blanket over her. He'd spent the night staring into the darkness overhead. Sleep hadn't come, and in the short gaps that it had, he woke in a sweat. Nightmares. He saw Meachum, standing there in the corner of his bedroom, whispering to a shadowed figure beside him. He knew it was because of what Hasting had said.

"You're saying whoever it is you're looking for knew the boy in the lake."

◆ ◆ ◆

When the sun was up, Rooker changed into a dry T-shirt and stumbled downstairs. "Christine Vandenberg just called." Millie put her cell phone on the table. "They're having a vigil tonight in the park."

"What exactly are they looking for?"

"I'd say hope."

"History repeating itself," Rooker said. "It all started with Amy. Now Nora."

"Maybe you should get out of the house. Thomas Vandenberg should be there. Maybe you'll find something. Maybe someone in the crowd who looks out of place."

"What about you? Where will you be?"

"I might be able to catch the end of it. But I want to see if I can do a little more digging into the dark net the killer is using. See if I can get anywhere with that."

◆ ◆ ◆

Rooker arrived at the town green just after 8:00 p.m. It was just like the clip he'd seen of Amy's vigil. A horde of somber faces partially illuminated by candlelight. Clear ponchos dragged on the concrete and a stream of umbrellas along the walkway, thought it wasn't raining yet. With the window cracked, he thought he could smell the pungent, earthy aroma that preceded rain.

As he slowed the car, he noticed a surge of posters. From every tree and post on the street, Nora stared back at him, young and vibrant, even in black and white. Under the photo were the harrowing black letters: MISSING.

Rooker parked on the corner, rolled up the window, and got out. The side street where he stood was hidden from the park behind a large building of dark brick with navy-blue window frames. The streetlight flickered dimly overhead but did nothing to brighten the spot where he stood.

He stuffed his hands into the warmth of his pockets and walked toward the turnout. There had to be two hundred people packed onto sidewalks and the green. He caught a glimpse of a tall white gazebo surrounded by pop-up canopy tents through the cracks in the gathering.

Rooker waded through the crowd. He turned sideways and gently knocked shoulders as he squeezed past cluster after cluster. He found himself surveying the faces near him, but there were far too many to keep track of. Maybe there would be one, just one, that looked out of

171

place. A face that would make Rooker's blood freeze and would awaken that feeling inside that told him something was wrong. Still, the person he was after had been at this for a long time. It wouldn't be so easy.

He did his best to eavesdrop on the conversations, but some were far too sad—sniveled stories and thunderous bawling—and some that had nothing to do with Nora Vandenberg at all.

He made his way to the gazebo. Christine Vandenberg was standing there wearing an exhausted expression, along with dark pants and a black coat where the waist tied in a bow. She looked like she was attending a funeral.

Beside her was a sign with Nora's face: a dimpled white smile, freckle-spotted nose, and hair that glowed like the sun. It wasn't one of the photos the news had been using. He had a feeling those had lost their appeal to the Vandenbergs.

When her eyes met his, he kept his hand at his waist, waved, and gave her a thin, sad smile. She turned her head and whispered to a face he couldn't see. That was, until the head turned toward him. It was Thomas Vandenberg.

The two of them came down the steps, and Rooker shook hands with the tall man. He had the squeeze of a businessman or someone who wasn't fond of you.

"Rooker, I'm Thomas. My wife has told me a lot about you."

"I hope only the good."

"Only the good." He smiled politely. "I appreciate what you're doing for our daughter."

Rooker nodded. "Mr. Vandenberg—"

"Thomas." He smiled again.

"I don't want to intrude, but do you mind if I ask you a few questions?"

"I answer questions all day at work," he said. "What's a few more?" After he put on the presentation of planting a kiss on his wife's cheek, the two of them stepped out of earshot.

"What can you tell me about Jacob Wyndham?"

"I've known Jacob for years," Thomas answered without hesitation. His voice was deep, one you'd imagine capturing the attention of a room. To Rooker, it sounded phony. "Over a decade. We vacation with him and his wife once a year."

"How long has he been your lawyer?"

"He's represented Vandenberg Enterprises since its inception. There was never any question."

"Why is that?"

"Because the man is brilliant. He's skilled at what he does, as I am with what I've built, and I'm sure you are in what you do. I've always tried to align myself with people like that. He's become family to Christine and me."

"What can you tell me about the court case you were involved in?"

His lips curled into a smile. "That's what I mean. Jacob is ruthless in court. He got the prosecutor to back down. And the allegations were dropped."

"Allegations that you were granting stock options rather than pay increases. And that you tried to hide it."

"Those were the allegations, yes." He smiled again.

"Nora is an only child, correct?"

For the first time, Thomas Vandenberg's eyebrows raised, and his smile curled to a scowl. "I'm sure you already know the answer to that."

He did. They tried a second time, but Christine miscarried.

"Were you grooming her to take over Vandenberg Enterprises?"

"I had hoped so. I didn't want to push it too hard on her. When I told her that's what I wanted for her, it didn't take. Instead, she got a job at J&L Co. It's mostly pharmaceuticals and medical equipment for hospitals and nursing homes. That's what she wanted, but I hoped she wouldn't like it."

Rooker uncapped a pen from his pocket and wrote *J&L Co.* on his hand in the darkness.

"Have you found anything?"

Rooker capped the pen and looked up into Thomas's blank face. "There are a few things; I just have to figure out what they mean." He turned the questioning back onto Thomas. "Your wife told me that Nora wasn't dating. Is that true?"

"If she was, we didn't know anything of it."

He nodded. Then pulled out his cell phone and unlocked it. "Have you seen a symbol similar to any of these?" Rooker held the phone up to Thomas Vandenberg and swiped the screen through the wiccan symbols. Thomas didn't react.

"No. What are they?"

Rooker decided to give a little. "Wiccan symbols. It has to do with pre-Christian beliefs. Witchcraft. Supernatural powers. Magic. All sorts of crazy cult shit."

"What does it have to do with my daughter?"

"I'm not sure yet. Maybe nothing at all," he lied. "It's just something my partner and I were looking into. Have you received anything in the mail that you found . . . odd? Maybe written to a different address?"

"No, nothing. Just neighbors bringing over Tupperware dinners. Casseroles. More food than we can store in the fridge."

"If I think of anything else, do you have a private line where I can reach you?"

"Here's my card." Thomas pulled one from his pocket and handed it to Rooker. "My cell is there."

"I'll let you get back to it," Rooker said and took one last look at the photo of Nora Vandenberg. He turned on his heel and started back the way he came.

Suddenly, he saw a television crew pull up. "Fucking vultures," he spoke under his breath. That's what they were. They fed on misery and death. Nora Vandenberg's disappearance was just another carcass. They found horror and aired it on the nightly news, along with a few minutes of a fluff piece to cap it off, just to remind people there was still a glimmer of hope for the world.

He understood them all too well. He'd reported on more fatalities than he could count on his hands and feet.

Through the light drizzle that swept in, he discerned the FOX News logo on the truck. A moment later, he watched her waves of auburn hair whip off her shoulder, a waterfall down her back. Once the lights hit her, she started fixing her hair.

Caroline positioned herself so that the vigil was her backdrop. He couldn't help but watch her. He couldn't even help what he did next. He pulled out his phone and texted: You look great.

He watched her pull her phone from her back pocket. She looked up from it and began scanning the crowd, but he disappeared.

He crossed the street. He watched Caroline a bit more and then focused on the crowd. His eyes buzzed gnat-like from person to person. That's when he saw it. A person watching him. He was almost sure of it. The face was cloaked by a dark hood, but he could *feel* the person watching him. He squinted. The rain had started, and it was making everything hazy. And just then, the figure tilted their head, took one step backward on their heel, and turned away. Rooker sprinted across the street. His height allowed him to peer over most of the crowd. He thought he could still see the back of the hood, and then it turned ever so slightly and dropped lower. Rooker moved faster. He tried his best to follow. Scanning the crowd left and right as he passed. At times, his head peering down to see if the figure had dropped anything. But whoever had been watching him had vanished.

He stood still. Let the rain beat down against his skull. When he'd stared at the crowd long enough—the candles that swayed and went out in the rain, the eerily illuminated faces of the news correspondents under their dark umbrellas—he decided he had enough for the evening.

He jogged back across the street, away from the crowd, and dialed Millie.

"There was someone here," he yelled over the rain. "I looked at them and they took off into the crowd. I couldn't see a thing, but I think you were right. They were here . . . Do me a favor—look into J&L Co. Pharmaceuticals and Medical Equipment. Nora was working there. See what you can find."

The wind had picked up, the rainfall now beating against the nape of his neck and his upper back. Puttering along with his head down, he listened to the hiss of rain and the pulsing thump between his temples. Despite the rumble in his stomach, he craved the bitterness of hot black coffee over food. The thought of driving home made him even more tired. He'd roll the window down to avoid drifting off to sleep to the whir of the wiper blades. He turned the corner under the last streetlight and soon was in darkness as he approached the Volvo and appraised the size of the puddle that had pooled by the driver's-side door. Water droplets and mist blurred the windshield and windows.

His foot squelched in the puddle, the water spraying over his ankle. The door squealed open. Rooker had already sat in the driver's seat and shut the door when he noticed something was wrong. Inside the car, he inhaled the earthly odor of rain. The glove box was open just slightly. He guessed whoever it was in the back seat couldn't get it to close. When he looked up to the rearview mirror, he saw a figure in a horrible mask sit up.

"Ah-ah. Don't move." The finger waved back and forth, slow and steady as a ticking clock.

Rooker raised his right hand cautiously. The other patted around discreetly for something beneath his seat.

"I drew something for you." The voice was gentle, lowered and muffled behind the mask.

Rooker looked down at the drawing that the stranger slipped onto the armrest between the seats. "Kind of you," Rooker said.

"If you don't drop this, Mr. Lindström, I will kill more. I will even kill you, though I don't want to."

"I can't drop it."

"Why not?" The soft voice spoke again. "You have nothing else. You can't honestly believe that saving some girl will offer you penance."

"Saving a girl from the devil himself just might."

Rooker heard a snicker from behind the mask. "You've killed someone, haven't you? What's the difference between killing one sheep and the entire herd?"

"I wouldn't know."

"They're already dead, Rooker. They must stand trial. They can't be saved, as much as I can't be cured. These witches hiding among men. You can't be the one to save them; you are merely a man trapped by shadows. You can't see them for what they are."

"And what are they?"

The figure hunched forward. Rooker could feel the eyes on him, chilling, behind the mask. "*Inhuman.* This is your last warning. Give it up, or you'll be sorry. And I won't be."

At that, Rooker heard the crack of his skull, the right side of his temple whacked by what he could only imagine was the pistol from the glove box. The last thing he saw was a droplet of water trickling down the windshield.

◆　◆　◆

"Rooker?"

"Hmm," he muttered. When he recognized the pain that spread across the right side of his face, he remembered the visitor in the back seat.

"What the hell happened to you?"

"Please, keep it down."

"Christ. I was worried sick all night, and you were out getting shit-faced?"

"Not exactly. But I'd assume my face does look like shit." He turned his face to her and gently touched the tip of his finger to the bloodied knot on the side of his head. He pressed harder against the hard lump, as though he deserved to feel the pain.

Her jaw dropped. "Shit! What happened?"

"A visit from our friend. I think I got it recorded. I keep it under the seat. Can you check somewhere down here by my feet?" Rooker's head swayed. Though his eyes were fastened shut, the world to him was spinning. "Concussion." He tried to use as few words as he could. "Might puke."

"All right, c'mon. Let's get you out of there."

He felt Millie under his arm, pulling him like deadweight. Eventually, he felt himself standing, and she leaned him up against the side of the car. He heard her get down to ground level, moving her hand around until she found it.

"Got it," she said.

"It's not going to do us much good. The things he was saying . . . he's delusional. Possibly a psychotic disorder. But from what I can remember, he didn't really give anything away."

"Did you get a look at him?"

"Mask. Couldn't see much of anything else. It was dark outside. Windows fogged up from the rain. Dark in the car. The damn lights don't go on when the door opens, so I couldn't see him before I got in."

"Do you remember anything about him?"

"Just the mask. Freaky. Part of it like one you'd wear to a masquerade, top and bottom of it. Black and silver. Middle of it looked stitched or glued on to it. Witch mask. Like an old hag. Halloween type."

"I'll find some Tylenol. Let's get you some rest."

Right then, his phone buzzed. He looked down at the message from Caroline.

Thanks (: Let's get that drink soon.

He closed the phone. "Dear God, please turn the lights off." He held his hand over his eyes to block out the sunlight. It radiated this morning—a fiery coral pink burned even behind his eyelids.

"Food or coffee?"

"Both."

Millie drove. When the car stopped, Rooker opened his eyes when she got out of the car and analyzed the big red sign. **DINER.** The neon letters were turned off in the daylight. He closed his eyes and opened them again when Millie put a warm bag of food in his lap and two Styrofoam cups of coffee in the cupholders. Despite the throbbing in his skull, Rooker's mouth watered at the smell of bacon, eggs, and potatoes. He thought he could smell a juicy burger and salted fries too.

When they got back to the cottage, Millie dumped a few white tablets into her palm and handed them to him. He took them with his coffee and scarfed down his meal for two, while Millie occasionally stole fries from his Styrofoam container.

"J&L Co.," she said. "You said Nora worked there. Well, the CFO, Roger Milton, just stepped down. There was a lawsuit against him for embezzling $4.5 million. His lawyer was a man named Gerry McAntis." The last thing he could remember was the clicking sound as Millie pressed "Play" and "Rewind" on the tape, along with that horrible mask.

Chapter 28

Rooker woke up to darkness. He was dreaming that Geralt was purring beside him, his fluffy white fur falling and rising. It wasn't until he lifted the sheet from his face, along with a cold compress that Millie must've placed on his head, that he realized it was his phone on the night table. Pawing at it, he realized the sun was still out, but Millie had draped heavy sheets over the windows.

"Hmmm," he groaned.

"No shot you're still asleep, Lindström," said Warden Hastings. "It's . . . two p.m. there."

"Yeah, well. I had a rough night."

"Yeah? Good or bad?"

"Which one does a pistol whip to the temple fall under?"

"Christ. The hell happened to you?"

"Hmm. Funny you asked." He scratched his head until he flinched at the pain in his face. "My partner asked me the same question when she found me. Let's just say the guy we're looking for got the jump on me. Been a while since I've taken a shot that hard."

"Frozen peas."

"Hmm?"

"My mother used to get a bag of peas out of the freezer."

"My father was a butcher steak kind of guy."

There was an awkward pause; then Hastings cleared his throat. "So, I've got something."

"Yeah?" The pain strained his voice while he struggled to sit up. He shifted over to where he could see the purple growth in the mirror. "What did you get?"

"There's an inmate here. Goes by the nickname Pounds. Because his name is Luis Barrios." He pronounced it *Lou-eees*. "Get it? LB. I'm sure it helps that the guy is six foot four and pushing three hundred. Anyway, the guy is a gang member: West Side Locos. Quite the rap sheet. Murder. A couple of counts of attempted murder. When they raided his house, he was running methamphetamine and fentanyl out of his kitchen. Possession of illegal firearms: short-barrel shotguns, large-magazine assault rifles, armor-piercing bullets. Because of the gang affiliation, he can't be in lockup with gen pop. A rival gang would try to kill him. Better yet, he'd try to kill someone.

"Now, the weird part is that you were right. Luis 'Pounds' Barrios got himself a new lawyer. The weirder part: he asked for him by name. How? Don't ask me."

Rooker sat up straighter. "Who?"

"A guy named Gerry McAntis. He has his own office there in Minnesota."

"Can you get an address?"

Millie looked up from her laptop. "As much as I hate to say it, don't you think it's time to call Tess?"

"Let's go take a look around. We can give her a call after."

"This isn't smart, Rooker. If it *is* him . . ."

"We're just going to take a look. That's all."

Gerald "Gerry" McAntis lived in a restored bungalow in Grand Rapids. Private cul-de-sac, homes spaced out, large yards, quiet. They parked the car at the curb on the street behind McAntis's home. The two skulked through a backyard and helped each other over a chain-link fence.

Rooker fished around for a spare set of keys beneath rocks and plants. Nothing. The doors and windows were all locked. No car parked in the driveway. He shined a flashlight through the panel in the garage. There was no car. But it was when he made out the storm-cellar hatch in the back, and the two handles sealed shut by a steel padlock, that he smiled.

Rooker pulled a pair of old eight-inch bolt cutters from beneath his shirt.

Millie squeezed his arm. "What the hell are those?" she whispered angrily.

"C'mon. We didn't come all this way for nothing."

"We aren't breaking and entering."

"The hell we aren't."

"Stop!"

"Millie. What if Nora's inside? We can't leave without knowing."

"We call Tess!"

"Did you hear that?" he asked. And in the next second, the lock snapped between the steel jaws of the bolt cutters. Rooker snapped on a pair of gloves and handed Millie a pair. As he grabbed the pieces of the lock and shoved them into his pocket, he told her, "Let's go."

Rooker jerked up on one of the doors, enough for the flashlight to shine down the cellar. Webs ran thick as yarn. He swatted at them while he climbed down the steps into the dark space.

The air was cool and damp. He extended a hand to a hesitant Millie, who ultimately walked down of her own volition. Rooker shut the hatch door above.

He sprayed the light over the gray basement floor, then at the shiny silk, webs like veins in the nooks and crannies of the ceiling.

Rooker said, "Do you know why spiders spin webs like these? To protect their habitat. Balloon from web to web. But, most importantly, to catch prey."

"Are we the predator or the prey in this scenario?"

"I think both." Had it not been for the many times Gunner had beaten him to a pulp, and the first encounter with Sadler outside the cottage, he would have joked about his record against serial killers being 1–0.

The basement was unfinished. He could see through wood framing to cheap black shelves lined with cleaning supplies and outdoor tools. An old stone double-laundry sink looked like it belonged on the set of a slasher film. Rooker found the staircase that went up to the first level. The two of them scaled quietly in the darkness. At the top of the stairs, Rooker found the handle for the door and turned it.

The door opened out to a hallway. It was dark, but not enough for him to shine the light and risk a neighbor seeing. The two of them crept through the rooms one by one. Kitchen. Stainless steel appliances, white cabinets, and marble counters. Takeout boxes in the refrigerator. Dining room. Mostly empty. Clearly it wasn't a place he used. Living room. Large flat-screen television mounted to the wall, a massive sectional couch and matching white recliner.

Then the bedroom. The bed was unmade. Chocolate-brown sheets and pillows were thrown all over. Satin, by the look of it. Sliding glass doors opened to a walk-in closet, where Rooker perused the drawers and suits and found nothing significant.

It was a bachelor pad.

When the two of them reached the office, Rooker drew the blinds closed. If he'd struck out in the rest of the home but was going to find anything, it would be in here.

"If he does have her, she isn't here," Rooker said.

He opened the drawers and began rifling through the desk compartments. Files. Client names. Maybe there was someone in here worth noting?

He opened his phone, turned the flash on, and took a quick photo of the names on the folder tabs. While he plucked the one marked *Milton*, Millie sat at the computer and moved the mouse. The screen came on. Rooker scanned the pages.

Millie clicked away on the keyboard.

"Whoa," she said. "Look."

Rooker lifted his head. "What am I looking at?"

"There's an application currently running on his PC."

"What?"

"ExpressVPN and Tor. Hold on." She clicked away fast. It wasn't long before she opened a page, and three blinking dots appeared on the screen. The name beside them was WICCAN. "Well, shit."

"It's him."

"Wait." She began typing, and sure enough the letters were falling to the right of the username. There was a photo folder unlocked. She clicked it. That's where she found images of Malin Jakobsson, Nora Vandenberg, and Amy Berglund.

"We need to call Tess. Now."

The two of them started to put the room back as it was. As they crept back through the doorway, two strobes punched through the glass window. Headlights. Rooker jumped to the right of the illuminated hallway. Millie moved across the hall out of sight.

"What kind of car did you say this guy drives?" he whispered to her.

"Jaguar."

Rooker peeked out just enough to appraise the vehicle. The lights were too bright, and he could only make out a silhouette, like a shadow in the darkness beyond the threat of light. He pulled his head back.

"I can't tell."

While the engine hummed, his heart ticked too fast and unsteady. But just then, the vehicle crawled in reverse and drove down the road.

"Let's get the hell out of here," Millie said.

Chapter 29

The two of them argued over who would call Tess the whole way back to the cottage. Eventually, Millie won. In the hope that Tess wouldn't answer, Rooker dialed her number. But she did.

He told her that maybe it was time to clue her in and asked her to come to the cottage.

Twenty minutes later, Tess pulled up with Martin Keene. Tess wore a half-zipped black windbreaker with the sheriff's department's emblem embroidered on the left chest and gray denim pants. Her radio and gun were clasped to her belt, and her badge swayed around her neck beneath the jacket. Keene's beard had grown out a bit, a few scraggly hairs over his lip. He donned a collared shirt that resembled desert sand, along with black trousers and boots; his badge hung around his burly neck. Though Rooker recalled fond memories as the two of them walked into the room, now they felt like strangers to him.

"You finally fall down those stairs?" Tess asked.

"Yeah, the hell happened to you?" Keene asked.

"This?" Rooker pointed to the colorful bruise protruding from his head. He tried to smile, but even that felt like his skull was being cinched in a vise grip. He winced and relaxed his face. "A run-in with the guy we're looking for."

"When?"

"I was at the vigil they had for Nora Vandenberg. I saw someone in the crowd watching me. When I stared back, they turned and disappeared into the crowd. I tried to follow, but I lost them. It was when I got back to my car that I noticed something was wrong. The glove box gets jammed. It was unlatched. But by the time I sat inside and noticed, it was too late. He was waiting for me in the back seat."

"What would he want in your glove box?"

"I keep a gun in there."

Tess sighed. "Jesus Christ, Rooker. Illegal."

"Yeah, no shit. I was hunted through these woods and nearly died. If you think I'm going anywhere without a weapon nearby, think again."

"What did he say to you?"

Millie played the tape for Tess and Martin.

"Shit," Tess said. "That sound?"

"Yeah. He got me good. But that isn't why I called. Remember Meachum had the phone in prison? We couldn't figure out how he got it."

"Yeah."

"There's an inmate in solitary, a couple of cells down from Meachum. His name is Luis Barrios. Goes by the name Pounds. It turns out, he was asking for a lawyer only a few months before the Sadler murders started. He asked for the lawyer by name."

A sound played from Tess's hip. She looked down at the radio and twisted a knob to silence it. "You're saying the lawyer got the phone in for Meachum? That's crazy."

"Is it? Because he works here in Minnesota." He watched Tess's face blanch. "His name is Gerry McAntis."

◆ ◆ ◆

Rooker had been drifting when the phone rang. It was after midnight. He unfurled an eyelid to see Tess's name and knew that whatever this was, it wasn't good.

"Yeah," he spoke and cleared his throat.

"There was a fire at the Berglunds' house. They've asked that you and Millie come to the scene." The line clicked, and her voice was gone.

◆ ◆ ◆

Rooker and Millie pulled up to the Berglund property. Local police vehicles lined the road. Six of them in total. The fire had already been put out. Rooker looked up at the corner of the home that had darkened. A wave of black looked to have infected it; the plague had spread toward the center before it was extinguished.

They got out of the car and began treading up the slope. Rooker imagined that with Amy Berglund's disappearance connected to the investigation, and the broadcast put out by Chief Larsson, it wasn't long after the fire was put out that the locals dialed the Itasca County Sheriff's Office. Riggs was chatting with a few rookie cops. Tess and Martin were already at the front steps. Martin tried to wave them back toward the road, but Rooker ignored him. As they got closer to the house, Rooker could make out the burn marks in the grass. They walked closer. And that's when he saw the crabgrass; the yellowish tinge that it once had was now black. It looked like ash, spread out in a circle. Small dead weeds lay like folded arms over the dead earth. For a moment, he closed his eyes. He thought his mind was playing tricks on him. But when he opened them and breathed slowly, he realized it *was* there. It was the same symbol on the letters addressed to the Berglunds. Same as the one carved into Malin Jakobsson's floor.

But what did it mean? Was the killer coming back after all this time to threaten Amy's parents?

"Ahem." The intentionally deep, phlegmy clearing of a man's throat made him turn his head. "You Rooker Lindström?"

Rooker looked over his shoulder and stared into the furrowed eyes of a veteran cop. Then he looked down at the nameplate on his chest. WYATT. His hair was shaved short, jagged as a comb's teeth despite it. Black soot covered the majority of his scalp as though that's where the fire had started, gray as cigarette ash on the sides. His lips tightened, along with his jaw as he stared from two wide-set, angry eyes. Rooker figured him to be somewhere in his fifties, but he looked to have kept up a habit of the weight room.

"Yeah, that would be me."

"The couple inside say they won't speak to us until they've spoken to you. Any idea what that's about?"

Rooker shook his head, even though he knew. *Quite frankly,* he thought while he stared at the man in uniform, *they hate you.* "No, sir. Not really."

"Can't say I can let that fly. This is police business, and from the looks of it, you aren't police."

Rooker smiled. "No offense, but I think you know exactly who I am." Rooker left the man standing there, and though his back was to him now, he could feel the leering eyes like some sort of cartoon heat vision.

He walked up the front-porch stairs. Red waited just inside the door. When it squealed open, he watched the flail of Red's tail back and forth, smiled, and patted him on the head. Rooker ambled a few steps until he could peek his head into the next room, which was where he found Charles and Eva Berglund.

"Rooker." Charles limped over and shook his hand. "I want you to meet my wife, Eva."

Rooker tried his most charming smile and nodded. "Nice to meet you, ma'am."

"Charles told me what you're doing for our daughter. Thank you."

189

"There's still work to be done."

"I looked you up," she said. "I hope you don't mind. You had a son."

He nodded again. Smiled. "I did. I can barely bring myself to look at his picture anymore. He was the best thing that ever happened to me. I know the cliché. But after . . . It was like I lost the best parts of me. Not sure if they're still here somewhere or if they're gone forever."

"There's still time to be a good man if you allow yourself to be."

From where he stood, he could see a rifle leaned up against the wall and a flashlight standing on the edge of the table beside it. He figured Charles had come downstairs at some point in the dark of night to investigate. "Did either of you see anyone?"

"No one. Didn't hear anything, either, until Red kept barking. I hollered from here, but when he didn't stop, I got ready to check outside. Then I heard the crackling—like something burning."

Red may have been an old dog, but Rooker knew one thing. Whoever had been here had been quiet enough that Red hadn't thought much of it until they'd started the fire. It was obvious that the protection symbol would have taken a while to pour in pitch-black. The killer probably splashed some on the edge of the home, lit it, and ran back to a vehicle off the road somewhere.

"What time did you wake up to Red barking?"

"Around midnight."

"Did the police mention if they found shoe prints anywhere? Maybe a vehicle nearby? Tire tracks?"

"Didn't speak to 'em. Don't plan on it neither."

"Seems like your guard dog still works."

Rooker went outside to find Millie on the front porch. Red snuck between the two of them. As Rooker stared out at the heap of police cruisers, some with the lights still on, it felt eerily similar.

"Looks familiar, doesn't it?"

He felt her eyes on him. "We won't let Nora die."

"Someone probably said the same thing about Evelyn."

◆ ◆ ◆

It was after 7:00 a.m. when Rooker's eyes flickered open. Millie's back was to him. She had burrowed herself under the blankets, snoring like his ex-wife beside him. With his hands steepled behind his head, he lay there beneath a small lump of covers, now wistfully awake.

There was a hollowness here. Charles was right; the walls in the home were thin. He could hear the low, rumbling chirps from the grass that reminded him of Geralt's purr. It made him think about just how beautiful the world could be, if it hadn't been for humankind. He listened to the badges walking around downstairs, whispering back and forth. Then, suddenly, there was the groan of old wood out in the hall. The slow, uneven steps that creaked.

Rooker sat up. He lifted the covers off him and snuck out of the bed. Skulking to the door, he poked his head out to see the officers standing around at the bottom of the stairs.

Rooker went downstairs and asked if the Berglunds were still asleep. Riggs answered him. "Eva hasn't come downstairs yet. Charles left a little while ago. Said that with everything that happened yesterday, he wanted to go for a drive. I said I'd go with him, but he wasn't having it. Something about how he needed some silence and his legs locking up if he doesn't move around."

"What were you guys talking about down here?"

"Call came in that they couldn't find the lawyer. Judge Adams signed off on the search warrant. They mobilized a team to find Gerry McAntis at his home. No one there."

Rooker looked outside. "Shit."

"What?"

Rooker could hear the cops from upstairs if he tried hard enough. That's why Charles wasn't home. He must have heard them.

As Rooker turned in to the other room, he looked at the end table where the flashlight had been last night. It was there. The rifle wasn't.

"Nice job, gentlemen. My guess: he heard you. You just told him who might have killed his daughter thirty years ago."

While Riggs's face reddened, Rooker called Tess. "You need to put out an APB on a 1970s Ford Icon F-100. White and beige, rusted on the driver's side. Can't be too hard to find. Belongs to Charles Berglund. He overheard your guy Riggs mention Gerry McAntis by name and took off."

"Shit, hold on." He listened to her spell Charles Berglund's name and give the make and model of the vehicle. "Where's he headed?"

"Wherever he can find McAntis. And Berglund's armed."

Chapter 30

September 28, 2019

He was due in court four minutes ago. On a Saturday at that. Imagine. Gerry was on good terms with Judge Browne. Even Roberts's surly ass. But today, a woman named Beyer had the gavel. It wouldn't be a good look to be late in front of a new judge, but he'd do his best to charm her. If he ever got out of this damn traffic.

A sideswiped van spun around onto the shoulder. The driver of the black Lexus sedan that had hit it was already out of the car. The hood folded up like an accordion. The cop on the scene—a guy named Sutton whom he knew well enough—had the black-haired female standing away from the chaos in the grass. She held her forehead with one hand and the side of her neck with the other. He thought he could see her trembling even from a distance. Sutton postured beside her, scribbling notes on a thin pad, looking like a middle-aged Denzel Washington.

He'd already suckered Sutton into giving the woman his business card. She was attractive and she drove a Lexus. He smiled as the thought of the term *ambulance chaser* wriggled its way into his mind. Business was business.

Traffic cones merged the two lanes into one. The cruiser's light bar flashed, the hues reflecting in flickers of red and blue over the broken glass on the road. And the line of cars crawled. He checked his watch, a silver Movado chronograph with a black face that ran him $1,300. Six minutes late now.

He made two calls. One to the clerk—a guy named Pérez—to do his best to stall. The other was to his assistant, to start everything if he was running too late.

As he inched past the accident, he cranked the stereo to This Is Led Zeppelin on Spotify. "Kashmir" played first.

The sky grayed. As he pulled up to the courthouse and parked, he tightened the loosely made Windsor knot and combed his dark hair in the mirror. He got out with his briefcase under his arm, slammed the door, and strutted toward the doors. He listened to the click of his loafers while he fiddled with the button of his jacket. When he looked up, two uniformed officers whom he knew, Leon Fisher and Tony West, approached him.

Fisher was a big guy with hardened facial features, rippling muscles, and faded ink that traveled just shy of the wrist on his right arm. He'd worked the drug task force for years and looked the part. In spite of having shared war stories over drinks with Fisher at a dive bar he couldn't remember the name of on Main Avenue, there wasn't the slightest hint of a smile on his face. Beneath the dark sunglasses that hid Fisher's eyes, his lips were tightened. He knew that now, Fisher mostly patrolled downtown in a cruiser. So what did he want?

West, he'd only ever made small talk with in passing. But he knew the white-haired, mustached man once had IA crawling up his ass for use-of-force violations. Despite it, the man had the look of the uncle who comes over on holidays just to eat and hog a recliner. His uniform was wrinkled and loose, which did little to hide the sagging flabs of flesh over his stomach.

Gerry nervously scratched his fingernails against his cheek. "Sorry, fellas. I'm running late for—"

Fisher looked down at the briefcase and then back up to his face. "Gerry, we were told to bring you in. Come with us."

He couldn't just leave. Gerry had documents in his briefcase that needed to be exhibited in court. He'd spent hours familiarizing himself with the documents that his assistant drafted, which he'd made a couple of tweaks to here and there. Not that they needed it; it was purely for what Gerry wanted to emphasize to the grand jury. It was what would keep his bonehead client, Roger Milton, out of prison. He looked past the two officers to the white Crown Vic parked in a spot. Past it, he scanned the faces of the people staring from the courthouse steps. He typically loved the feeling of walking up the steps, dressed for battle. Especially the sneaking glances he'd receive and the smile he'd exchange. But the loose crowd that was forming, their watchful eyes, felt like needles penetrating the pressure points of his skin. "What the hell is this, Fisher? Told to bring me in by who?"

"Harlow."

He'd known Tess Harlow to be a cold, no-nonsense type. Obsessive about proving herself. Pretentious. She was lead detective of the task force that had caught Gregory Sadler. What on earth would she want with him?

"*Harlow?* She on her period again?"

West smiled. Fisher didn't. "Let's go. I don't want to have to cuff you."

His eyes went wide. "Cuff me? On what charges?"

He stared at West, whose hand was closed around his belt. He found it odd how close to the service weapon his fingers were. "Let's just take 'im, Fish."

Fisher ignored the comment. His unblinking stare was one of menace, aimed at Gerry as though he was expecting him to run. Hell, it made him want to. "Amy Berglund, Malin Jakobsson, and Nora Vandenberg."

195

Gerry searched their faces in disbelief. What scared him the most were their faces. West looked as if he wouldn't mind rag-dolling him to the ground. And Fisher . . .

They weren't joking. He was someone who typically didn't budge, especially when he knew his rights. But right now, he felt his shirt glued to the pits of his underarms. "What the fuck is this? I'm not going anywhere with either of you—"

As he turned on his heel toward the courthouse, he caught a figure in his peripheral. Swinging out from behind a parked SUV was someone with a large rifle. Gerry watched in astonishment as the old man's mouth moved. His face was hooded, shadowed by a frayed cap pulled low. Gerry couldn't pinpoint the scream that he heard, but as he flinched, the bullet tore right through him. He collapsed. His skull ricocheted like a rattle off the hot pavement. He turned and stared through hazy eyes; the shimmer of tears clouded his vision. His mouth opened wide. His shirt felt damp. And in the next second, two more shots whip-cracked. He watched the barrel muzzle flash and the old man flail backward. Gerry's right leg jolted as a fire stormed throughout his kneecap. Even if he could bear to search for the entry hole—which he couldn't—he was frozen.

As he lay dying, he looked past the hand where the watch said he was now sixteen minutes late. He stared at the old man dead on the ground. Fisher came into view and kicked the rifle away from the old man. Gerry thought he could hear the words clearly now.

This is for my daughter.

Chapter 31

The first 7.62x51mm round shattered Gerry McAntis's left clavicle. As the trajectory of the bottleneck cartridge shifted, the projectile nicked his subclavian artery and severed the subclavian vein. McAntis bled out in less than a minute.

The second GSW was a three-inch hole that tore through the cartilage and bone in Gerry's patella. Both shots were fired from an old M1A semiautomatic rifle manufactured by Springfield Armory. When Rooker saw it tagged as evidence, he ID'd it as the same rifle as the one he saw in the Berglund home.

Tony West's service weapon was a Smith & Wesson M&P 9mm. One 9mm Luger round ended Charles Berglund. The bullet was sent center of mass, penetrated his liver, and exited his back. Tony West called for a bus and a trauma unit, but Charles Berglund was DOA.

Two wet circles on the concrete were what remained of them now.

Tess was the one to inform Eva Berglund about her husband. She sobbed. And then she crumpled into a ball on the hard floor. By the time Keene went to her, her face was already damp. With her nose and mouth webbed with snot and tears, she screamed at the top of her lungs, "Get out of my house!"

And they did.

◆ ◆ ◆

Tess sighed. Leaning back in her office chair, she rubbed her hand wearily against her forehead.

"Boss," Keene said to her.

She held up a finger. "Give me a minute, Martin."

She pushed her tousled hair into her face and hid behind her hands. Her shoulders trembled.

"It can't wait, Tess," Keene said gently. It was rare that he called her by her name inside these walls. "Got something strange."

"What is it?"

"So, the stuff we found at the McAntis home. We've got prints that don't belong to him."

"Where?"

"Seems mostly in the bedroom and en suite bathroom. Small. Belong to what looks like two different females."

"Gerry was known for being quite the playboy. That's nothing new. Any ID?"

"Not yet. Two more things. One, the neighbor said there's a lock to the cellar hatch at the back door. It wasn't there. If it was snapped off, whoever did it took the pieces with them. And when Xander dusted for fingerprints, he found this." Keene handed her a photograph. It was a close-up shot of one of the drawers in the office. "Glove marks. Nitrile."

"Someone was inside his home."

"Seems so."

What the fuck is going on?

"I have to make a call."

"To who?"

"Larsson. Someone has to keep the old prick away from the cameras."

The conversation left her fuming.

Chapter 32

"You know what they say, *Mother.* Two birds, *one stone.*"

He squeezed her face in his hands, lean yet powerful hands like cold barbed wire. Her face trembled. But she wouldn't dare try to bite him. *Not again.*

What a miracle it was. Charles. *Poor old Charles.* Tormented for thirty years waiting for the authorities to find his daughter's body one day. But that day never came. And it never would. The man died thinking that he'd killed the man who took his daughter from him. What a fool.

And Gerry. *Gol-lee Gerry.* That loudmouthed oaf. He'd never have to listen to his spew again. He smiled at the thought of working in the office alone now. No more obnoxiously loud telephone calls. No more repulsive belching. No more of that damn squeaking hand gripper. No more slaps on the arm or awful Tender Nob drinks.

Blissful quiet.

At the edge of his mother's bed sat Hartley Caldwell in pitch darkness. It was four in the afternoon. The blinds were drawn. But today, he'd need to spruce the place up a bit. The police would be paying a visit soon to discuss Gerry. He practiced his lines for the unearthly quiet that lay in the bed.

I don't know, Officer.

We didn't speak much outside the office.

Hartley sat up from the edge of the bed to his mother's whimper. He said over his shoulder: "Oh, hush, Mother. Isn't that what you told me? *Oh, hush!*" With the tip of his finger, he wiped a tear from his mother's cheek. Then he touched it to his tongue. He patted down the wrinkle in the bedsheet where he'd sat, tucked the blanket beneath the thin mattress, and sauntered out of the room.

He stood before the door. Pressed a hand to it like he was feeling for the heat of fire behind it. He closed his eyes and breathed.

Good morning, Warrel. Morning, Warrel. He practiced different voices and tones in his head until he got it right. Then he opened his eyes and slid the key into the door, turning it until it clicked. For a moment, he waited. This was never in the plans. He knew the man downstairs shouldn't be here. Still, when he saw how easy it would be to take him, he couldn't help himself. It was like his body unleashed itself from his brain and was acting on its own accord.

For you, dear Rooker.

Hartley descended the stairs, plunging into the darkness. The way down was committed to memory. Twelve stairs. The snap-creak at the third wooden step from the bottom. Thirty-degree turn to the left. Five more steps to the light cord that swung after a pull. The light switch at the top of the stairs hadn't worked since he purchased the home. He'd decided not to fix it. He liked the feeling that the darkness gave him, the way it wrapped like a cold sheet around his skin, the chill of it that invaded his body.

He heard him. The guttural squeal, muffled. His voice was trapped behind the tape, yet he understood every word perfectly.

"Help! Please help me! Please!"

Slowly, his footsteps slapped on the cold concrete. Around people, he designed his walk to be ordinary: head down a few foot measurements in front of him, one quiet step of the leg with the gentle sway of the opposite arm. No one would take a second glance at him. Down here in the darkness, though, he relished the sedated cadence of his footfalls.

Slap . . . slap . . . slap . . .

He felt like he was the only person for the shadows to see.

In the center of the room, the chair was bolted to the floor. It was an old jury chair. Too bad for Mr. Haney, Hartley was judge and jury.

The man of the hour, a celebrity to some, sat naked, his wrists tied to the chair, his ankles bound together.

"Good morning, Warrel." The man froze, as though liquid nitrogen had been force-fed through a feeding tube. His words—maybe his presence—were enough to turn him to ice. Despite the snot that was glued to the tape, it tore from his mouth with ease. For him, at least. A red rash coated Warrel Haney's upper lip. Little black needles of hair stuck to the strip of tape.

He stood in front of him, unseen. "You're the only one who seems to understand, Mr. Haney. The witch trials—your article. You understood."

"Yes—yes, I did! I have my followers. I'll get the tabloids to publish everything you say word for word and—"

"Hush, Mr. Haney. This is a court of law. There *will* be order, understand?" He laughed and paused and lowered himself to stare into the face of his latest toy. He inched closer until he could smell the oil from his glands, the fear that leaked from his pores like milky pus. "You write lies, mostly. You spread them like a plague. Your fans are white-supremacist types for the most part—hillbilly UFO chasers and Area 51 fanatics. Gun-rights activists. Moon-landing doubters and flat earthers. People who want war but are too afraid to fight in one. Isn't that right?"

Haney nodded hysterically.

"But in this case, there was truth to your words." He yanked the silver cord. The center of the basement was illuminated by a spotlight—harsh yellow light, surrounded by darkness.

"*Please!*" His face trembled. Sweat bubbled along the man's thinning hairline. His eyes squeezed tighter. "I haven't seen your face. I'll do whatever you say—"

"*Oh, hush!*" The words fell short of his mother's tone. He tried them again. "*Oh, hush!*" Better that time. More venomous and detached next time.

The man went silent.

"Now, Mr. Haney. I'll need the log-in and password to your site and your Facebook page. Email too."

"Yes—anything! Take it."

Haney gave him everything, even the six-digit alphanumeric passcode to his cell phone.

Upstairs, knuckles rapped at the front door. He pulled the tape tight across the thin lips and bloated cheeks of Warrel Haney. "I can hear your heart, Mr. Haney. Try to scream and I'll cut it out of you."

Chapter 33

Harlow took a deep breath. She listened to the chain rattle on the other side of the door before it opened.

"Mr. Caldwell?" She lifted the badge from her chest. "My name is Detective Tess Harlow."

"Detective, nice to meet you. I remember you from the television—the Sadler case. Would you like to come inside?"

"Please." She ignored the Sadler comment.

"We'll just have to be a little quiet. I've been taking care of my mother for years, and she's in the other room resting."

"Absolutely."

Hartley Caldwell was a gaunt man with a wide-set grin and pencil neck. Unlike his colleague, Gerald McAntis, he didn't seem to have any sort of reputation.

From what she heard, Caldwell was a quiet, professional man who mostly kept to himself.

He led her halfway down the hall on the right to a gray sofa where it appeared no one ever sat. She took a seat. He sank into a rocking chair across from her but sat perfectly still.

"May I ask what happened to your mother?"

"She suffered two strokes, actually. As a result, she developed apha-sia. The doctors said she'd never regain the ability to speak. At first when I brought her home from the hospital, I was in denial. I hired a speech therapist to come to the house, but it didn't work. So I take care of her, and sometimes I hire someone if I need to be away for work."

Suddenly, she thought of her own mother. It had been more than a month since she last worked up the courage to see her. She'd driven to the nursing home. Even walked in through the sliding glass doors. She'd given her name to the person sitting behind the desk. But she hadn't gone to see her mother.

"WHAT HAVE YOU DONE?" The words beat like wings, like a gnat landed on her forehead; her hand gestured to it and brushed the thought away. If anything, it appeared she may have a headache. "Sounds like she's lucky to have you."

He only smiled.

"When did you start working for Gerald McAntis?"

"Two and a half, maybe three years ago."

"What did you do for him exactly?"

"When he was feeling good, he'd call me his caddie. *'You know the course and choose the club; I take the swing.'* That's what he'd say. I mostly conduct research and draft legal documents. Help him with develop-ments and case planning. He didn't listen to many people, but I'd say he did respect what I had to say."

"Had you seen any kind of change in his behavior lately?"

"Not that I can think of."

"How well would you say you knew him?"

She watched him consider the question. "I'd say I knew *of* him. I knew he frequently slept with different women, but I didn't know or meet any of them. I'd say he was witty, intelligent, but could be a bit unprofessional at work."

"How so?"

"Drinking during office hours. The way he'd speak about clients, the opposing legal team, or jurors."

"Did he ever say anything about Roger Milton?"

"Some things that are protected by attorney-client privilege. What I can tell you is that he called Milton a bull—he'd simulate Roger having intercourse like one over his desk. He often made comments about the attractiveness of Milton's secret girlfriend at the time, Ximena Hernandez. Anything else would have to do with findings in the case."

"What can you tell me about Luis Barrios?" She hurled the question at him like a baseball at a pitch-back net.

He squinted. "Sorry?"

"Luis Barrios. He goes by the nickname Pounds."

He cleared his throat. "I'm not sure I know the name."

She didn't buy it. There was something off about Mr. Caldwell at the mention of Barrios. The pause before his answer a little too long. "He wasn't a client?"

"Not to my knowledge."

"Luis Barrios is an inmate at Pelican Bay State Prison—multiple murder charges. He's locked up in solitary confinement for violent tendencies and gang affiliation. Mr. Barrios asked for a lawyer by name. He asked for Gerry McAntis." She paused. "Can you tell me how an inmate in solitary confinement could have come up with an attorney's name who works out of Minnesota?"

"If he didn't already have a lawyer, he would have been able to get a public defender. I can't tell you how an inmate who I don't have any recollection of would have gotten Gerry's name."

Chapter 34

After Detective Harlow descended the porch steps, he chained and twisted the front door locks and stood back to watch her from out of sight. His hand balled into a fist.

With her in mind, he hurried to the bathroom, stripped, and started the shower. Before he stepped inside, he played music from an old-fashioned speaker that he placed on the toilet lid. "Good Vibrations" by the Beach Boys played. He wasn't particularly fond of the song.

I love the colorful clothes she wears. And the way the sunlight plays upon her hair.

He climbed in the shower and let the water pummel him. His mind raced, while he stood perfectly still over the hair-clogged drain. But when the chorus started, he turned his face up at the spout of the showerhead, the tiny black dots where the water sprayed, and fastened his eyes shut. Behind his eyelids, he saw tiny spots of rage. He screamed at the top of his lungs.

After he got out and changed, he went back to the door. Holding his palm to it, he could feel Mr. Haney's presence. It was there, but it was weakening.

It's almost time, Mr. Haney. The rage inside him was like a flare, only just beginning to burn bright. It wouldn't go out anytime soon.

He opened the door and was face-to-face with the darkness. The refreshing cold of it tingled his spine. He ambled down the steps.

Twelve stairs. Thirty-degree turn to the left. Five more steps to the light cord.

A large black dresser, with a modern face and an oil-like sheen, sat against the wall. Behind the bulky silver pulls on the drawers were his tools. Along with the pistol he'd stolen off Rooker Lindström.

Hartley Caldwell snapped on a pair of black latex gloves. As each glove *thwack*ed against the lumpy bone in his wrist—echoing like the snap of a finger in a barren room—Mr. Haney flinched. He slammed the drawer shut. Again, Haney twitched.

"You little shit!" he hissed. "*Shit!* No. *You lit-tle shit!*" That was better. More like the way his mother would say it.

How did they find out about Barrios? He'd only gone to see him the one time. Were they onto him? Then he thought of the bank records. Nothing there that could come back to him. Flight records. He'd taken a red-eye flight from Range Regional Airport in Hibbing to Rogue Valley International Medford Airport. A close second option was Eureka, California, but better to be safe and avoid having a ticket say he flew to California. Once he landed in Medford, with a fake ID he paid for with a stolen credit card, he rented a vehicle at a Budget Rent a Car. Pelican Bay State Prison was a little over a two-hour drive from Jackson County.

By taking Warrel Haney, he had screwed the pooch. No worries, though. There was time to get rid of him and go on with his quiet life. If it came to it, he could run. But enough of these games.

"Nora Vandenberg sat in that chair," he said. "Would you like to see her?"

"HMM-MM!" the man with wax skin muttered beneath the silver tape.

He jerked another drawer open. He pulled a roll of plastic sheeting from it. He held one end and let the other slink down to the floor. He let it go, and go, before he snipped across the end with a pair of scissors. He laid it on the ground and spread it all around the chair. It wrinkled and puckered beneath his steps.

"Do you know what the perfect murder is, Mr. Haney? Imagine killing someone and never giving them a body to find. They send out search parties for them, day and night, and you join. They have these pathetic vigils, and you blend in with the crowd. You have a chance to offer your sympathies to the parents. And all along, you're the one responsible. And this time"—he smiled—"you get the father who has longed for his daughter for thirty years to shoot and kill someone you detest. You understand?"

Haney nodded.

He tore the tape from his mouth. "Open your eyes, Warrel."

He didn't.

He yanked the metal string. The bulb burned overhead; harsh yellow light flooded the two of them. "I said *open them*!" He pecked at the fleshy eyelid of Warrel Haney until it trickled red. It wasn't long before clear-blue tears mixed with it. Haney stared down at the clear plastic.

"No, please!"

"Look," he told him. "What do you see?"

Warrel's right eye fastened shut. The other surveyed the room through a trembling squint. He watched Warrel Haney look around at the mirrors, at least twenty of them in a circle around him. Then he turned his face up to the symbols on the walls.

Hartley pointed to each one as he recited, "Eye of Horus. Eye of Ra. The Horned God. The ankh. Fire. Water. Air. Earth. The pentacle.

"My mother was a hippie. She had me young. I was her accident. She said she loved my father, but he took off the very day he laid eyes on me. She always resented me for that. *'You scared him away, you lit-tle shit!'* She drew symbols. Practiced witchcraft."

Not far beneath his mother's bedroom, he jabbed the point of a pen into Warrel Haney's right eye. "I SEE YOU!" he screamed. "I SEE YOU!" Haney let out a piercing cry. He convulsed in the chair. Hartley twisted the pen around. Like he was fishing for something in a stew. And he yanked it out. The eye detached from the socket, the end pink and stringy like bubblegum stuck to the bottom of a shoe. Seconds later, he grabbed a knife. With an imprecise but swift, powerful motion, he hacked at the throat of Warrel Haney. A gurgle left his open throat. But after the second, and the third, and fourth, there was only the silence of blood dripping down to plastic.

Chapter 35

September 28, 2019

His phone rang. It was Caroline.

"Hi," he said, curious.

"That favor I owe you. A call just came in. They asked for me. I know the police were looking into Gerry McAntis before he was killed, but I don't think he's who you want. This caller . . . there's something wrong about him. *Scary.* Do you have a pen?"

"One sec." He pulled the pen from his pants pocket and bit the cap off. "Go ahead."

The call ended with a warning from Caroline to be careful.

Rooker filled up at a Cenex and drove north on the MN-48 out past Suomi. It connected with Itasca County Rd 253 Bridge. Millie drummed her fingernails against the glass, but Rooker ignored it. While he gripped the steering wheel, he glanced at the ink on his hand. Once over the bridge, he pressed his thumb into the button on the dash that tracked his mileage. The only thing left to do was drive 14.6 miles and take the exit onto a dirt road like the message said.

Sure enough, it was there.

Rooker pulled off the exit. After a couple of minutes, the pavement turned to dust. The shocks in the Volvo were no match for the bumps. He pulled up to an abandoned barn and put the car in park. An old barbed-wire fence surrounded it, though most of it had come down. The barn was made of rotting brown wood, and the steel roof seemed to bleed rust. There was a human-size hole in one side where a small section had caved in. A small window in the loft would offer a good vantage point for anyone awaiting approaching cars. The window was dark, and Rooker saw no sign of movement anywhere, but he had the skin-tingling feeling that he was being watched. He went to open the glove box but remembered his gun was gone.

"Shit," he hissed. Had he remembered, he could've brought the old Glock 17 that he had stashed in the house.

"It's all right. I've got mine."

The sky was falling. Dusk would be unfolding soon.

Rooker waded through the wild golden grass that came up to his waist. Millie followed behind until they reached the wall. He nearly put his hand to it until he saw a horde of what looked like thin maggots or translucent ants. Termites.

They ducked inside, and the odor made him want to puke. It reeked of death and shit-sodden hay.

Their steps fell over cold ground and remnants of hay. The dampness was trapped here, as Rooker felt now without a weapon. But he stayed close behind Millie as she peeked the corners in a shooter's stance. After she'd cleared the bottom level, the two of them looked up the length of the ladder.

"You've got the gun," he whispered to her.

With that said, Millie scaled the warped wood. Rooker watched her get up to the middle, when one of the pegs snapped beneath her foot. It echoed off the walls.

As she steadied herself, Rooker asked her if she was all right.

"Just fine. I'm the one with the gun, remember?"

He watched her grab the rung above the one that had snapped and hoist herself up. The top half of her vanished. He listened to the click of her flashlight and could see it sweep over the floor from below.

"Clear," she said.

Relieved he didn't have to climb up after her, Rooker milled around the barn and peeked out through one of the broken windows on the far wall.

That's when he saw the shape of her.

That's when they found Nora Vandenberg.

"Millie," he said without taking his eyes off her. "Come down."

The tree was dead. It was an old oak tree. Tall grass sprouted wildly around it. Limbs bent like broken bones, all snapped at horrible angles. Arthritic. One branch hung lower than the rest. A heavy beige rope hung from it. It looked like climbing rope. He knew it was one that could have been purchased from any hardware store. As he walked closer, he saw where the rope frayed against the branch, either when the body must have swung or the killer pulled on the other end.

It made him wonder if she had still been alive when she was brought here.

He looked up at the dark-brown discoloration, red on either side: ligature marks. They were deep. It meant she'd been tied up for a long time.

She'd been tortured. Her left foot was scorched black. The right one swollen like a sickly raisin. Purple welts covered her body, where he assumed she'd been pelted by rocks and stones.

It was consistent with what the killer had sent in the envelopes to the Berglunds.

Stoning. Drowning. Hanging. Burning.

And then he thought for a moment, on the fact that Nora Vandenberg was dead—and that they were, indeed, hunting another serial killer.

Millie hung up the phone. "Tess is on her way." She looked sad, defeated. But as Rooker stared at Nora's bare body, at the pain she had endured, his fist clenched to a ball so tight, his knuckles were ready to pop.

Chapter 36

September 28, 2019

Tess had the entrance to the dirt road cordoned off with crime scene tape. She stationed a deputy named Ervin just outside it and said that if anyone came by, to get their ID. Then, after she told Rooker and Millie to stand back, she ordered a few work lights to be brought out to the scene. They'd be working in the dark soon. When Rooker saw them, he thought they looked like two-headed monsters. Once they turned on, he listened to the electricity hum through them. Ugly, grim shadows casted over what was meant to be dark now. What wasn't meant to be seen.

Millie leaned closer to Rooker. "We need to call Christine and Thomas."

He nodded.

At 9:00 p.m., the first television crew pulled up outside the yellow tape in a white van. Sure enough, as Rooker walked toward the source of the noise, Caroline Lind and a burly, goateed man holding a lighted tripod stepped out of the van.

When Rooker rounded the corner and watched Tess moving hurriedly toward them, he muttered the only thing he could think of: "Uh-oh."

Tess stood on the other side of the tape. "This is a crime scene. You need to leave."

"Is it really Nora Vandenberg?" Caroline sounded unfazed.

"Maybe you didn't hear me, Ms. Lind. This is the scene of a crime—"

"The killer called me. I'm the reason you found her—"

"If I have to ask you again to leave, you'll be escorted in the back of a police cruiser. Clear?"

"Crystal." Caroline smiled.

Tess marched over to Rooker and dug her heel into the dirt. "Keep her far, far away from all of this. If she interferes . . ."

"Got it."

"I won't hesitate to throw her in the back of a squad car."

"Noted. Anything else Millie and I can do?"

Tess sighed. "I met a man who works with Gerry McAntis. Name is Hartley Caldwell. The guy gave me a weird feeling. Claimed he didn't know who Luis Barrios is. I'm not sure I buy it."

"I'll call a favor in with Warden Hastings. See if the guy recognizes him."

At 9:25 p.m., six more networks pulled up in trucks and vans. Caroline must have tipped them off. If she wasn't going to get what she wanted, she'd make the night a living hell for Detective Tess Harlow.

As he dialed Hastings, he watched Keene cautiously remove items from a kit and swab and scrape beneath the victim's fingernails. Rooker knew exogenous DNA could be collected if she had been able to get her hands on her assailant. By the looks of her, though, he imagined she never got the chance.

He got voice mail and left a short message: "Hastings, I need a favor. I'm emailing you a photo. I need a guard to take it to Pounds right away and see if he recognizes the guy. It's urgent. Thanks."

Rooker took a screenshot of Caldwell's bio pic from the law firm's website and sent it to Hastings. As he pocketed his phone, he heard Tess yell to Keene, "After we get photos and bag the evidence, get her cut down and out of here."

"You got it, boss."

Rooker wandered over to Keene to ask if the luminol the detective had applied in the barn had turned up any traces of blood. It made him shudder to think that the substance would make any blood trails glow neon blue, like the barn had been the site of some demented rave.

"Hey, Martin. Anything in the—"

"Sorry, Rooker. This isn't the Sadler case. You and Millie need to head home now."

Chapter 37

Tess couldn't see much of anything, which she knew was a bad sign.

"Boss," Keene said to her. She already knew what he was going to say. "No traces of blood found in the barn."

Tess sighed. Although the smell wasn't bothering her, when she inhaled through her mouth, it felt as though she was eating it. "She was tortured somewhere else and then brought here."

That meant the only shot they had at gathering evidence was that which they'd find on the victim's body.

"Looks like it. That mark on her neck . . ." Keene trailed off. "It's a lot fresher than the ones on her wrists."

"Hangman's fracture," Tess said. "That may have been what ultimately killed her."

"That means he brought her here alive."

◆ ◆ ◆

"You've brought me a peculiar case, Detective," said Isaiah Hayes, scratching his head while he peered over bifocals at her. He had the balding crown of scorched earth, one where all that was left was white debris and flaky ash. He donned a white lab coat and a blue surgical mask. "A dormant killer. One thing he has more than you, tenfold: *time*."

"Yeah, we seem to be running out of it." She checked the imaginary watch at her wrist.

"If he did in fact kill Amy Berglund and Malin Jakobsson, it's been thirty years since his first victim and eight years since he last killed, *that we know of.* I can say with confidence that Ms. Vandenberg's injuries are nearly identical to those of Ms. Jakobsson. Two victims found so close together in time, dead eight years apart. Doesn't that strike you as fascinating?"

She didn't answer.

"Unfortunately, the crime scene isn't much of one."

"What does that mean?"

"It means that, yes, your victim was killed where you found her. But aside from that fact, almost nothing in my findings will help you."

"What are you saying? How can there be nothing?"

"There were zero fibers, zero signs of prophylactic or seminal fluid, or any fluids, for that matter, on the victim. I don't believe he kills for sexual gratification."

For the first time since Tess walked into the room, Isaiah Hayes gently pulled back the cloth. Beneath the veil of a white sheet, Nora Vandenberg appeared to be made of glass. The room hummed, a combination of fluorescent light and suffering. A fear was growing inside Tess. One that she couldn't define.

"I'm not one to tell you how to do your job, Detective. But you may want to look at someone who has medical knowledge. These wounds . . ." The shake of his head matched the gruesomeness of the act. "Her left foot has fourth-degree burns. That typically leads to life-threatening infection. It destroyed every layer of skin, down to the bone. Extensive nerve damage. Her muscles, tendons—the foot would never heal. It would have to be amputated.

"The right foot seems to have been submerged in water for a time spanning multiple days. It doesn't sound all that bad, but after days of it, the skin would begin to break apart and develop open sores. Again, you're talking dangerous infection.

"Then ecchymosis—the dark welts all over her body—where the victim suffered blunt-force trauma. In this case, she sustained these wounds over an extended period of time.

"Now, modus operandi. There are impulse killers. Premeditated killers. I guess you already know all this, but I'd say it's evident your killer goes through this process as more of a ritual. He's taken his time with her. What I can't say is whether or not he intentionally preserves the victim's face."

"Preserves?"

"Nearly every inch of her body has sustained unimaginable trauma. But her face doesn't have a single scratch on it.

"Whoever you're after . . . they must've been giving her antibiotics to not only prevent infection but to keep her alive."

Tess's hand covered her mouth. She pulled it away. "What can you tell us about TOD?"

"So, the C2, or the upper cervical spine, has been fractured. Edema, or swelling, of the neck. You can see here." He drew an invisible line with his index finger. "The fall didn't kill her. Cerebral hypoxia and global ischemia. The flow of oxygen and blood are cut off from the brain. Tardieu spots in the eyes, these red-and-purple markings where the vessels ruptured. Time of death, somewhere between two a.m. and four a.m."

Chapter 38

Just after three in the morning, Millie pounded her third energy drink: 160 mg of caffeine and allegedly zero sugar in a tall black can with a neon letter *M* on it. Tess once told her they'd stop her heart one day. But now, she was even more inclined to rebel and drink them.

She stared at the tabs she'd left open. Pressed the tip of a finger into the dull ache behind her eye. It could have been the caffeine, maybe the hours in darkness staring at the bright screen. Oh well.

She was reading about femicide, the gender hate crime where women are killed just for being women, the databases and statistics of women killed by men, when she heard a loud bang outside that lifted her from her seat. She froze. Waited.

Silence.

She slid the drawer out slowly. Her hand vanished into the darkness of it. Wrapped around the cold steel. She raised the pistol and listened to the hammering of her pulse.

While her finger hovered—trembled—over the safety mechanism, the wind wailed again, like a heavy breath on her ear. She felt the brisk air slip inside the poor insulation of the old windows, and the chill invaded the room. She listened to the rustling outside. The clink and clatter of the rusty chime on the front porch. And just then, the loud bang again, a loose shutter whipping against the side of the house. She left the HK45 on the table beside the keyboard and closed the drawer.

While she stared at the grooves in the barrel, her mind traveled back to when she'd told her family she wanted to be a cop. She was only a little girl then. Maybe twelve years old.

She could still see her mother in a pair of jeans and striped sweater sitting on a little three-cushion sofa. "Women don't save the world, Mill. Women comfort men who come home after a long day of making the world worse."

Though Amy Berglund's disappearance happened just before Millie was born, she grew up knowing every detail about her, just as everyone else did. The girl became a legend. Parents used what happened to her as a lesson, to show kids the dangers in the real world. It was a way to tell them not to go out alone and not to stay out late. Don't talk to strangers. They all thought that Amy must have.

She must have done *something* wrong for her to disappear.

Millie never bought into that.

Sometimes, bad things just happened.

She studied the case through high school. Even into her years at the academy. She'd have dreams during the night of finding her alive. But it was far too late. First Malin, now Nora . . . no way Amy had escaped the same killer.

Millie pinched the bridge of her nose hard. Paced back and forth. She'd been delaying the inevitable. It wasn't fair to Christine and Thomas; she should have told them by now. She should have driven over to the house once they had a positive ID, but she couldn't bring herself to do it. For the first time, she'd have to bear the brunt of a family's grief. She'd never had to deliver a death notification and was suddenly glad about that. It was after three in the morning, but she had to get this over with. As she fought the tremor in her hand, she dialed Christine Vandenberg and nearly winced when she answered.

"Christine . . ." Millie swallowed hard. Instantly, she thought of how she couldn't save Nora and fought the urge to cry. "I'm so sorry. We found Nora's body. She's gone."

Christine Vandenberg burst into a scream of tears. Muttered a string of incoherent words before the line went dead.

Despite her sigh of relief, she didn't feel a weight off her shoulders.

She'd finally gotten her chance to prove her mother wrong. But Nora was dead. Millie had failed.

Chapter 39

September 30, 2019

Rooker pulled a garment bag from the depths of a storage closet. The suit was the one thing he always put away as neatly as possible. It had only been a few months since he'd worn it last—at Evelyn Holmberg's funeral. Here he was again, recycling the same dark suit, for Charles Berglund. Another death he felt responsible for.

And then he thought of Nora. He wondered if he'd have time to dry-clean the suit before her funeral.

Rooker and Millie trailed the fifteen-car procession in the Volvo at a steady crawl. There was a police escort, with a Crown Vic in the lead, to deter gawkers from disrupting the funeral. They all moved in somber unison, hazard lights flickering. Rooker listened to the steady whir of the windshield wipers. Rooker thought about Eva and how the seventy-nine-year-old widow would keep up the house and all that land alone. Really, he worried more that she'd die soon of a broken heart. As he turned in to the cemetery, he followed the procession past aisles of headstones until he saw the blurry taillights in front of him. He stopped the car and shut off the engine.

Millie broke the silence. "People once thought a rainy funeral meant that whoever passed away was going to heaven."

His brow twitched. If there was one thing he hated, it was when people tried to make death out to be a good thing. Light wasn't meant to be found in the dark. Rooker spoke, still staring at the red of the brake lights. "It's a funeral, Mill. The only place the dead go is into the ground."

"Well, some say it's good luck."

"Is this where I'm meant to feel lucky?" Rooker looked at the gravestones through the window that had begun to fog. He wiped it away with a cold palm. The dead flowers—red rosebuds—the dull, broken petals appeared to have been stepped on. "Because if it is, my *luck* feels like someone called heads or tails on a coin flip that has neither."

The two of them got out. Millie smoothed out the skirt of her black dress with one hand and shook open a dark umbrella with the other. Rooker preferred to let the rain hit him like sucker punches and thrashing kicks he couldn't brace for. Like most days, today, he felt he deserved to take it. Rooker watched the people getting out of their cars, afraid of the rain. They were mostly in black and charcoal suits, some that didn't fit nearly as well as Rooker's did. Any suit he owned was tailored to his measurements. If he was forced to wear one, he'd look good doing it.

The cemetery stretched the length of two football fields, though for the most part it was lumpy and full of divots, like a bad golf fairway. Despite the rain that hazed his vision, he analyzed the gathering of people as they walked. And then he felt a hand on his arm, and the rain stopped beating against his hair. As the rain fell against the umbrella, he closed his eyes and imagined fuzzy radio static.

"Ready?" Millie said beside him.

He sighed. "As I'll ever be."

They followed the other mourners. The earth was sopping wet. A few people slipped and nearly went down to the ground. But eventually, everyone was standing by the six-foot hole in the earth.

While the priest recited a psalm that went on and on about God at your side, Rooker scanned the expressions of the people around the black casket.

"You really think he'd come here?" Millie whispered.

"He was at the vigil for Nora."

The air beneath the umbrella's vortex was raw. While he stared past the rain that fell in cloudy beads from the umbrella, eventually he met the tired gaze of Eva Berglund, who only stared. It wasn't a look of anger. It was 100 percent pure, unlaced sorrow. The face of someone who had lost everything. Rooker had seen that face countless times, staring back in the mirror.

The hearse was an early-2000s Cadillac. In the dull gleam of the black hood, he could make out the shadows of the swaying trees. Wearing a pressed black suit, the driver stood with his back against the driver door, his hands steepled with rehearsed sympathy across the belly of his buttoned jacket. He had the clean-shaven face, the sadness in his eyes, the look of a man who made his living off the dead.

He caught her in his periphery. Really, she'd caught him. In a black gown, she stood alone by an elm tree. The dress, her petite figure—for the first time, she looked breakable. He pictured her as a ceramic doll, shattering to a thousand pieces in slow motion. He stepped out from beneath the umbrella and walked to her. His footfalls slapped hard, the heavy soles of his black shoes clacking against the split concrete.

As Caroline smiled, he watched her cheek dimple and the shine of gloss at her lower lip. She smelled of pomegranate.

"Lovely day," she said.

"Perfect for a funeral. What brings you here?"

"I wanted to pay my respects. I hope he wouldn't mind my being here," she said.

For what little time he'd come to know Charles Berglund, he figured the man wouldn't want most of these people here. Maybe just Eva and Red. "Judgment is made only by the living. The dead no longer care what we do."

"Always so morbid." She smiled again.

"When you've seen the things I have—"

"Well, that's one reason I'm here too. I was hoping we could catch up. Are you free tonight?"

"Why not. I'll come by around nine." He didn't wait to see if she looked pleased with herself before he turned and headed back to the service, avoiding Millie's gaze as he shimmied under her umbrella.

As he watched the casket being lowered into the ground, Rooker's mind raced. What unnerved him the most about the killer was his *patience*. So few deaths—that they knew of, anyway. So many years between them. Thirty years between Amy Berglund and Nora Vandenberg. *Thirty.* It made no sense. How would it be possible to catch someone who'd been hiding this long?

He knew he was missing something. Like he was staring into a blank face, and it was up to him to form the features.

Chapter 40

September 30, 2019

Before he went to Caroline's, Rooker pruned the edges of his beard, rinsed off quickly in the shower, and picked up a reasonably priced bottle of red wine and a handle of gin. He remembered the taste of a French 75—or something similar—on her lips.

His change from the package store rattled in the cupholder between the seats. When he pulled to a stop at the curb in front of Caroline's home, he shut the engine off. The small digital numbers above the scratched leather on the dash read 9:04 p.m.

All the lights were off. *Strange.* He'd said nine o'clock; he was sure of it. He reached into the glove box for the Glock 17—he'd replaced the one that was gone with Sundgren's. He got out and shut the door silently. Rooker loped up the front steps, gun in hand, where the motion detector light kicked on.

The door wasn't all the way shut. His fingers gently nudged it, the groan of it fracturing the silence.

Shit.

He took a few steps inside, and the dark swarmed him, crawled all around him, and invaded his pores. Oftentimes in darkness so black he couldn't see, he would cover his throat with the L of his hand, as if the shadows would grow fingers and choke him to death.

His palm moved blindly over the wall. The calluses snagged on the wallpaper. He found the two-way switches on the wall and flicked them all up until the light vanquished the shadows.

Fresh lilies stood tall in a glass vase on a table placed against the wall of the entryway. If there was any kind of person who would buy themselves flowers, Caroline fit the profile. At least he hoped she'd bought them.

He knew better than to call out her name. Still, that didn't stop him.

"Caroline?" he called out at the edge of the staircase. He waited a few moments. Standing still, he listened to the hum of silence, the thumping in his chest. He raised the gun.

He turned into the living area. Rounded the corner to the kitchen. He switched the light on. Listened to the steady drone of the refrigerator. As his eyes swept the room, that's when he saw it. A small notepad intended for little reminders or shopping lists. Red.

As he walked closer, he recoiled.

Next to the notepad was a ballpoint pen, the tip of it spearing an eyeball with pink veins lying wetly on the counter.

The red paper had a message in large black letters: I SEE YOU.

"Fuck." He sprinted upstairs and cleared the rooms. When he set foot in Caroline's bedroom, he found two mirrors propped up at the foot of the bed a few feet apart and facing each other. He put the gun down on the bed and made two calls. The first was to Tess, the second to Millie.

"You okay?" Millie asked.

"Just peachy."

"You know what I mean."

"Yeah, believe me. I know. With my track record—"

"Stop there. We'll find her."

"I know we will. But I need to start finding people *alive*."

He heard her suck in a breath. Then she said, "When Tess's team gets there, you should go to the station. I'll meet you there. There's no more time for pettiness—we all need to work together."

He agreed and hung up. He went downstairs and forced himself to take another look at the eyeball. He'd been so distracted by the gore, he hadn't looked closely at the iris.

Caroline's eyes weren't brown. And neither were Nora's.

Whose was it?

Chapter 41

Rooker found Millie sitting at her old desk—*Tess finally got her wish,* he thought. Her face was hidden partially behind her laptop screen, and the bright light of the display played across her forehead. It felt so familiar. A sadness started in the pit of his stomach, seeing her back with the team, back where he knew she belonged. He tried to quiet his pity party with a sharp clearing of his throat.

Keene and Sterling were standing at their desks, chatting. Riggs was sitting. For a moment, he pictured the detective formerly known as Elias Cole, twisting and twirling that pen between his fingers. Whitlock was cracking his knuckles, then his jaw. Tess was pacing back and forth on the phone before she ended the call and pocketed it.

A search warrant had been granted to access the street cameras between the broadcast building and Caroline's home. According to station security, Caroline had left at 8:10 p.m. The killer must have tailed her back to her place.

Naturally, Millie was the one put in charge of the footage. Cameras picked up the two cars. The first was a dark BMW X3 SUV. It was registered to Caroline. The second car was a dark Jaguar F-TYPE. After running the plates, it came back as registered to Gerald McAntis. The killer was driving Gerry's car.

Chapter 42

In the black sky, it was impossible to see where the smoke plume ended. He focused his eyes on where it began.

Twenty minutes had crawled by before they'd received a call about a burning car. Now Rooker was about twenty yards back from the Jaguar with his arms folded across his puffed chest. Through a squint, he took a step closer and thought he could feel the heat on his shins like from an open oven door. What remained of their best lead was a ball of fire and a puff of smoke that seemed to climb the tallest above the rooftops. Red and yellow flames crackling—flickering in his eyes—the storm sputtering out from the windows. Scorch marks ate at the paint. While the wind carried the tune of fire, he felt Millie's shoulder against his biceps and untightened his muscles and relaxed his jaw.

"They found something," she said loud enough to clear the roaring flames. Something within the car clanked. Then a screech of metal melting down, and something like a shotgun blast, before there was a miniature explosion, thankfully contained beneath the hood of the Jag. "There must have been a switch car. They don't have a make and model yet. But they found tire tracks, impressions that they can match in SICAR. It's a database that keeps thousands of tread patterns. They should be able to match it and narrow down the vehicle." He watched

everything unfold in slow motion. A team of three firefighters in full
gear spilled out of the red truck, manning a single powerful hose. As he
watched the water spray back and forth, hissing like a fighter jet far off
in the distance, he couldn't help but think there was no time.

Nora had been taken only weeks ago. The eye made him wonder
who else the killer had taken. Whoever it was, he believed they had
been taken after Nora. Whether they were taken before or after she
was killed, he didn't know. He couldn't. But what he felt rattling in his
bones was that something had triggered the killer, the dormancy period
between kills, or the "cooling-off period" when a killer returns back to
normal life.

For a moment, Rooker saw his father hunched over the kitchen
sink scrubbing his hands raw. White and cracked and brutally strong.
Suddenly he wondered if every time he'd seen his father get worse—
the escalating verbal abuse, throttling Rooker into a fetal position
of submission—that was just the period when his father would go
dormant, back to a "normal" life, before it would be too much and
he'd kill again.

Rooker drummed the back of his phone and jumped when it
buzzed. It was Hastings, finally returning his call.

"It's about fucking time."

"Christ. I can't just interrogate inmates whenever you want. They
still have rights. And Mr. Pounds needed a little incentive to look at
more photos. Apparently, the food in SHU is not up to his refined
standards."

"Spare me, Hastings. Pissing without privacy in a box the size of a
closet. Their rights were taken a long time ago."

"So, you weren't calling in another favor? Got it."

"The best restaurant you can find. Michelin star. Run up the tab
on my dime."

"That it?"

"Both the *LA Times* and the *New York Times* want a story from me. Maybe I can find a way to say what a great job you're doing over there."

"Okay, Lindström," Hastings said. "When we showed Pounds the photo of Caldwell, he stared as if he knew the guy. Then he said, 'Kinda looks like the guy. When I saw him, gringo had a mustache and looked a little older.' When I questioned him about asking for Gerry McAntis by name, he said, 'That's what I was told to say.'"

"What? Told by who?"

"He said it was in a note he got in his mail. And no, we don't have it—it's long gone."

"Thanks, Lamonte. I owe you."

"Sure as shit do. Good luck."

Rooker walked back to the Volvo, where Millie was tapping away on her laptop in the passenger seat. He got into the driver's seat, and when she looked over at him quizzically, he shook his head wearily and called Tess on speakerphone.

"Harlow," she answered.

"Tess. I think you're right about Caldwell. Luis Barrios seemed to recognize him. He said it could have been Caldwell who visited him after he called McAntis's office, but the guy had a mustache and looked a little older. I think Caldwell wore a disguise into the prison and somehow handed the phone over to Barrios—who then got it to Meachum."

"Why would he go through all of that? He hadn't killed anyone in eight years. What does Meachum have to do with all this—and triggering him to start again. And why Nora? Did the two of you find any connection between the Vandenbergs and Meachum?"

"No. But I think Caldwell knew Sadler. I don't know how or how well. It could have been Sadler who recruited him to get Meachum to start calling me. So much of this has felt personal—the 'come out and play' note and now taking Caroline of all people . . ."

"Rooker, all this on the word of a gangbanger in solitary? And it's not even a positive ID."

"Look, I'm trying to help."

"I know." She sighed. "I'll get the team together and check out Caldwell's home. If you're wrong about this, I'm done for."

Chapter 43

Tess Harlow breathed slowly, listening to the ambience of torn Velcro and hushed voices in the cargo area of the van. Level IIIA Kevlar vests were designed to withstand handgun fire, up to .44 Magnum rounds, full-metal-jacketed rounds, and armor-piercing rounds. Tess had already slipped two ten-by-twelve steel ballistic plates into the front and back pockets of her vest just in case. The inserts were used more in active military situations with rifle fire, but when it came to being shot at, she didn't fuck around. They added roughly another fourteen pounds to the six-pound vest. But it gave her the versatility to be protected and still be mobile, and that put her mind slightly more at ease. The fact that she may be shot at within a matter of minutes didn't.

While she surveyed the front of the house for movement, she picked at the scar on her finger or adjusted the vest like she was wearing football pads. With a long, unblinking stare, she clamped her jaw tight as though it were wired shut.

Nothing.

Come on, you prick.

Keene sat beside her in the driver's seat. Sterling, Whitlock, and Riggs were in the back. Once their movement ceased, she knew they were ready.

"Martin and Sterling on me; Martin, you breach the door if anything goes wrong. Whitlock and Riggs, back of the house. Let's go."

"Why do I get the rookie?" Whitlock scoffed.

"I said let's go."

The five of them slipped out of the van and into the night. Whitlock and Riggs moved low, their booted footfalls nearly silent in the thick grass. She was the first to the door. Keene stood beside her. Sterling peered through one of the windows and then moved to the porch steps out of sight. She rapped her knuckles against the wood hard. It took only a matter of seconds.

A shadow covered the peephole. Someone was standing there.

"Police!" She ducked out of view. Shoved Sterling back with her palm in his chest so he wouldn't be seen. People get shot all the time through that damn hole. Usually, it was the person on the other end looking through who would get a bullet to the face, but she wasn't taking any chances. "Open the door!"

The door cracked open. The chain was still latched.

"Open it now!" The chain clinked and rattled against the doorframe.

Keene shoved the door open, and a girl with long frizzy hair fell back against the wood floor. Fear and tears welled in her eyes.

Before she'd realized it, her pistol sights were centered between the girl's large breasts. She turned her cheek to the room past her and pointed her gun there. Tess whispered, "Where is he?"

"Mr. C? H-he's not here. He left a couple of hours ago."

"Who are you?"

"Cynthia. Albright."

"All right, Cynthia. It's okay. I'm going to have you escorted out to the van. Once we clear the house, you can come back and grab your things. Understood?"

She nodded furiously, the tears falling faster as her head jolted.

She pressed the button at her hip. "Riggs, there's a girl. Get her out of here. What do you do here, Cynthia?"

"Mr. C has me take care of his mother when he's busy."

"Okay. Thank you. Detective. Riggs is going to come around and take you outside now. Can you tell me anything about the house?"

"There's a door down the hall that's always locked. I'm not allowed down there. He says his mother is dangerous and never to give her anything sharp."

Riggs came around front and took the girl out to the van. She told him to keep Whitlock on the back of the house.

The three of them swept the level of the home quietly. Tess found the old woman sobbing hard in an old bed. From the looks of her face, it was a muted scream. Her face reddened. A vein bulged in the pit of her forehead. As she thrashed and flailed and kicked, Tess became certain that she was trying to scream.

"Everything is going to be all right," she told the woman as she backed out of the room. "I'll come right back."

She craned her neck to the staircase, and Keene and Sterling surged forward. Moving behind them, boots hardly thudding, they checked the primary bedroom, a bathroom, and an office space. There was a computer setup, files out but neatly arranged, and a locked safe. Once every room was cautiously checked, she decided to come back after they cleared whatever room lay behind the padlock.

The three of them descended the stairs together. Keene smashed the lock repeatedly with the butt end of the pump-action shotgun. When it snapped, he kicked the door in and tried the light switch. It didn't do anything. Instead, they flicked on their flashlights; Tess held hers firm in her left hand, wrists interlocked beneath the magazine well of her SIG Sauer. She held the flashlight like an ice pick; the technique was developed by a marine in the seventies.

If the P226 hadn't already injected cold into the veins of her hand, the ominous darkness—*snap*. She sprayed her light around the bottom of the stairs. Then at the space behind them.

Nothing.

Just the old wood beneath Keene's and Sterling's boots.

She took the bottom stairs slowly, listening. Her pulse thumped in her temples. The black room beckoned her. She willed herself to move into whatever was waiting for her.

As the light shined over cabinets, she scanned the cement floor and found an old chair bolted into the ground. *A jury chair?* It looked like it belonged in a courtroom. A dull metal cord attached to a light bulb hovered overhead. She moved to it and gave it a good yank.

A cylinder of light fell over them. The room wasn't entirely lit, but she could see. White modern cabinetry with massive silver steel pulls. Mirrors. Maybe twenty of them. Arranged in a circle. Seven of them had a single letter drawn on the glass: I SEE YOU.

Tess looked up to the symbols on the walls above them. She stared at the same symbol they'd found on the envelopes sent to Charles Berglund. The same symbol they'd found in the floor of Nora Vandenberg's bedroom. The pentacle in the photos of Malin Jakobsson's bedroom.

"Boss," Sterling whispered.

"Yeah."

"Got something—someone, actually."

She twisted her neck to find a shape balled up tight in plastic.

"Clear." Keene came around from under the stairs.

Sterling pulled a glove from his back pocket, slipped his fingers inside fast, and rolled the clear sheet back. As she watched, she started to see features. Male. Shy of six feet. Heavyset, maybe two hundred, two hundred twenty pounds. Dark hair. Thinning crown. But once Sterling rolled the body over and the face was visible . . . the blackened, bloody hole in his eye socket . . .

She took a small step back. "*Fuck.* That's Warrel Haney."

She stared into the eye that was there hanging open, milky and dead. It reminded her of a shriveled olive.

Sterling whistled. "No shit." His whispered words lifted in surprise. "What the hell would he want with Warrel Haney?"

She thought on that for a moment. "I don't know. Haney went after Rooker in the paper. Maybe he wanted Rooker to feel responsible for another death."

"Well, now we can be certain we've got the right guy," Keene said. "Know how to crack a safe?" he asked Sterling.

"Got an axe and a crowbar somewhere."

"I'll get CSI out here and get him bagged. No offense, Sterling, but I'll get someone to open the safe," Tess said. "I'd like to see what's inside, and not in a hundred pieces . . . The safe has a fingerprint reader and a combination. We can lift a fingerprint here surely, but the combination is a whole nother story. If I can get someone to crack the combination, great. But otherwise, we get someone with a thermic lance. Some of 'em get up to 8,000 degrees Fahrenheit. Should just cut through the steel like butter."

"Boss." Keene spoke. As she turned to him, her gaze following the floating particles in the flashlight beam toward the top of the stairs, she noticed the little red light and tiny black lens. "Looks like he knows we're here."

Chapter 44

October 1, 2019

Rooker killed the engine half a block from the abandoned home. Even after several price reductions, no one was willing to purchase the property, not even to demolish it and rebuild.

Millie's leg jackhammered in the passenger seat. But he knew that if he addressed it out loud, her fear would only become more real.

"You wanted your shot at fieldwork, right?" He did his best to joke.

Millie smiled weakly. "That I did." He watched her pull her pistol, check the round in the chamber, and secure it in the back of her pants. Her leg stopped.

Rooker was carrying the old Glock 17 that he'd stashed in a drawer behind his favorite chair. It had belonged to Peter Sundgren, and it was the gun he'd used to fire two rounds into Gregory Sadler before the two of them plunged into icy waters. From there, Rooker had used his hands to kill the man.

Tonight, he hoped he wouldn't need to use his hands or the gun.

They watched the home for a moment before they got out of the car. There was no FOR SALE sign staked in the earth before the old Berglund residence. The grass was in the middle stages of regrowth. Someone, perhaps the city or a neighbor, was giving it a trim every now and then. He imagined it would have unsightly wild grass sprouting tall as cornstalks. Maybe busted windows, bubble letters tagged and empty spray cans in overgrown bushes.

In reality, it looked like a home that had aged. Instead of hanging skin and purple veins and crow's-feet, there were grime-blackened windows, leaves crawling out of the gutters, and dirty, cracked hardboard siding. Old white paint had flecked and grayed. As the two of them scaled the steps, short wires reached out like talons from the busted doorbell.

Rooker tried the door.

The knob wiggled loose. Enough to where there was a crack of a sight line into the room. He ducked down and couldn't see anything. As gently as he could, he nudged the door open. A sinister creak, worse than the old stairs he'd replaced at the cottage. The noise, and the jarring groan and scrape of his first featherlight step inside, sent a shiver down his spine.

"No sense trying to be quiet," he whispered to her. "If anyone's here, they know we are too." He pressed a weightless palm between her shoulder blades and brought the pistol up from his side.

The air was stale. A pungent odor seemed to infest the walls—a concoction of damp wood and mold and sweat.

He was out of his element. He knew that. He wasn't some ex-military guy or part of a SWAT strike team. He wasn't professionally trained in firearms. He was an ex-husband and a former father. He wrote articles in an air-conditioned office. A double homicide in Valle Vista. A murder-suicide a block away from the Ramona Bowl Amphitheatre. In his line of work, the toughest parts were getting the first words of a story onto a page. Staring at a blinking cursor, trying to find the perfect words for a grabby headline. Hell, the commute in city traffic.

But he did know his way around a gun. And he could take a hell of a punch and dish one twice as good.

Rooker took a high hold on the pistol grip in his left hand. His right hand wrapped around below it. With his arms extended, the barrel in line with his left arm, he pointed it at the ground a few feet in front of him. While he peeked his head in and out behind corners and doors, his finger hovered over the trigger guard.

Suddenly, he thought of Amy Berglund. Which room was hers? But at this point, it didn't matter if there was some symbol to find. He didn't need to search deep down to know that Amy Berglund was dead. He just knew.

His only priority now was locating Caroline. Finding her before too much damage was done. Before he could etch another mark in his mind—just like the tally in Meachum's cell—for another of his victims.

"Come on," Millie said. He followed her down a hall to a door that was open a crack. She clasped a firm hand to it and pushed the door wide enough for the two of them to slip inside. It was the cellar. Pitch-black climbed like a baleful smoke, cold and devouring, all around him. He squinted, and his mind tricked him into seeing something move. *Wait, did something just move?* Instinctively, Rooker flipped the light switch on the wall. When nothing happened, under a chattered breath he whispered, "Worth a shot."

Rooker went first. With his back pressed against the wood railing, he sidled the stairs one at a time. Halfway down the staircase his eyes began to adjust, and he found her.

Caroline sat motionless in an old wooden chair in the center of the room. Her head hung down, her forehead nearly to her knees. Her perfect curls were matted and frizzy, hanging over her face.

"Caroline," he whispered. He moved toward her. "Hey." He dropped to his knees and shook her. She didn't budge. Her hands were tied behind her. "Caroline." He moved the hair out of her face and saw a gash above her right eye. He tapped her cheek.

"Hmm." It was her. The noise. It came from her.

"Caroline?"

"My head . . ."

"I know. Where is he?"

"He—he heard something . . . upstairs."

Rooker looked at Millie.

"He was going to kill me. Wasn't he?"

A low rumble started from the curb a few houses down, and when Rooker ran to the nearest window, he made out a dark vehicle behind two white beams, the headlights puncturing the darkness like a needle piercing skin.

"Not today," he said softly. He peered into her eyes and smiled. "Let's get you out of here."

Maybe he wasn't cursed after all. She was alive. There was still time to keep her that way.

"Sorry I didn't make it for drinks." She slurred the last word, like she'd had a few too many. The ties around her wrists snapped too harshly when Millie cut through them with a pocketknife. Her hands slackened, and Rooker let Caroline fall forward against him. She groaned when he lifted her across his forearms against his chest.

"I'll call for an ambulance," Millie said.

"Nuh-uh," Caroline muttered. "Afraid of hospitals."

But when Rooker told her he'd stitch it and leave her looking like Frankenstein's monster, she gave in. When they reached the top of the stairs, he felt Caroline go limp, merely weight in his arms.

But not *dead*weight.

◆ ◆ ◆

They followed the ambulance to the ER. As the EMTs wheeled Caroline into the hospital, Rooker watched her head slowly turn, her knee-weakening gray-blue eyes roll open.

The next time he saw her, about thirty minutes later, the wound above her brow was stitched with black sutures in a shoelace pattern. He figured that wasn't the technical term, but that's what it looked like to him.

It had bled and gushed through several gauze pads. Trickled beneath it down her cheekbone. Bright red blood. She'd been asleep for most of it.

"My knight in shining armor?"

He gave a weak smirk. "Far from a knight. Can't say I've seen one in jeans and a T-shirt."

"Yeah, well. You saved my life."

"Before you, I'm pretty sure I was batting zero."

"Not anymore."

He hesitated. "I want you to stay with me at the cottage. Just for now."

"You think he'd come after me again?"

"I do. Which is exactly why I'm keeping you close to me. When I'm not around, you'll be under police protection."

She stared at the ceiling and sighed. Then looked back to him. "I don't think a camera crew has ever been inside the famous Lindström Manor. If you give me a tour and the exclusive"—she smiled—"it's a date."

"You do owe me one of those."

"All right, handsome. Break me out of here, then."

"Soon. Tess's team has some questions for you. After all, you're the only witness they have to a serial killer; it might take a while."

◆ ◆ ◆

Back at the cottage, Millie was sprawled out on the couch beneath only half of the blanket, the laptop open just a crack, climbing and falling with her breaths. Rooker shut the door quietly so as not to wake her, but it didn't work.

"Hmm." Her eyelids opened a crack, about the same amount as the laptop lid.

"Go back to sleep," Rooker whispered. The locks on the door clicked into place. Rooker took the laptop from Millie, placed it on the table, and covered her in the rest of the blanket. Letting Caroline scale the stairs first, he placed a hand on the small of her back.

He gave her a T-shirt to change into; the shoulder of her blouse was stiff with dried blood. When he checked himself in the mirror, red stains coated the inside of his arm. He changed his shirt too.

He knew that now wasn't the right time. But when would it be?

He turned away while she changed. "What can you remember about the vehicle he took you in?"

"I never saw it." He could hear the rustle of clothing going over her head. "There was a hood, maybe a mask over my face. It smelled like burning rubber. You can look now."

He turned back toward her. "Did you ever see his face?"

"Yeah. Are you planning on sending out a sketch artist in the middle of the night?"

He could hear the frustration in her voice. "I think you're forgetting the fact that I don't have a badge."

"True. I guess it just feels a bit like an interrogation."

He stopped himself. "Sorry."

"It's okay. I get it. I'm just usually the one asking the questions."

"Sometimes I forget I'm not a journalist anymore." He pulled up a photograph of Hartley Caldwell and faced it at her. "Was this him?"

Her glance lasted no more than three seconds before she turned away. "That's him. Who is he?"

Rooker pocketed the phone. This was the tricky part he was afraid of. He sighed. "I'll give you everything. Just not yet. *After* we get him.

This guy wore a disguise and got into Pelican Bay under a fake identity. If we put his name out there, we think he'll run."

"Why Pelican Bay?"

"To get contraband in for an inmate."

She craned to look at him over her shoulder. "Tate Meachum."

He nodded.

Gazing out over the quivering treetops miles off in the distance, he followed the blinking lights of a Boeing 737 commercial airliner, descending from the stars. He let himself stare at the little white shimmers until the memory of his boy captivated by the telescope Rooker had gotten him for his seventh birthday became too vivid and overwhelmingly painful. Instead, he looked out through the black bars, then beyond the broken wrought iron gate, wondering if Caldwell would come for him now as Sadler had. Caldwell may not have wanted to kill Rooker the last time they'd met, but now he had a funny feeling in the darkest pit of his stomach—the one where he expected only the worst—that things had changed.

He recounted Martin Keene's words: *"This time around, you're a pawn, just like us."*

I'm not so sure, Martin.

Like a cold whisper, the darkness called to him. He fought the urge to go to it, to do anything except sit around. Even if it meant patrolling the house perimeter, making rounds like a military watch. But right now, the smart thing to do was wait. While he listened to the slow breaths and light snores from the bed, his eyes fixated on the long stretch of gravel drive. For someone who left everything behind for a life of solitude, he wasn't doing a particularly good job of it. With his track record, he told himself he needed to keep these people further away than arm's length. To keep them safe, he needed to be miles, states, maybe even countries away.

In spite of that and the toll his presence took on others, for some odd reason he felt safer knowing Millie and Caroline were close by. The cottage was locked up tight. If he knew himself, he'd be awake into the morning, the pistol within reach.

He thought again of the hooded man in the stormy vigil crowd. The man behind the mask in the back seat. With his jaw clenched, he tapped the Glock 17 hard against the side of his leg.

Come on, you fuck. I dare you *to come out and play.*

Chapter 45

Tess wore safety goggles and stood from a distance watching the sparks fly like a fiery rain. At first, the ear-splitting grind had infused a chill in her bones. Now, the constant high pitch and the smell of burned steel sent her head pounding. She dumped two ibuprofen tablets into her palm that she gulped hard with bottled water.

The building had old vintage-blue siding that appeared weather-stained and three steel garage doors that were open, with two older muscle cars up high on steel lifts. One was a '78 Ford Mustang Fastback, polar-white with two blue racing stripes. The other was a rusted '69 Dodge Super Bee. Above the door read ERNIE'S GARAGE in bold white letters. All capitals. After Ernie Jacobs Sr. died from lymphoma, his son took over the business.

Ernie Jacobs Jr. was a man you'd look over and almost expect would work with dangerous machinery. With his mangy gray beard, he wore black sunglasses, a dark-gray Harley-Davidson tee with dark cargo shorts, and a black trucker cap stained white with old perspiration. His jagged smile was one that wasn't totally unpleasant but void of hygiene and surely routine dental visits. When he first saw her, he'd wiped at the wet circles blotched under his arms, and the sweat that trickled fast down his sun-beaten face, and extended a hand.

She had taken his hand anyhow.

Body odor and marijuana were the first two smells she got off him.

"You don't need what's inside, I can burn through her in a few minutes."

The *T* had been lost in the words *don't* and *what's*, and the *H* in *her*. Still, she'd understood him just fine.

"Sorry, Ern," she'd told him. "I need to see what's in there."

She was hopeful that whatever was inside the safe would help them locate Hartley Caldwell. She didn't need the contents to go up in flames.

His sunglasses looked less like welder's gear and more like ones that came from a spinning rack in a convenience store. He'd left them on and put on a pair of thick black fire-resistant gloves.

While she paced back and forth, her phone rang. She plugged the hollow of her ear with a finger and answered. Sterling told her that Mrs. Caldwell was awake in the hospital and that she'd want to hear about her medical records.

She told him to keep the woman calm and find the best way to communicate with her. She'd be on her way soon.

She waited out the fiery storm that fell all around Ernie. She watched him power down the machine and grab a long steel pry bar before he called her over.

He leveraged his weight and dug it into the edges of the safe and jimmied and pulled. It loosened. The gap between the door and the safe growing. And it snapped.

He dropped the pry bar. She pulled on a pair of gloves and searched inside.

Perfume bottles. Three of them.

She inched closer and read the three bottles. One was Chanel N°5. It was old. Really old. The topper was glass, but it looked like a dusty diamond.

The next one was smaller, with a gold liquid and black stopper. Flora by Gucci.

The one on the end was much newer. There was no dust. It was a clear bottle—16.9 oz.—with a similar glass topper as the Chanel perfume.

Santal 33. Le Labo.

There was something behind both bottles toward the back, folded crisply. She reached her hand back there and pulled it out into the light.

They were newspaper clippings. One dated thirty years ago. Another dated eight years ago. And one that was only a few months old. They were the headlines for three missing girls. Amy Berglund. Malin Jakobsson. Nora Vandenberg.

Chapter 46

Rooker never slept. When he felt his eyes growing heavy and his head sagging, he got up and moved around the room. Listening to the dissonant snores from beneath the balled covers, he struck up a conversation with himself in a whisper until the snores stopped or Caroline stirred fitfully. He watched her kick the blanket from her feet as an infant would and smiled.

Once the snores continued, he'd start again.

For a portion of the night, he'd stared at the Glock 17 he'd placed on the windowsill. He peered out blindly into the shadows. And he listened to the sounds of the home: the creak of the floor wherever his weight shifted, the groans of the trees outside, the yips and howls from somewhere out there in the distance, and the melodic tune of grasshoppers and tree frogs and cicadas hiding in the grass.

Just after 8:15 a.m., Rooker heard Millie stirring downstairs and Caroline opened her eyes.

"Your bed isn't that comfy." She wiped the specks crusted at the edges of her eyes.

He smiled. "No, it's not. Can't say I afford myself many luxuries these days. Coffee?"

"Sure. By the way, I think your house is haunted."

Funny. Even though the home legally belonged to him, he'd never thought of it as *his*. "I think you're right. Stay," he told her.

"Hmm. Yes, sir."

He ambled down the stairs to find Millie scrambling eggs in a bowl and watched her pour the yellow mixture into a hot pan.

"Morning," he said.

"You're right. That couch kind of sucks."

"Told you." He pressed the button on the coffee machine.

"Did you consummate the marriage last night?"

"Shut it," he said and watched her giggle. Just then, he felt the vibration from his pocket. He opened his phone and read the text from Tess.

Glad Caroline is okay. Got the safe open. Headlines from when he took them. Three perfumes. Chanel No. 5. Flora by Gucci. Santal 33. Mean anything to you?

"Tess got the safe open." He stared down at the phone. He typed back: Santal 33 was Nora's. A gift from Christine Vandenberg.

"And?"

"They found newspaper clippings, seems like. From when he took them. Found a bottle of Santal 33, the perfume Christine said she bought for Nora."

"Anything else?"

"Don't think so."

"What was the name Caldwell gave at the prison?"

"Hastings said it was under James Cohen."

"I'll see if I can find anything under that name."

"He probably already knows we talked to Barrios. I think that identity is burned, and he knows it."

"Probably right, but I'll give it a shot. Maybe Tess will let me take a crack at the computer in his office."

"I think that would be our best move."

◆ ◆ ◆

Rooker pulled up to the old Berglund home. A couple of people were watching from the street, as were a few television crews. He knew they would double down on the history of the home; tragedy was the fastest way to get ratings. Luckily for Rooker, it was a familiar face he saw stirring around the front of the home.

"Yo," Vic said from beyond the police tape. "Just like old times?"

Rooker smiled. "If you wouldn't mind."

Vic raised the tape, and Rooker ducked under. "Thanks."

"No problemo. What were you doing here anyway?"

"When I got a look at the grid mapped out, the pin for Caroline's home, the pin where the Jaguar was torched, I realized the street with the old Berglund home was nearby. It just made sense to me that maybe that's where he was."

"Not bad, man. Next time, make sure you call for some backup, though."

"Yeah, I seem to have that problem, don't I?"

"Some would call it a death wish."

"What would you call it?"

"Not sure. Maybe a man who still isn't sure whether he wants to live or die. Let's go inside."

While the two of them closed in on the door, Vic spoke again. "We pulled partials from the front door. Yours and his. Got some full prints in the basement where he planned to keep her. They're Caldwell's."

"Show me her room."

Sterling led him into a damp room at the end of the hall with graffiti tagged on the door. The cold came in through a fist-size hole in one of the windows. He looked down at a rock in the corner of the floor, along with stringy brown pellets. Rat droppings.

"We found a few scurrying in the basement," Vic said to him.

Rooker surveyed the room. Lucky for him, it was empty of furniture. He didn't need to toss the room around to go searching for a symbol. Still, at first glance, he saw nothing.

That is, until he saw scratches between two planks in the wood floor. "Sterling," Rooker said and hunched down on his knees to assess it.

Sterling knelt down beside him. "The hell . . ." He unfolded a knife from his pocket and slipped the blade beneath one of the boards. It wiggled, and Sterling pried it free. When he flipped it over, there were five symbols—old, judging by the faintness of the outlines—carved into the wood.

"No way . . . ," Sterling breathed. "You think . . ."

"Do I think he carved this thirty years ago? Maybe."

Chapter 47

October 2, 2019

Detective Tess Harlow hated hospitals. She despised them as much as she did the assisted-living building where she'd stuck her mother like a cardboard box in an attic.

After signing in and pulling her badge from her chest like a diamond necklace for the desk person to appraise, she sauntered down a wide corridor that gave the illusion that it was never-ending. Her footfalls clopped over shiny white tile. Artificial white light hummed overhead from square ceiling panels. Passing a gift shop, she rolled her eyes at the racks filled with get-well-soon cards and floral arrangements, the colorful plushies and stuffed animals and bright balloons beyond the glass. She did her best to stare ahead, not at the white walls, or the gray handrails, or the empty blue seats and vacant wheelchairs, or into the rooms she passed.

Based on her first visit with Hartley Caldwell, she'd had Mrs. Caldwell instated in a unit that housed other stroke patients.

She still didn't know how wrong she was.

The end of the corridor forked into a left and right hallway. She cocked her head to the left and saw Martin Keene standing with his back against the wall, his arms folded across his stocky chest.

He nodded at her. "She's awake. You want coffee?"

"No, thanks. If I wasn't awake already, I think this would do the trick."

"I'll get the doctor."

A minute later, a woman in scrubs, standard hospital blue, hurried toward her with a serious expression.

"Detective Harlow?"

"Yes, Doctor."

"Do you have any idea what this woman has been through?"

"I was told she developed aphasia from sustaining two strokes—"

"I'm sorry." She stopped Tess. Her lips tightened. "*Who* told you that?"

"Her son."

"Absolutely not. Detective, this woman has sustained abuse for several years. *Torture*, if you will. Forced to be bedridden, so much so that she has bedsores and her muscles have atrophied to the degree of a syndrome called sarcopenia. She's lost a significant, *significant* percentage of skeletal muscle mass, as well as motor function. Not only that, but she does not suffer from aphasia. Her tongue has been cut out."

The room beyond the door suddenly felt like a place she couldn't enter. It might as well have been a dark cloud of chaos, funneling and spreading, intended for her. There were times on the job that felt like they'd taken a part of her humanity. Excised a piece of her soul. There was a feeling inside, the one that told her not to go in there, that this would take more from her than she could give.

Tess ventured a small step forward, only enough as if her shoelaces were tied together. "How do we communicate with her?"

"Her hands are cuffed. That much seems to be true: she is a danger to herself. We had planned to use a communication device that utilizes speech software. That is, until we saw that her tongue had been removed and she is legally blind. In her better eye, her field of vision is less than 15 degrees, her visual acuity 10/200. You'll be allowed to ask your questions, so long as they do not agitate her, and she'll handwrite her responses on a pad."

Tess nodded. Keene opened the door, and she moved past him into the room. Keene followed behind once the doctor made her way in.

She stood on a square of linoleum and felt alone.

"Mrs. Caldwell. My name is Detective Tess Harlow. I found you yesterday in your home."

She waited out the scratch of the pen. As she looked down, she read the words

Thank you.

"Mrs. Caldwell, can you tell me where I would find Hartley?"

The old hand trembled. It was as if all the heat in the room vanished when she heard her son's name. She read two jagged letters.

No

"Did he do this to you?"

Yes

"Why?

I was a bad mother.

"How?"

I told him it was his fault his father left us.

She dragged her left index finger and scribbled out the last word she'd written and wrote

me.

"Did Hartley ever introduce you to the women he took?"

Amy

"Was there ever a girl, Nora?"

No

"A girl named Malin Jakobsson?"

No

"A man, Warrel Haney?

No

"Okay, Mrs. Caldwell. You're doing great. What can you tell me about Amy?"

She was popular. She was friends with Hartley's cousin.

Tess looked at Martin, who only stared back in disbelief. "Hartley had a cousin?"

Yes. They went to school together.

"What was her name?"

Vicky

"Can you tell me her full name, please?"

Victoria Reynolds. She was two grades below Amy.

Tess scribbled down in her own pad. *Victoria "Vicky" Reynolds.* Then she looked at Martin again, who nodded his understanding and left the room.

"Is she your sister's child?"

Yes

"Can you tell me where your sister lives? Or where Vicky lives?"

No. They think I died.

"Can you think of any place Hartley would go?"

Here. To punish me.

Out in the hall, Tess caught her breath away from everyone. She typed a message to Rooker: Caldwell has a cousin. Her name is Victoria Reynolds. She goes by Vicky.

Not even a minute later, his response vibrated in her hand: Holy fuck. I have a plan.

Chapter 48

Rooker fought the phantom itch like a bugbite at his wrist. While he stood outside in a plain navy tee and black jeans, he fidgeted with the contents of his pocket. When the door opened, a bell hanging above it let out a metallic ding, and he folded the newspaper in half and tucked it under his arm.

For a random Wednesday, it was surprisingly busy. The booths were mostly filled, as were the silver barstools.

With his cap pulled low, he took a seat under a dim light in a corner booth. He stared out beneath the brim of the hat and recognized Victoria Reynolds in a black shirt beyond the patrons seated at the counter. Vicky. Or in Amy Berglund's yearbook: V.R.

The Wednesday-morning crowd was mostly seniors: men with silver hair and dress shirts tucked into pleated pants hiked far too high. And then there was a man with a trucker cap and a plaid shirt jacket, keeping mostly to himself. It was Riggs.

Victoria worked the old men at the counter like a seasoned pole dancer, with a playful smile that had lost its youth. Staring over the edge of the laminated menu, he made out Vic Sterling two booths down. Sterling winked.

This time around, Vicky came to his table first.

"Know what you want, hon?"

Without looking up, he responded, "What do you recommend?"

"The chicken and waffles. And the blueberry pie is out of this world."

"I'll do both. And coffee. Black."

While she took the menu out of his hand, he stared at her from beneath the brim of his cap. "Coming right up." As she walked away, he wondered what it was exactly, thirty years ago, that her hands had done.

He observed Sterling again, who fit the look of a diner patron perfectly. He could be a movie extra. At first and even second glance, he didn't appear to be someone outfitted with a pair of steel cuffs or a police-issued 9mm Glock who was ready to block off Vicky if she decided to make a run for it.

There was no telling if Vicky was in contact with Caldwell. A wire-tap on her home phone would take too much time at this point. Time they didn't have. But now that Caldwell had disappeared, maybe he'd show his face here.

That's why backup was outside in the blue van, reversed into a parking spot in case they needed to make a fast exit.

When Vicky came back around with his coffee, he ignored her and kept his face hidden in the black letters of the newspaper. It wasn't until she returned with his order that he stopped her.

"Vicky." He cocked his head up to look into her eyes. Her head twitched, and her eyes grew wide and froze on him. "Have a seat, please."

"You again?" She took a step back. "Look, man. I told you everything—"

"But you didn't, did you? I just have a few more questions to ask you, and then you'll never see me again." He smiled and slid a $100 bill across the table, along with a pack of cigarettes. She sat cautiously. "Smoke?"

"Yeah, but you can't in here."

He pushed the pack to the edge of the table. Then slid the two plates of food in front of her. "Eat up," he said and sipped his coffee. "Don't want it to go cold. I ordered it for you."

"What the hell is this?"

"That depends on what you say. Tell me what I want to know and maybe this won't be your last meal as a free woman."

She glanced at the other customers, then back at Rooker. Her eyes burned through him. "Fuck you."

"Ouch. Okay. I'll start." He turned the newspaper clockwise so she could read the headline. "You didn't tell me the full story."

"She's been dead *thirty* years." She scratched at her ear nervously.

"Do you know where I found this?"

"The library," she quipped sarcastically.

"In a safe. A safe that is . . . let me check my notes. Pry-resistant steel. A 500-DPI optical sensor biometric fingerprint reader."

"Sorry, don't know shit about safes."

"That makes two of us. But do you know where I found it?"

"Beats me."

"At your cousin's house."

Her face stiffened. She looked down. He tried to read whether it was to the left or the right. He remembered something about looking left meant the truth and to the right was a lie.

"Why did you lure Amy into the woods for him?"

"What? Are you serious?"

"Hartley Caldwell killed Amy Berglund. Why did you lure her into those woods?"

She didn't answer.

"Did you help him kill her?"

"Man, I didn't do anything."

"If you don't tell me, you're going to take the fall with him. They'll say that you helped kill her."

She didn't answer.

"Where is Hartley?"

For a moment, she didn't answer. But then she said, "How do I know you aren't wearing a wire?"

He nearly laughed. "What? Like taped to my chest? I think that's just in the movies. Want me to strip down in front of everyone here?"

"Lift your shirt, then."

He let her pat his chest over his shirt and peek down his collar.

"You're going to make contact with him."

"Look." Her eyes wandered. Her voice fell to a whisper now. "He threatened to kill me if I ever talked. Hate to say it, but I'm more afraid of him than I am you. He's smarter than you. He won't fall for me reaching out to him out of the blue. Anyway, I haven't seen him in years."

"They can pull your phone records, bank statements, the GPS on your car. If they find out you're lying to me . . ." He shook his head. "I don't care how smart you think he is. Your shift is over. I have detectives on every exit. If you try to run, they'll take you out in handcuffs. You'll be humiliated in front of all your colleagues and Wednesday regulars. Play nice, and I'll let you walk out with me."

He watched her. She knew she couldn't run. She stood, and he overheard her explain to the stocky woman with arms like ham legs that she wasn't feeling well and had to leave.

"Can I get this to go?" He smiled at the woman, who stared back with a guarded expression, probably worried for Vicky. He left the $100 bill on the table.

◆ ◆ ◆

Carrying the two to-go Styrofoam containers along with the newspaper and pack of Camels, Rooker stayed close behind Vicky. As the bell above the door chimed, the muscles in his chest and jaw tensed. In his mind, it was the sound of the bell, the moment the last bit of water splashed against his mouth guard, and he stood from the stool.

While Vicky slumped into the back seat of an unmarked car, Rooker held the door open. He ducked his head so he could see her face. "What did he do with Amy's body?"

Vicky Reynolds stared straight ahead of her, at the headrest of the passenger seat.

"No worries. We'll talk later." He shut the door.

Rooker handed the flimsy off-white cigarette pack to Tess. "Did you get it all?"

"Loud and clear."

Chapter 49

October 2, 2019

Hartley Caldwell wore a blond wig made of human and synthetic hair and used an over-the-counter comb-in dye for his eyebrows. Twenty dollars for a small package of hair dye. But a good wig was pricey. The one currently covering his entire scalp ran him more than $1,200. With a hand-tied, full-lace cap, it had the natural appearance of growing hair. Each strand of hair was placed and knotted perfectly to a mesh cap with a careful hand. Despite the five-star reviews and glowing consumer ratings, at first it had the itch of a poison-ivy rash. After he'd blow-dried and styled it, however, the comfort was nice. And he hardly recognized himself in the hotel mirror.

The executive suite cost just under $400 a night. More with room service and taxes after checkout.

He looked over the aluminum RIMOWA carry-on suitcase and Italian brown leather travel bag. The clothes inside still had tags on them. By the time he'd finished his shopping spree, he'd spent close to $10,000 on designer retail brands that he'd never worn before, let alone been interested in: Armani, Louis Vuitton, a beige Saint Laurent button-down collared shirt with a palm tree design. Today he'd wear a dark-navy two-button Dior suit with black suede loafers. It was all part of his disguise. A couple of high-priced outfits and a first-class ticket to South America. Once he passed through customs, he'd ditch the clothing, maybe sell everything at a pawn shop, then change his disguise once more and find a place to stay for a while.

In spite of the high he was on, knowing he'd evaded the police, the string that tethered his mind to his mother kept pulling at him. He hadn't terrorized her long enough. *Witch.*

Now he pictured her, hair graying, face aging, staring back at him from the mirror glass—malicious and nasty and cruel—and how badly he wished he could kill her before he vanished for good.

His mind flashed back to a memory from his eighth birthday.

His mother's bedroom was what some would call vintage; she kept an old antique mirror on the south wall across from her bed, standing on thick yellow shag carpeting. Beside a bed that was never made was an end table that housed bargain liquor and an ashtray filled with stubbed-out joints rolled with cheap marijuana.

He stood in the mirror beside his mother, sickly thin as a boy, with bones growing much faster than the weight and muscle could pack on. The doctor said he was healthy, just young and filling out. It seemed that for him, that only meant vertically. The puffy black spots beneath his sad eyes matched his curly black hair and looked like bruises on his waxy-pale skin. Even in those years, he knew that life as a boy was meant for getting dirty and running and bicycling and screaming.

That wasn't the life chosen for him.

He stood there, with his blue straight-leg jeans and tighty-whities coiled around his ankle bones.

Though she was slurring, he understood her perfectly as the words bubbled off her lips. Her mouth was wet with spittle and liquor. He tasted warm brandy. "You hear me? He left us because of you. One look at you was all it took." Her voice started out low and calm. It wouldn't stay that way very long.

"I'm sorry!" he whined while she held his member.

"You know how he left?"

He did. Still, he didn't answer. He tried his best not to cry, knowing how it would set her off.

"He packed a bag in the middle of the night; it was the night I brought you home from the hospital. One suitcase. Every single thing of his, gone. His clothing from the closet. Even his pillow. I never heard a thing. And it's all because of you!"

He felt a sharp pain and flinched. He tried not to cry.

"Oh, hush!"

It hurt more. When she pulled her hand away, she showed him the red blotch between her two fingers. The red beneath her fingernails.

"My love . . ." She stopped. "Open your eyes and look!" She smacked him there hard. "Look at what you've done. Look at what you *are*. One look at you and he ran!"

"Oh, hush!" he spat, perfectly in his mother's tone. He flicked himself hard on the penis. He smiled and said it again. And again. And then he laughed.

When a knock at the door came, he froze. He listened to the thump of his pulse, to the silence that crackled before him.

Knock. Knock. Knock. "Housekeeping," the soft Hispanic voice said through the door.

"No, thank you," he called back. And then again, he said more for himself than for the housekeeper, *"Oh, hush!"* Despite the brows that furrowed, his face was blank. It looked like his mother's when she was upset with him. She was always upset with him.

He changed into the Dior suit and put on a Hamilton watch—wore it on the wrong hand—and buckled the pin.

The airport was a thirty-minute drive from the hotel. A shiny black limousine would pull up to the front any minute now.

He opened his door and pushed the aluminum roller bag, the leather travel bag slung over his other shoulder, down the empty corridor to the elevator. He stepped inside, pressed the button for the lobby, and checked his watch again. The small hand reached just past the number eight. The other just before fifteen.

He avoided his gaze now in the steel reflection. He didn't want to see Hartley Caldwell now. He needed to see a perfect stranger. Instead, his head hung to the floor. But when the carriage came to a stop and the doors opened, he lifted his head and smiled.

From the doors, he could make out the silver accents of the stretch Lincoln, glistening in the morning sun. His heart fluttered.

As he passed the concierge desk, he forced a pleasant wave, but his smile fell once he felt the vibration in his pocket. He pulled out his new phone and stared down at the message notification.

USER-115 sent you a message.

The username and chat room were ones created by him that he'd given her. It was meant solely as a last resort and only meant to be used if something went horribly, horribly wrong. He hadn't heard from her in ages. Not since he threatened to kill her if she contacted him or if she ever went to the police.

Despite that, there had been many nights where he'd contemplated tying up the loose end that was his cousin.

But when he opened his phone and read Vicky's message, expecting it to say that the police had found her, he looked down in quiet shock.

Your mother died.

Chapter 50

October 3, 2019

Rooker. Rooker.

The voices called out for him. But their calls landed on the decomposed ears of the dead. He lay buried beneath the earth, frozen.

Rooker.

Get up, Rook.

The last voice . . . there was only one person who called him that. *Mom?* This time it was closer. Like a soothing, warm tone close enough to tickle the strands of hair tucked behind his ear, to press its lips to it.

And then the hands . . . bone . . . reached for him. Putrefying soil and blackened blood rained down over him.

His body jolted. More startled to consciousness than jump-started, his eyes flicked open. "Shit." He wiped the dampness at his lip and did his best to clear the rasp from his voice. A shaky hand scratched at the pounding in his chest, appraising his clean shirt. "Sorry."

His body felt heavy. He was light-headed, skull pounding. It felt like he was coming down with a virus, but it was just exhaustion. Leaning back in the chair, a crack erupted up his spine, and he did the same to the joint in his neck.

At her desk, Tess was in her own world. Her unfocused eyes on the screen of her computer monitor.

While he pressed his thumb into a spot of his forehead and ran it in small circles, Millie dumped two ibuprofen pills into his palm, which he swallowed dry.

"Thanks. Anything?" he asked.

Millie checked Vicky Reynolds's phone again.

She shook her head.

Nothing.

"He's connected to the chat room," he said. His voice was sleepless, monotoned to a degree bordering on rehearsed. "If he's online, can't we trace him?"

"Not on this. They communicate securely over a virtual private network. I could give it a try, but he would know it wasn't Vicky who had the phone. Probably best to see if he falls for the bait or tries to communicate with her."

The bait, Rooker knew, was their best hope at locating him. Tess had Caldwell's photograph sent out to every police station in the state, as well as the border states. It only served as a reminder that Hartley Caldwell had managed to get into a supermax prison with a disguise and a fake identity. It had been almost thirty-six hours since Caldwell had Caroline in the cellar of the old Berglund house and escaped.

He could be anyone by now.

But hopefully not *anywhere*.

Rooker knew in his bones that despite his comments to Caroline, Caldwell was far different from Sadler. In stature, Caldwell was slightly older and gaunt, bordering on sickly. Sadler was younger, far more powerful, with a law enforcement background in firearms and combat. In spite of all of that, there was something about Caldwell that made the skin on Rooker's arms pimple and tingle with cold, the little prickly hairs stand tall.

It was the gaps between his kills. The fact that Caldwell had remained dormant for decades. He wasn't a man who needed to kill. All this time, tormenting his mother could have satiated his fix. But what Rooker hoped was that his affliction toward his mother, the false message about her passing, would cause him to slip up. Still, he couldn't allow himself to be convinced.

With his brain feeling jet-lagged and his fingers jittery, he wolfed down a strong cup of coffee and poured himself one more. Gazing into the lukewarm liquid, he imagined a starless night sky.

"When's the last time you got some sleep?"

He felt Millie's eyes on him, and his smirk was lost behind the rim of the paper cup. "You just saw it."

She rolled her eyes. "I mean a good night's sleep."

His fingers like spider legs slinking, tapping along the edge of the white ceramic mug. "Well then, that I can't remember."

Waiting now felt like a standstill, like a ringing silence when two sides at war waited out the smoke and tended to the wounded.

Rooker was sure that for the rest of the day, he'd be running on caffeine and will.

At a loss for anything better to do, Rooker scrolled through the latest news in the *Valley Chronicle*. He'd often go to the site to see what his old reporter friends were up to—and what homicide cases he'd be covering had his life never been flipped upside down. It wasn't long before he zoned out. That is, until his laptop speakers let out a single *ding*, one he'd never heard before. Searching for the melodic chime through the open programs, he found it.

It was from the PHENOMENA website.

A new story had just been published.

His heart lurched a foreboding beat. Leaning forward in the chair, he sturdied his feet in the skin-thin carpet beneath him, as if otherwise he was going to fall, and fall. While he opened the article, a numbness invaded his chest, like a bucket of ice dumped over his insides.

> To those who may not hear the truth: cut out the ears.

To those who cannot speak the truth: carve out
the tongue.
To those who will not see the truth: cut out the
eyes.
It is time for death to the sorceress.

Once the witches are stolen from their homes,
Burned and drowned and hanged and stoned,
Mankind will again walk in the light.
For all the rest who hide in the night,
Forever be trapped by shadows,
The deaf, the mute, and the blind.

To those who hide among us,
To the man trapped by shadows,
I SEE YOU.
-WICCAN

Chapter 51

October 3, 2019

His photograph was circulating through every news outlet in the country. Rooker Lindström and the detective unit led by Tess Harlow were the least of his worries now. He wasn't listed as just one of the FBI's ten most wanted fugitives; he was listed as number one. Watchers would be posted all over the airports, plainclothes types that would be tough for him to spot. Maybe even canines tasked with picking up his scent from an article of clothing left in his closet.

He'd ditched the limo driver—best not to have people staring his way, wondering who it was who would step out—and was now at a rest area in Minneapolis. A Greyhound bus line would take him back to Itasca County.

Several times, he'd reconsidered his decision. He could be on a flight right now, sitting on a beautiful sandy beach somewhere in a matter of hours. Who was he kidding? He'd never sat on a beach a day in his life. Nor did he have a complexion that could withstand the sun.

On the surface, Caldwell's body language was calm and cool as he turned in to the restroom when he thought he'd been made. A police officer in a dark-navy uniform had looked his way more than once. A portion of his high-and-tight haircut was streaked as silver as the badge clipped to his upper left chest. His face was well shaved, aside from the thick brown mustache above his lip.

With the belly on the cop, Caldwell knew he could outrun him. But running drew attentive eyes. It would bring backup his way. Once the door swung shut behind him, he hurried and crouched low to check the stalls. There were three of them. All three were empty. *Lucky.* He pushed the one on the end open. Then he checked his appearance in the bulky silver mirror before he positioned himself over one of the urinals and unfastened the button and zipper of his pants.

It reeked of urine. He could tell by the spattered shine on the floor where it had landed. He was certain he was stepping in it.

When the door creaked open, he stared straight ahead at the dirty beige tile. His right hand slipped down into his pocket and unscrewed the cap of the hotel pen.

He pulled the lever, and the toilet flushed. The gurgling reminded him of Warrel Haney while he died. He zipped his pants and secured the button back in place. Once he looked up, he saw the officer with one hand on his utility belt. It was dangerously close to the holster.

Caldwell manipulated his face into a warm smile. "Officer," he said. He moved over to the sink, where he pumped pink cream soap into his palm and turned the faucet handle. While he rinsed the soap from his hands, he looked up to find the stern expression in the mirror, hovering behind him.

"Is something wrong, sir?" he asked the man. Then he read the letters on the silver nameplate: FOSTER.

He didn't answer. He only continued to stare. His hand inched closer to the holster. "Put your hands behind your head."

"I'm sorry?" He looked sincerely at the man in blue.

"I said put your hands behind your head!"

"I think there's been a misunderstanding—" He turned toward the powerful man, and while the large arms went to restrain Caldwell, he pulled the pen from his pocket and jabbed the point of it into the man's throat. He pried it loose and skewered the flesh again and again until the man started to wheeze and collapsed to the ground.

Caldwell pulled him toward the far stall, then unclipped the utility belt holding the police radio and gun and stuffed it all into the bottom of his bag. Next, he pulled the officer's pants off and pulled his underwear down around his ankles and sat him on the toilet. Then he unbuttoned the uniform top and tossed it in the bag along with the badge and tie. Caldwell locked the door and climbed beneath the next stall and went back to the sink. Once he wiped the blood from the floor, he started washing the blood from the grooves in his fingers and between his knuckles when someone else entered the bathroom. A tall, lanky man hobbled in, wearing a plain wrinkled tee with jeans torn at the knee, chocolate-brown sandals, and a fitted black Minnesota Twins baseball cap—the kind the players wear on the field. When he noticed the flecks of red and the bubbly liquid in the drain, Caldwell said, "Nosebleed." Smiling, he went on scrubbing his hands and listened to the man's stream against the nasty pink urinal cake.

Once Caldwell wrapped up, he tossed the pen into the trash bin and exited the restroom. Sauntering through the aisles of the convenience store, he grabbed a hat and pair of sunglasses off a rack and tossed them onto the counter along with cash. While the man leisurely plucked change from the register, he fixed the fake gold chain around his neck and adjusted his faded blue tank top hanging loose off his shoulders.

Caldwell was repulsed by the thick hair up his forearm. While the man fixed his cap, he stared at the raw skin tags and the sweat-twirled hairs under his arms.

"Keep the change," he said and turned his back to him.

He opened his phone. Launched the messenger application. Jabbing his fingers into the screen, he typed out a message to USER-115.

> Midnight. Where we took her. Come alone or I'll kill you.

He pulled the cap low over his head, pressed "Send," and walked onto the bus.

Chapter 52

It was after 6:00 p.m. when the message came through. The first time Vicky's phone had buzzed—and everyone had jumped—it had been a concerned and anticlimactic voice mail from one of Betsy's servers, Patty. This time, however, even the way the phone swiveled back and forth from the vibration seemed sinister. It was the message they'd been hoping for.

Millie opened the phone and called the message out to the team.

"The woods," Rooker said with a hand clamped over his forehead like he was blocking out the sun. "Thirty years ago, Vicky lured Amy into the woods for him. That's where he wants to meet."

"He'll kill her whether we're there or not," Tess stated.

"We don't know that for certain," Rooker said.

"We can't just use her as bait."

"Why not? She led Amy Berglund to her death in those woods."

"Yeah, and I'm not about to do the same to Vicky Reynolds."

"Tess," Sterling spoke up. "With Vicky, we got a shot at the guy. Put her in a vest. If we don't use her, the guy's good as gone. Same if he finds out we got her. Maybe we set up a trap out there for him. He never even gets close to her."

Without realizing, she dug her fingernail back and forth into the grooves of her scar. "Larsson can't know." She hesitated. "If things go wrong, it's over. I want everyone to know that. Say Vicky gets injured or one of us . . . if we don't get Caldwell tonight, this case goes to the Feds. You'll all be handing over everything you've worked on. If that's good for everyone . . ."

No one said a word. Her answer was in their faces.

"All right then. Let's do it."

In the midnight hour, the woods looked both dead and alive. The tops of the trees vanished into the pitch darkness. The moon offered illumination in patches, as clouds rolled by overhead. Muggy winds hissed against Rooker's back.

Rooker had dressed in black: a featureless shirt with sleeves, along with jeans and his old pair of boots. The vest was snug, but when Tess gave it to him, he didn't protest. He'd been shot once and would do anything not to experience that level of pain again.

She didn't know about the gun he had tucked into the back of his waistband.

The damp air was thick; it felt as though it were draining the oxygen from his lungs. His underarms were already saturated with sweat. He footed carefully, trying to avoid stumbling through the gray mist that coated the earth to just above the lowest eyelet of his boots. It was a disorienting feeling, not being able to see his own feet or the uneven ground.

"Hell of a night for this," Rooker whispered to himself.

The wind rustling the leaves made it tough to hear anything. And one wrong step and something would snap beneath his boot. If Caldwell were close enough, he'd hear it. The biggest problem of all was that Caldwell probably knew these woods better than anyone. He imagined that's why he'd chosen them.

He hunched low to the ground. Adjusted the vest as it shifted upward against his neck. Even Vicky Reynolds was wearing a bullet-proof vest beneath her buttoned flannel top, along with a GPS tracker and a wire. If she made contact with Caldwell, they would close in on him. Rooker was given strict orders to stay put and stand down if anything did happen. He knew there was little chance of that. If Caldwell was alive enough to talk at the end of this, he had questions he needed answered.

Not far from him on his right, Martin Keene's large back was pressed against a tree. He wore his vest over a black shirt, along with dark jeans and boots. Rooker assessed his slow, uneven breaths, which reminded Rooker to breathe himself. Somewhere out there was the rest of the team. Millie, he knew, was behind him. Somewhere. Tess, Sterling, Whitlock, and Riggs were out of sight already.

After crouching forward for so long, his legs rubberized, felt as if they'd caught fire. The lean muscles in his thighs and calves started to cramp until he shifted his weight quietly, and he knelt behind thick brush.

He's not coming. He checked on Martin. Then felt the cold legs of something crawling up his neck before he saw the string of spider silk and swatted it away. While his head oscillated slowly, he thought he saw Riggs in the distance, adjusting the cap on his head. And that's when he thought he saw a figure, a shape moving somewhere behind Riggs. Rooker squinted through the blackness, and when he was sure, he yelled, "Watch out, Riggs!" There was a quick whipcrack, and Rooker watched the muzzle flash, right as Riggs's head burst open.

Fuck. Rooker's arm bent to reach around his back. His fingers closed on the cold steel. He started to pull the pistol but stopped when he watched Martin Keene fire twice at the shape that was now zigzagging through the trees. Despite the powerful squeeze, the pistol jolted in his gargantuan double-handed grip, a bright spark as if the barrel had burst into flames. It was too late. The figure had vanished.

The woods echoed the gunfire.

"Stay there," Keene ordered Rooker before sprinting through the trees and sliding to the ground where the limbs of John Riggs contorted. Rooker thought he could see his eyes open. Keene closed them and slid his own back up against a tree. His vested chest climbed rapidly, the stress painted on his face. Rooker moved as low and as quietly toward him as he could. At a tree about ten feet from him, he saw the hole where the bullet had exited the front of Riggs's head.

"I told you to stay—"

"Heard you," Rooker whispered. "Not going to sit back and watch you die too."

The two of them heard a crunch back the way Martin had come. Keene swung out and raised the pistol at chest level to find Millie in his sights before he lowered the gun off her.

She looked down and whispered low. "Shit. Riggs—"

"Shh." Keene put a finger to his sweat-beading upper lip. "No more talking."

A screech. Somewhere deeper in the woods. *Pop. Crack. Crack. Pop. Pop.*

The three of them took off in the direction of the scream. There was no doubt that it was Vicky Reynolds. That noise . . . it couldn't have come from Tess. Could it?

The three of them jumped through brush and trampled down vines that snagged on Rooker's clothing. Prickers and thorns cut through his skin and a piece of flesh at his cheek, but he kept moving. At a dead sprint, the wind felt like it was pulling the blood from his face, but he did his best not to touch it. When they wrapped around a fallen log covered in moss and leaves, they saw the tensed back of Vic Sterling. There was a three- or four-foot hole there where the earth caved in like a gully. He was ducked down beside a warped and gangly excuse for a tree.

"Where is he?" Keene asked.

"The damn woman ran." Sterling let out a shaky breath. "We had eyes on her until she took off running and we lost sight of her. Somewhere, Caldwell grabbed Vicky."

"Which way?" Keene wiped the sweat from his eyes.

"Back east toward the road. He may have left a getaway car there somewhere. I'll call it in, get police on the road there."

"Where're Tess and Whitlock?"

"Don't know just yet. Let's go back to the rendezvous point. Caldwell's gone. Let's just hope he hasn't found the tracker yet."

There was stony silence as the group made its way back to the clearing they'd used as a staging area. Once they were safely at the vehicles, Millie and Keene huddled over his phone.

Rooker heard a few twigs snapping and saw Tess and Xander emerge from the woods.

"They're on the move," Keene shouted to them. "GPS has her due west of the woods when the tracker stopped."

Tess's face was all business. Sweat trickled down her cheeks, and her lips tightened to a thin line. *"Goddammit."* She clicked the safety mechanism on her sidearm and holstered it at her hip. "Why the hell would she run? And *how in the hell* did he get out of here?" She started to pick at the jagged layer of skin at her finger.

"Fear," Sterling said. "Say she stayed, the two outcomes in her mind are: die at Caldwell's hands or go to prison as an accomplice to murder."

Keene cleared his throat. "Boss, he got Riggs."

"What?"

"Riggs is dead."

She put her hands on her hips and let out a shaky breath, the sweat flying off her trembling lips. Rooker was certain the tears would come soon. Whether it was now or when no one was around. "Pull up the audio," she said.

Millie fiddled with her phone and said in a grim tone, "He disconnected it. Listen."

The audio played. Static first. Then Vicky's voice. "They made me do it. Please. Your mom is alive. I'll take you." More static. He must have felt around her clothing or yanked it.

Then they could all hear when he pulled the microphone to his face and said: "I SEE YOU. I SEE ALL OF YOU."

"All this, and Riggs is . . . gone," said Tess numbly. It was evident she couldn't bring herself to say *dead*. "And Caldwell is gone."

"We got him to come back," Rooker said. "Vicky's using her last bargaining chip to stay alive. But he won't keep her alive longer than he needs to. He'll want to see his mother. Maybe kill her once and for all."

"Martin, get an ambulance out here and police outside the mother's room. I've gotta go tell another set of parents that their child is dead . . . on my watch."

Chapter 53

"Where is she?"

He felt her tremble away from him in the passenger seat. "I . . . I think—"

"I asked you a question." He spoke without turning his head to her. The words he uttered were cold and slow. "If you can't tell me where she is, then what use are you?"

"The hospital!" She tucked her knee to her chest and cradled it with her arm. Her body was pressed back against the door as far away from him as possible. If he opened the door, she'd fall right out.

"What floor? What room?"

"I—I don't know! They didn't say!"

He shook his head. Flung the hat in the back seat. The sweat had dried in the blond wig. In spite of the heat whirring on the furthest red setting, it did little to dry the sopping wetness of the clothing adhered to his skin. He shut it off.

He felt her gaze on the pistol in his lap. Maybe she thought she could get to it. He was going to kill her. But he didn't want her death to be of no use to him. He'd wait for now.

Suddenly he looked up to the mirror between them and saw his mother. He shut his eyes and gritted his teeth so hard, they hurt. "Oh, hush!" He heard her words from the back seat. Then he heard them come from his own lips.

"Please!" she begged beside him. "Don't hurt me!"

"Oh, hush!" he told her, just as his mother would. His eyes flicked open, back to the whir of the wipers. "You're going to get into the hospital for me. You'll do exactly as I say. Or you'll die. Understand?"

She nodded frantically.

"You'll end up just like *she* did."

He didn't need to say more. He knew she'd know exactly whom he meant. The woman she'd brought him, like a gift wrapped in glittery paper.

When he pulled up outside the hospital, he circled the exterior sharklike before he stopped the car in a space in visitor parking. He dropped the pistol by his feet. Then he slid his seat back as far as it would go, grabbed his bag from the back, and tossed it in her lap. He made her unzip it. Then he started pulling parts of the uniform out piece by piece.

He changed his clothes. Picked the gun up from the ground.

When he finished, he looked up at the windows that were lit, and at the large capital letters glowing red. EMERGENCY. "Ready?" he asked her.

"Ready for what?" For the first time since he'd grabbed her, he looked into her eyes and smiled.

"See those doors right there?" He waited for her nod. "All I need you to do is walk over there."

"Tha—that's it?"

"That's it."

For a split second, the darkness in the car flashed with a spark of white. He had pressed the gun to her leg and fired.

Chapter 54

October 3, 2019

"Did you hear me?"

Rooker nodded, despite knowing she'd repeat herself.

Tess stared him in the face. "You don't go inside the hospital. If you see anything, you call me. You do not pursue."

"I heard you."

Tess began to walk away when an officer ran up to her in a frenzy. "Detective Harlow," hollered a pale-faced man around six feet tall with parted orange-brown hair. With one hand he yanked down on the neck of his black tactical vest, his other hand gripping a Colt M4 Carbine rifle, his finger stretched along the trigger guard. "We have a situation."

"What kind of situation?"

"GSW. The vic is a woman, Victoria Reynolds. Says your guy had her."

"*Shit!* What happened?"

"He parked in the visitor lot. Told her all she had to do was walk right here through the doors. Then he shot her in the leg. She limped, screaming bloody murder, until someone got a wheelchair to her and rolled her inside. Not sure she's going to make it. The bleeding's bad. Real bad."

"Shit," Tess said. "It was a distraction. He's gotta be inside. Police still stationed outside her room?"

"Some of 'em, I think. Pretty sure some took off looking for him when the gunshot was reported. They were talking about moving Mrs. Caldwell."

"Don't. Vicky doesn't know where she is, so neither should he."

"What if he found out, though?"

Tess hesitated. "If he sees her while she's being moved, he'll kill her and anyone who gets in his way before he's put down. Tell them to stay put and guard the room. I'll take the nearest stairwell up to her floor."

"By the way, Detective. The vic said he's wearing a police uniform."

When the automatic doors slid open, Rooker watched Tess go inside with the feeling that he was watching her run into a burning building.

"Let's go." Millie unbuckled her seat belt and opened her door.

"What? Are you crazy?"

"Since when do you listen to anyone?"

"The place is crawling with cops. He'll never make it to her."

"You forgetting what we just heard? He's dressed like a cop. Who's to say anyone recognizes him before it's too late?"

"Bad idea, Mill."

"Oh, c'mon. I've been trained for situations like this. I can help them."

"Not without a badge, you can't."

"Well, I'm going. With or without you."

She got out of the car and started moving toward the doors. "Goddammit! Wait!" Rooker got out of the car and followed.

The automated doors slid open. The reception area was empty. The two of them moved through, past the massive desk and examination and treatment rooms.

They found the door to the stairs. Millie lifted her pistol from its holster and swung open the door. Three women were hunched there beneath the stairs. Rooker could see the colorful-print scrubs over Millie's shoulder. "Come on," she told them, and the three of them slid out from beneath the staircase. She held the door open, checked the end of the hall, and told them to run outside. Once all three made it out past the doors and into the protection of the police outside, she shut the door and they started up the stairs. The stairwell was pale-white walls with chrome railings and gray steps that reminded him of wet cement. With her back to the handrail on the wall and her arms extended, she turned her attention to the flights of stairs above her. She found her footing without looking and scanned the area above. Rooker held the Glock 17 in a two-handed grip now, lowered in front of his midsection. Every now and then, he'd glance behind them and over the railing to the bottom of the stairs.

When the two of them reached a door, Millie pried it open slowly. While she held it open, Rooker peeked past her, down both directions of a long stretch of corridor. Aside from an officer at each end, it was empty. He pulled his head back. She let the door shut slowly against her foot before they continued on.

Rooker and Millie had come to the same unspoken understanding. If they didn't see a number of police on the floor, Mrs. Caldwell wasn't there. But while he thought it, he knew that Hartley Caldwell would know that too.

When they made it to another floor, again, Millie checked the hall. She shook her head and let the door close before they moved on. That's when the door above them blasted open, and they both aimed their weapons at the source of the noise. A couple of crying nurses in V-neck scrubs ducked their heads and held their palms frantically in the air.

Millie and Rooker lowered their guns and moved quickly up the stairs.

"Stay there," Millie told the two nurses. "It's not safe to go back down yet."

Rooker checked the other side of the door and saw at least ten officers spread out. He pulled his head back. "This is the one."

"I can't have the two of you on this floor."

The nurse with straight dark hair nodded, while the one with wavy red hair cowered between her own knees.

Millie called an officer over and told him to guard the two women. She then told him she was a member of Detective Harlow's task force before he let her pass but stopped Rooker.

"I know who you are." He pushed him back toward the door, and Rooker shoved the hand away.

"Don't touch me if you know what's good—"

"He's with me. Without him, we might've never caught Sadler. And without him, we wouldn't have found Caldwell."

Rooker fixed his shirt while he eyed the officer.

"Fine. He gets shot, it's your ass. Not mine."

Rooker and Millie stepped into the hall and saw Tess at the end against the eastern wall. Sterling and Keene stood beside her.

"What do you think?" he asked Millie.

"I think he's here." Her face turned slowly. She was scanning the face of every cop in the hallway. "Somewhere."

"We know Caldwell has black hair and pale features. How far would his disguise go? White hair and wrinkles? Blond hair and blue eyes? Tan?" Rooker couldn't see a single face that reminded him of Hartley Caldwell.

When the two of them walked down the hall, the look on Tess's face was one of unsurprise and anger. "The hell did I tell the two of you? I said stay put, didn't I?"

"Yes, you did," Rooker said.

She shook her head. "Mrs. Caldwell is in a room at the end of the corridor." She stopped when her radio chirped at her hip. She pulled it up to her face and pressed the "Transmit" button. "Say again?"

"Harlow?"

"Go."

"Before Vicky Reynolds passed out, she said 'foster.' Not sure if it means anything to you."

"Not yet. Thanks, though." She clipped the radio to her hip.

Vic asked, "The hell does that mean?"

Keene spoke. "Foster child?"

"No," Rooker said. "The last thing Vicky Reynolds said was that he was dressed as a cop, right? How many names do you see when you look around? Maybe that's the name on his nameplate. Foster."

"Vicky Reynolds was good for something after all." Sterling raised his eyebrows.

"Have all these rooms been cleared yet?" Millie asked.

"Not yet. Listen up," Tess hollered. "Suspect is armed and dressed as a cop. We have reason to believe the name on his tag says 'Foster.' I want this place cleared. Now." Then she turned her attention back to Millie and Rooker. "You two get out of here."

Millie started to walk away. Meanwhile, Rooker couldn't help but stand his ground. "If he's here, he has to know he's not getting out alive."

"So be it."

"That's not what I'm saying. He'll do whatever it takes to get to his mother. He'll entertain a firefight. Just be careful."

She nodded.

Millie leaned against the wall at the top of the stairwell, listening to two female nurses in scrubs try to make small talk with a tall deputy. His nameplate read: GARZA.

It was the first thing she checked.

"What's happening?" the one in lilac-colored scrubs asked.

"Can't you tell us anything?" the other said.

He held an authoritative hand in the air. "Please, this will all be over soon. I just need you to be quiet." Millie noticed the two women only went silent at the notice of his wedding band.

What the hell is taking him so long? She shifted her weight from her heel to the ball of her foot. Rooker should've been right behind her. Just as she thought to open the door against the deputy's wishes, she heard the clink and clatter of something metal bouncing around and the hard thud of boots clomping up the stairs.

The figure was lean. Light-blond hair came into view on the landing below. Eight, maybe ten stairs stood between them. "Stop!" Garza yelled. "Hands!"

"What?" the man hissed. He hunched low. Huffed and puffed. "Too many . . . goddamn stairs . . ."

Millie couldn't see the man's face. Just his broad shoulders hunched forward. Garza's hand inched toward his holster. "I said show me your—"

The figure recoiled. Stiffened. In that moment, she read his nameplate and her jaw dropped.

Foster.

Crack. The stairwell flashed. Garza's head jolted back. Now, Caldwell had the gun pointed at her.

Rooker was headed back toward the door to the stairwell when he heard a blaring crack and two synchronized screams. "Millie?" He rushed to the door. But when it swung open, he saw a tall body sprawled on the ground before two nurses. Then a man came forward, with his forearm jutted into Millie's throat and a pistol pressed into her temple. He concealed most of himself behind her, hidden from any clean shot, but a portion of his face was enough for Rooker to see him smile.

"I'll kill her."

Tess yelled, "Everyone stand down! Do not fire!"

"Take me to my mother or she dies!"

Rooker's pistol clanged against the cold tile floor. He kicked it forward and raised his hands desperately. *Shit! Let her go, you son of a bitch.* "Why now, after all this time? Amy Berglund was thirty years ago. Malin Jakobsson eight years ago. Why kill now?"

"Oh, Rooker. The hypocrite. Death is your only reason to live. You should be thanking me."

"Where is Amy's body?"

He didn't answer. Only a wide-set grin.

"Why didn't you just kill your mother?"

His face blanched. "That would be too easy."

"You could've done it all these years—"

"It would have been too easy *for her*. She doesn't deserve *easy*. She deserves to suffer."

"Why kill Nora?"

"Why. Why. Why. Why. Why are monsters born every day? Nurtured in their mother's belly. What would the mother do, say, if she knew what the child would become?"

"Is that what they were to you?"

"Is that what *I* am to you? A monster?"

"How did you know Gregory Sadler?"

Caldwell smiled. "Keep the killer talking. Maybe he'll make a mistake?"

He hesitated. If he didn't ask the right questions, he was going to watch Millie die. But if he could keep Caldwell talking, he'd slip up eventually. A mistake that would allow someone a clean shot. "Did you know Gunner too?"

Caldwell's smile fell. All that was left was a blank expression and empty eyes. "You just don't get it, do you?"

"What's that?"

"You think it's all about you."

"Fucking right it's about me. Sadler came for me. You got the phone to Meachum that started it all. You sent that message to me at the station. It's never *not* been about me."

"And *you* think *I'm* the one with the delusions?" He put his lips next to Millie's ear, the darkness in his eyes still aimed at Rooker. "How would you like to watch me kill Mr. Lindström in front of you?"

But Millie had been waiting for Caldwell to slip up too. He must have loosened his grip a bit, turned an inch or two in the wrong direction, because she did it—she wriggled free. Rooker almost laughed, but when she went for the gun, the room erupted into chaos. Rooker dove to the ground, and when he looked up, he watched bullet after bullet tear through Hartley Caldwell. When the gun slipped from his dead hand and his body flattened to the ground, the room rang so loud, he thought maybe his eardrum had burst.

Then he saw Millie. She was lying on the ground too. But not in a stunned or protective way. She was stone-still. He crawled to her and saw the messy hole in her back. He turned her over and looked down at another hole in her chest, this one spilling blood. He pressed his hands over the wound. He didn't want to admit to himself that it was too late. He lifted her just enough to slide his leg under her so that he could hold her. He pressed his face into her neck while he cradled her head.

His back trembled. His head too.

"You're asleep," he whispered in her ear. She looked how she did when she'd fall asleep on that godawful couch. "You'll wake up soon."

He could barely see her through his tears now. In a lonely room down the corridor, beyond a door guarded by two police officers, a woman lying in a hospital bed wept along with him.

Chapter 55

October 6, 2019

The stack of mail clattered like a baseball on the porch steps. He rolled his eyes and sighed at the sound. When Rooker carried it inside and sifted through it, he found a check from Christine and Thomas Vandenberg, along with a handwritten note thanking him and Millie for doing everything they could to save Nora.

Did we do everything we could?

He thought back to the rainy night of the vigil. With the cloaked figure of Caldwell in the back seat, the gun on him. Maybe there was a moment he could have done something . . .

That was the issue. After the fact, there were always maybes. Maybe he could've somehow overpowered him. Maybe he could have distracted him. Maybe if he'd been shot, even killed, someone would have been able to catch Caldwell that night, and Nora wouldn't have died. Millie wouldn't have died.

But even the pessimist he was thought, deep down, the two of them had done everything they could to save her.

Rooker folded the check in half and stuffed it in his front pocket.

Later that morning, Rooker stepped inside the home of Millie Langston for the first time, where it felt as if every living trace of her was gone. There was a glare inside the old farmhouse that made his eyes water. His three-day-old headache throbbed. He stopped on a creaky floorboard, studied tiny particles floating in the beam of light, and couldn't help but think of her.

Despite camera footage and twenty-some police eyewitnesses, word had spread in small-town circles that he'd killed the former detective and private investigator—one of his only true friends—Millie Langston. It hurt him more than he could say. Still, he didn't bother to refute it. It didn't matter anymore how he felt. She was gone.

He'd never forget watching her be taken away. The noiselessness of her body lifted onto the stretcher. The eerie, peaceful expression on her face. For the last sixty hours, the image had stood at the forefront of his mind like a strange figure at the foot of his bed. He hadn't slept. Every waking minute it haunted him, along with the old memory of his mother dying, her hand going limp and cold in his. Rooker tried to think back to his fondest memories of the two of them: Millie and his mother. But it was a game of tug-of-war in his mind, the morbid thoughts the more powerful side, inching the rope further and further away. For moments, Rooker imagined his life in a state of Alzheimer's bliss. Such an ugly disease. But if only there was something that would help him forget all the pain.

Upstairs, her bed was made. On her desk, he found the box that housed her Smith and Wesson .357 Magnum and smiled sadly.

"You did it, Mill" was all he said. The words came out shaky. If he said any more about her catching the man she'd been after since she was a girl, about finding out what happened to Amy Berglund, about catching her own Buffalo Bill, about her being as badass as Clarice Starling, about being the best partner he could have ever asked for, he'd fall apart.

If she could hear him—wherever she was now—she'd understand.

Rooker removed the check from his pocket and placed it on the box.

Downstairs on a white table-clothed dining room table that stretched the length of the room, he found something that made his eyes narrow. Strings had been cut from it. It was something wrapped in paper that had been rewrapped. At least two feet tall and just as wide. When he folded the paper back, he saw the black metal sign with white letters that read:

MANOR INVESTIGATIONS

Just as his legs buckled, Rooker pulled a wooden chair out and sat down. He folded his arms, placed his head between them, and sobbed.

Chapter 56

October 7, 2019

She'd woken up every hour to the same nightmare. Woods. The hole in Riggs's head. Millie on the cold tile, dying.

By the time she accepted consciousness over seeing those images again, she told herself it would be a while before she dreamed. For now, she needed to endure this nightmare.

Despite her frame of mind and the queasiness, Tess wolfed down a protein bar and a cup of black coffee. When she walked into the office, the nightmare continued. A miserable thumping, drums banging between her temples. She could barely keep her eyes open. And even when she saw the wispy white hairs and displeased face of Chief Jim Larsson, she did little to change her expression.

She tried to ignore him, sauntering past him into her office, but he followed. "Detective, if you don't mind."

"Hope you're not delivering more of your scrapbooking, Chief." She gestured at the framed clipping up on her wall, still tilted to the left.

"Not today, Tess."

"Take a chair, Jim." Really, she hoped he wouldn't.

"I won't be staying long," he said.

No surprise there, she thought. *Thank the heavens.*

"I've known you for some time, huh?"

She ignored the comment. "What can I do for you, Chief?"

"I'm sorry, Tess. I've gotta pull you."

She stood straight. "*Pull me?* Are you serious?"

"Look, your father would've been—"

"Don't you dare tell me how proud he would have been. Two serial killers. Tell me another detective team around that's done what we've done. Both of them caught."

"You mean both dead."

"The hell's the difference? They're not out on the streets killing women."

"And what about Victoria Reynolds?" He paused. "She was in your custody, and she was taken and shot. It's a miracle she's still alive. I'm sorry about what happened to your team—to Riggs. I am. I'll give you till the end of the week. Finish up your report and I'll get you working on something else."

"Something else," she repeated with a smirk. "Who wants me gone?"

"I'm not saying anyone wants you gone. But there's been quite a few people on this team who are no longer . . . with us. People notice that at some point. And those people decide that action needs to be taken."

"And what about you? Why do you get off scot-free? You're the chief, right?"

"Watch it, Ms. Harlow—"

"Don't worry about demoting me. I won't need the week. I'm done." She heaved one of her father's old mugs at the wall behind him and smashed the porcelain frame to pieces. The sound reverberated off the walls. "Give Keene my position. If you don't mind, I'd like to pack my office without you in it." She moved along the desk and stood by his shoulder now, speaking to the edge of his wrinkled cheek. "You *worthless* old prick."

◆ ◆ ◆

Tucking her shortened locks inside the ski mask, she unlatched the door and lifted the pistol from the passenger seat. She switched the safety off. Tonight, there was no distracting tight dress or carefully applied makeup. Tonight, she'd threaded a suppressor attachment tight onto the end of a stolen FN 509 pistol.

She knew where every camera was.

In the rearview mirror, she stared at the three holes in the beanie, peering into eyes that no longer looked like her own. When she'd stared long enough that they reminded her of her mother's—vacant—she bit her lip. Had it not been for the gloves, she would have gouged her nail into the scar at her fingertip.

Instead, she got out of the car.

The smell of her own sweat permeated the warm knit material. She'd parked in semidarkness away from the streetlamp. Jan Cullen climbed out of a rusted Pontiac Trans Am and stumbled up the steps to the door of his town house. Clyde Miller, in the driver's seat of the Trans Am, idly sparked up a joint, then let his arm hang out the window. Once the door to Cullen's place shut behind him, she moved through the shadows. She'd rehearsed the next part in her mind, replaying it over and over, wondering if she could really do it. In the cloak of night, she watched Miller's face in the side mirror, the glowing tip of the joint a beacon, until she got up next to him—and fired one quiet bullet into his head. He slumped forward, and the joint rolled down his lap onto the seat between his legs.

Tess moved up the stairs quietly and got into position beside the door. She knocked three times and waited.

"Yeah, man. One sec," Cullen called out. When he opened the door, she swung out, stuck the pistol into his chest, and shot. He collapsed.

Tess stepped inside, closed the door, and stood over Cullen. A dime-size hole trickled red from the left side of his sternum. She heard her mother's words, this time in her own voice.

"WHAT HAVE YOU DONE?"

"What had to be done," she whispered. Then a little louder. "What had to be done. What had to be done."

Chapter 57

On the old wooden front porch, Red lay on his belly, his big paws sprawled out in front of him.

By the time Rooker pulled up the length of the driveway in the Volvo, he still hadn't figured out the words to say to Eva Berglund. Mulling over it the entire way here, all he could see was Charles Berglund's dead face. After all these years, they'd caught the man who killed her daughter. But in doing so, it had caused her husband to kill an innocent man. Maybe the Berglunds were as plagued as Rooker was, marked by darkness and death, never the protagonists of a happy ending.

To his surprise, Rooker scaled the steps to not a single peep from Red. Not a growl, not so much as a lift of his head.

He could hear Charles's voice now. *"Not much of a guard dog anymore, huh, Red?"*

Rooker wanted to smile but couldn't. His knuckles rapped at the aluminum of the storm door. At the bottom, the screen netting was torn where he'd imagined Red dug his nails. "Mrs. Berglund?" he called out.

He knocked again and waited. "Eva?"

Nothing.

He pulled the latch on the door, and the second door nudged open. "Eva?" he called out again. Rooker walked around the bottom level of the home. The silence rang between creaking steps. Above the fireplace was a framed photograph on an old mantel. There were three wooden picture frames spaced out, but this one was much cleaner than the others, like it had just recently been dusted off. Rooker looked at the photograph of Charles and Eva posing behind Amy. Their smiles radiant, not a care in the world. Ignorant to the evils within it, the evils that would take their daughter from them.

After he'd scoped out every room, he started up the stairs. He stuck his head into a guest room and then checked the main bedroom. Both were empty.

The bathroom door was half-closed but appeared dark inside.

Plunk. He waited a moment. Then it was there once more. *Plunk.*

Upon pushing the door open, he felt a cold liquid swarm around his shoes. He hit the light switch. There was Eva Berglund, submerged in the dark water, fully dressed.

Plunk. The waterdrops echoed hollowly. Her hands were purple and pruned, steepled over a thin, translucent-orange vial on her chest. Prescription pills, maybe painkillers. She'd drifted to sleep.

But as he stared, his vision hazed. The water blackened. Thickened as if it came to life. The putrid stench of death on her. Clumps of dirt and dark beetles and white larvae spilled from her matted hair. Eva Berglund's neck turned in dreadful clocklike ticks, and she peered up at him with dead eyes. He turned away.

No. It's not real. Stop . . . stop!

With his jaw clamped tight, he dug his thumb into the center of his forehead and faced her. Despite the aching thrash of his heartbeat, one that was pulsing too fast, she returned to normal.

Her body had slipped down into the tub; Rooker pulled her up and halfway over the side. He knew it was far too late, yet he flipped the chrome lever, and the water started to drain. He turned the water completely off.

Rooker went outside and patted Red on his wart-spotted head. He called Tess, who sighed wearily and told him she'd call the local authorities.

Soon after, Officer Wyatt pulled up in a marked Chevy Tahoe. He walked up to Rooker and crossed his arms over his chest.

"Mr. Lindström, no surprise I find you here."

"Good to see you again too."

"Can't say whether you're the unluckiest bastard I've ever met or if you're Bad Luck himself."

Rooker turned toward the house once more. When he looked back at Wyatt, he raised his eyebrows, smiled weakly, and nodded.

As he walked back to the car, he thought of his favorite quote about luck, which had stuck with him from his first reading of Thomas Harris's *Red Dragon*. Since then, he'd read it at least a handful more times. Jack Crawford said it about FBI profiler Will Graham: "Because it's his bad luck to be the best."

Only Rooker was no Will Graham. He wasn't so much gifted at this as he was subjected to it. Tragedy was his fate. He was born into it, nurtured by it. Wrapped in it, like a dying bird in another's wings. It was a miracle that he wasn't dead yet, the crows and the vultures pecking at his organs. Now, reflecting on one of his favorite authors only came with thoughts of death. And the thought of Millie.

The engine of the Volvo ticked, then rumbled. As he stared at the scene, the lights flickering atop the vehicles, the police ambling around the burned lawn, the gurney being carried inside, his gaze stopped on Red. He watched him for what felt like a long time. The old dog lifted his head and stared back.

He reached over to the passenger side and rolled down the window. Then as he whistled loud, he ignored the eyes on him, including

Wyatt's. Red got up from the porch and trotted down the steps toward him. Rooker fought off the urge to cry.

Strays, he thought. *What is it with me and these damn strays?*

When Red was close enough, Rooker swung the door open and the old dog hopped up into the passenger seat and pressed his face into Rooker's.

"Yeah." Rooker choked up. His voice quivered. "I know, Red. Let's go."

Knowing Geralt wouldn't be thrilled, Rooker pulled the door shut and let Red hang his old wart-spotted head out the open window.

TWO YEARS LATER

On a Saturday night at Lindström Manor, a cold breeze whispered through the black world, and the television quietly played ESPN's live broadcast of a welterweight title bout between Terence "Bud" Crawford and "Showtime" Shawn Porter. Rooker was in the middle of typing up the finishing touches to an article for the *Los Angeles Times* when his phone started to buzz. And buzz. And buzz.

So many notifications that the display on his phone froze. While he held two buttons on the iPhone to restart it, the highest-paid news anchor for FOX, Caroline Lind, strutted into the room in her undergarments and a sleep shirt.

Her expression was one he hadn't yet seen from her. Even after carrying her out of a room where she was meant to die. This was far worse.

His face blanched. "What is it?"

"They found a woman's body. Late last night."

"Who's 'they'?"

"Riverside PD. Some kids found her at the edge of a drainpipe; there are storm drain tunnels that run for miles beneath Hemet. The Feds were called in."

He knew about the sewers that drained into the San Jacinto River. What he didn't know was why Riverside PD had contacted the Bureau this early. Something had to be wrong. Rooker pictured them in his mind, strutting around the crime scene in their blue windbreaker jackets emblazoned with three yellow letters.

"The fingernail was busted. It turned black. There was a time carved into it."

Rooker's chest capsized. He closed his eyes. "What was the time?"

"11:37."

Rooker changed the channel to the news.

"But why a drainpipe? Meachum never left a body in one. His victims were always found in their homes."

"In the house I owned with my ex-wife, I had this huge bookshelf made. It covered three walls behind my desk. It was my favorite part of the house. Every Michael Connelly book in order. The first novel he ever wrote is called *The Black Echo*. I had a signed first-edition hardcover. It's about a body found in a drainpipe at Mulholland Dam."

"What are you saying?"

The banner at the bottom of the television read: GRUESOME HOMICIDE IN HEMET. The picture zoomed on a body zipped up tight in a black bag. Siren lights in the darkness. Crime scene tape.

"I'm saying either Meachum told someone about the inside of my house or he didn't kill my son."

Rooker was going to do something he vowed to never do. He was going back.

Home.

ABOUT THE AUTHOR

Photo © 2021 Steven Woodfield

Pete Zacharias received a BA in English with a concentration in creative writing. He is a lover of Nordic noir, dark thrillers, and anything spy, and credits Michael Connelly's *The Poet* as the novel that inspired him to become a writer. Pete is the author of *The Man Burned by Winter* in the Rooker Lindström Thriller series.